W9-AZE-354

POACHING MAN & BEAST

MURDER IN THE NORTH WOODS

BY RICHARD L. BALDWIN

To My friend, Terry,
Best wishes
Rich Baldwin

© Buttonwood Press 2006

Copyright © 2006 by Richard L. Baldwin

All rights reserved. No part of this book may be reproduced or transmitted
in any form or by any means, electronic or mechanical, including photocopying,
recording, or by any information storage and retrieval system, without
permission in writing from the publisher.

This novel is a product of the author's imagination. The events described
in this story never occurred. Though localities, buildings, and businesses
may exist, liberties were taken with their actual location and description. This story has no purpose other than to entertain the reader.

Published by Buttonwood Press
P.O. Box 716
Haslett, Michigan 48840
www.buttonwoodpress.com

Printed in the United States of America

OTHER BOOKS
BY RICHARD L. BALDWIN

FICTION:

A Lesson Plan for Murder (1998)
ISBN: 0-9660685-0-5. Buttonwood Press.

The Principal Cause of Death (1999)
ISBN: 0-9660685-2-1. Buttonwood Press.

Administration Can Be Murder (2000)
ISBN: 0-9660685-4-8. Buttonwood Press.

Buried Secrets of Bois Blanc: Murder in the Straits of Mackinac (2001)
ISBN: 0-9660685-5-6. Buttonwood Press.

The Marina Murders (2003)
ISBN: 0-9660685-7-2. Buttonwood Press.

A Final Crossing: Murder on the S.S. Badger (2004)
ISBN: 0-9742920-2-8. Buttonwood Press.

The Searing Mysteries: Three in One (2001)
ISBN: 0-9660685-6-4. Buttonwood Press.

Ghostly Links (2004)
ISBN: 0-9660685-8-0. Buttonwood Press.

The Moon Beach Mysteries (2003)
ISBN: 0-9660685-9-9. Buttonwood Press.

The Detective Company (2004; written with Sandie Jones.)
ISBN: 0-9742920-0-1. Buttonwood Press.

Unity and the Children (2000)
ISBN: 0-9660685-3-X. Buttonwood Press.

NON-FICTION:

If A Child Picked A Flower Just For You (2004)
Buttonwood Press

The Piano Recital (1999)
ISBN: 0-9660685-1-3. Buttonwood Press.

A Story to Tell: Special Education in Michigan's Upper Peninsula 1902-1975 (1994)
ISBN: 932212-77-8. Lake Superior Press.

Warriors and Special Olympics: The Wertz Warrior Story (2006)
ISBN: 0-9742920-4-4. Buttonwood Press, LLC.

ACKNOWLEDGEMENTS

I want to thank Dr. Dan O'Brien, Veterinary Specialist with the Michigan Department of Natural Resources for his explanation of animal necropsies; Mike Johnson, Conservation Officer, for his plot suggestions; hunters David Rollins, Gary Simons, and Jeff Woodworth who provided a wealth of technical information; attorney Frank Kolasa for sharing his expertise as a trial lawyer; and the Buttonwood Press team: editor, Anne Ordiway; writing consultant, Karen O'Connor; proofreader, Joyce Wagner; and cover designer and typesetter, Sarah Thomas.

Finally, I wish to thank my dear wife Patty for her belief in me, her love and support. I am so blessed to share life with the most beautiful human being on the face of the earth.

*This book is dedicated to
Michigan's conservation officers
and all employees of the Michigan
Department of Natural Resources.*

POACHING MAN & BEAST

MURDER IN THE NORTH WOODS

BY RICHARD L. BALDWIN

SEPTEMBER 30

For weeks Zeke had looked forward to the opening day of bow hunting season. A hunter for almost thirty years, Zeke loved everything about the hunting season: being outside in the fall; the quietness and beauty of nature; and the excitement of the hunt. For the past twenty years he had been the lone hunter on an eighty-acre farm northwest of Trout City, Michigan, land that was owned by a boyhood friend, Thomas "Tommy" Wilds.

On this day before bow season, Zeke Simons drove his blue Ford pickup to the Marathon station in Clare to get gas, an ice cream cone, and deer bait. He was on his way to Trout City, a small community 30 miles east of Traverse City. As was his custom, Zeke would arrive mid-afternoon at the Wilds' home. After greeting his hosts, Tommy and Jane, and unpacking, he scouted his hunting area, making sure that deer still used a trail on the farm, a natural path from woods to cornfields.

Zeke placed his bait in a small opening, set up his blind, and returned to the Wilds' home where Jane prepared a delicious meal and then left the two men to talk into the evening. For a few hours, Zeke and Tommy shared drinks and memories beside a log fire in the Wilds' log cabin home.

1

Unlike Zeke, Tommy was not a deer hunter. In fact, he didn't hunt at all, but he supported hunting. He wanted the herd thinned since he, like most farmers, often lost crops to the deer who devoured them as if they were grown for their consumption.

At 46, Zeke was handsome and clean shaven, with a full head of black hair. He was muscular to such an extent that many would assume he was a professional athlete. Zeke was a weight-lifter with practically no body fat. His muscles were largely the result of good genes; his father, a professional hockey player, played defense for the Boston Bruins.

Zeke and his wife Angie lived in Mason, a small community south of Lansing, Michigan's capital city. He was an attorney, a graduate of Cooley Law School. Peers described Zeke as intelligent but confrontational, thorough but somewhat immature.

Angie Simons was 44, an attractive woman who might be termed striking. She wore her blond hair long and usually sported three rings on each hand. She dressed fashionably but understatedly whenever she was in public. A world-renowned judge of show horses, Angie spent a great deal of time traveling around the country. At home, she volunteered countless hours at the Michigan State University animal barns. She loved animals of all kinds, having decided as a student at MSU to devote her life to the care and protection of animals.

The Simons had no children and lived in a modest ranch home in the country. As respected members of the community, they could be depended upon to support local events and fund-raisers. Each

Sunday, Zeke and Angie sat in the same pew in St. James Catholic Church at the 11 a.m. service.

Angie and Zeke often had long and sometimes intense discussions, bordering on arguments, about whether hunting was a sport. Zeke saw it as a necessary activity to thin the deer herd, while Angie saw no logic in blatantly killing innocent animals living in their natural habitat. Over the years, they had grown to accept each other's philosophies and attitudes, and, even though they were miles apart on this particular subject, they loved each other.

OCTOBER 1

Zeke rose with the 5 a.m. alarm to a crisp and cold morning. There was little, if any, wind and the forecast was for a cold and sunny day. Tommy prepared his traditional farmer's breakfast of French toast, eggs, bacon and hash browns, and the two drank coffee while they ate the hearty meal. Zeke had a feeling that this would be his lucky day. After he dragged the last bite of French toast through the sugary syrup, Zeke began his final preparations before heading out into the darkness.

Zeke layered for warmth and then applied his No Scent. He painted his face and filled his fanny pack with the items needed by any bow hunter: a knife to gut the buck; some rope; identification; and numerous other odds and ends. He made sure he had his tag so that when he bagged his prize buck he could legally wrap it around an antler or leg.

Tommy brought Zeke his bow and a thermos of coffee. After Tommy's annual good-luck wish, Zeke walked into the darkness and began the trek to his blind to await the excitement of sunrise and his new opportunity to bag a prize buck.

As Zeke approached his blind, he was startled by movement in the brush about thirty yards to his right. Thinking it an animal of some sort, he stopped dead, hoping it wasn't a skunk; an upset skunk was the one thing that could really ruin a hunt.

Suddenly, an old man emerged from the brush carrying a rifle and as startled to see Zeke as Zeke was to see him.

"Mornin'," Zeke said. "Where you headed?"

"Not headed anywhere. I'm hunting this area."

Both men straightened up in confrontation. Zeke, wanting to appear dominant, spoke first. "I think you're mistaken about where you're supposed to be. And why've you got a gun on the opening day of bow season?"

The other hunter grunted, "Don't think so. This is my area to hunt. I got here first. I got this here rifle because I'm hunting small game, if it's any of your business."

"You're on private property!" barked Zeke, striking the first blow of the inevitable confrontation.

"I've been hunting here for ten years or so," replied the man, who was probably about 75 years old. He was overweight and grizzly-looking.

"You're on private property, and only I have permission to hunt here," said Zeke sternly.

"You don't know where you are, mister," the old man said derisively. "This is public land — we're within a half-mile of the county line and the creek. You should have studied a map before you headed out."

The hunters stood about five yards apart, neither seeming willing to retreat. The two men held their ground. Turf is as important to a hunter as double-digit gains on the Dow are to a stockbroker.

"Listen, I've been coming here for 20 years," Zeke said, getting riled. "This is private property, and I don't want to get physical, but if you don't leave now, I'll have to bust your ass, understand? Now get out of here!"

"The only one leaving is you. I was here first," countered the angry hunter.

Suddenly it occurred to Zeke that he should use his persuasive skills rather than his strong voice and dominant physical presence to win this skirmish.

"Listen fella, why don't you save yourself some pain, turn around and head north into the federal forest? We could argue all day but we'd ruin the hunt for both of us. I'm not going anywhere. My blind is over there, my bait is down that deer trail, and as I said, if I have to take you out, I'll do it." Zeke removed his hunting knife from his fanny pack, making sure the old man saw his threat. Zeke stood tall and moved closer to the old man. They resembled two rams staking claim to their territory and a ewe.

The old man knew he was no match for the younger and stronger adversary. He took the threat seriously, but he needed to get in the last word. Leaning into Zeke's face, he snarled, "The next time I find you in my hunting area, I won't be using words to settle the argument." The old geezer stood firm for a few seconds, then stepped back four paces, turned, and plodded north.

Zeke's heart beat at a good clip. His anger had once again reared its ugly head; one of these days he supposed he should learn to curb it. Flying off the handle had gotten him into trouble often in his life, but he had never taken seriously the suggestion that he get professional help. He really didn't believe he had that bad a problem.

A half-hour before, he had been heading for what he imagined would be a perfect dawn and the taking of a prize buck. Now, he had won an encounter with a hunter, one with a rifle; the thought crossed his mind that the old man might move behind a tree and put him in the crosshairs of his sight.

Glad the old man was gone, Zeke settled into his blind and tried to forget the confrontation. Inside he was warm, trusting his No Scent to fool the deer into believing no human was near, listening closely for sounds of movement or twigs snapping.

The old man moved to the north but remained on the property. His .22 caliber rifle was the excuse that he was hunting small game and not poaching deer, and he had planned to use Zeke's bait to his advantage. He knew that the bullet from the .22 would have to pierce the deer's heart, with not much room for error. He hoped the deer would be still and his aim would be perfect, his .22 resting in the crook of a tree branch.

Both men waited for their prey. Eventually, patience paid off when a prize buck and two does meandered along the feeding trail, apparently oblivious to humans stalking them.

The 12-point trophy buck with a wide spread walked along the trail, stopping frequently to sniff. He looked left and right, as if expecting to be threatened by man or beast. Zeke decided to wait, bow in hand, until the buck got closer to his blind; the trio were predictably heading for their usual feeding area.

At the moment Zeke drew his bow string taut, the deer scattered into the woods. Disappointed at the missed chance, still Zeke knew that there would be more opportunities to get his trophy. The deer should follow their routine trails, and it was simply a matter of time until another opportunity presented itself.

Over the next hour, Zeke saw other deer, but he decided to wait and use his tag on the 12-point buck. The encounter with the old hunter faded into the back of his mind and he remembered why he loved to hunt. He enjoyed the color changes in the trees, appreciated quiet, and liked the sounds and smells of being in the middle of God's country.

Suddenly the peace was interrupted by a gunshot. Zeke wasn't surprised: opening day for bow season fell during hunting season for small game. It was also possible that a deer hunter was sighting his rifle in anticipation of firearm season. Zeke knew the rifle wasn't a 30-06 or similar firearm, since the sound wasn't loud enough.

He did think of the old man and their confrontation in the pre-dawn hour. The sound came from the north, where the federal forest began. If the shot was fired by the old man, he was probably off the Wilds' property, shooting at a squirrel or rabbit.

At 10 a.m., Zeke decided to go back to the Wilds' home. He'd been up late last night talking with Tommy and he'd gotten up extra early to have breakfast and head out to his blind. Jane and Tommy both had commitments, so Zeke had the house to himself, having been told to make himself at home. When he got back to the house, he stretched out on the couch and took an hour's nap.

As Zeke slept, a 12-point buck was hoisted feet first, to a rafter in Howard Richards' barn, a mile-and-a-half west of Trout City. It was the prize buck, the envy of any hunter. But, this buck had been killed with a .22 rifle. It looked like Howard had gotten away with something. He didn't care much for the government, or for laws or rules. He basically believed that animals were on this earth for man to hunt for pleasure and to eat for survival. Laws simply got in the way — created by bureaucrats in Washington and Lansing.

After a nap, Zeke drove to Trout City, thinking he'd leave the cooking to the short-order cook in Mickey's Bar. He didn't know anyone in Mickey's, and he wasn't one to strike up a conversation with strangers, so he took a seat at a small table about ten feet from the bar and ordered a beer, a hamburger and fries. While he waited for his beer to arrive, he couldn't help overhearing some of the conversations at the bar.

As he dipped fries into a mound of catsup, he couldn't believe his ears. The voice of the old man at the bar was similar, if not the same voice he had heard before dawn. He listened as the old man told those around him about a 12-point buck he had shot near the Wilds' farm that morning. The old man's buddies seemed to enjoy the story, feeling as if they had taken part in the shot that felled the buck.

Zeke felt adrenaline shoot into his stomach as he was overcome with intense anger. He knew that the old man was not near the Wilds' farm, but had been on it, in Zeke's territory, and now he had his deer. Zeke decided right then that the old man would pay a price for shooting his buck.

After the old man left, Zeke approached the bartender. "Does that guy usually brag about shootin' deer out of season?"

"Howard Richards brags about everything," Danny Willard replied. Dan was a middle-aged bartender who knew everybody in Trout City and for miles around. "He's his own man. Laws and rules weren't written for him. He lives in a world all his own."

"Gets away with it, does he?" Zeke asked, shaking his head.

"Most of the time, yeah, guess he does," Dan replied, wiping the bar top. "Couple years back he got pissed off at a bunch of high school kids using mailboxes for batting practice. He hooked up a rig so that when the bat hit the box, it triggered a shotgun aimed right at where the speeding truck would be. That explosion killed two kids."

"He was prosecuted for murder, I assume?" Zeke asked.

"Nope, not around here. That's self-defense, protection of property. Most folks around here were proud of Howard. Nobody would ever stand up to them drunken kids, but Howard figured out a way to get back. Cops and courts weren't doing nothing, so he done it."

"Was there a trial?" Zeke asked, astonished at what he was hearing.

"Nope. Judge gave him a talking-to about finding better ways to settle problems, but he walked free and got pats on the back and a round of applause when he walked out the courthouse door."

"Did the parents of the kids who were killed sue?" Zeke asked.

"No. They didn't have money for lawyers."

"Really?"

"Yeah, that's the way it is around here," Danny replied.

"So, this Howard, when he wants to hunt, he just hunts? When he wants to kill, he just kills?" Zeke asked, taking out some paper and a pen.

"That's right. He lives in the 'County of Howard,'" Danny replied with a smile.

"Howard Richards?" Zeke asked. "That's his name, right?"

"Yeah."

"Where does he live?"

"Peavine Road. Why, you going to go talk to him?" Danny asked.

"Nope, I don't talk to crazy people," Zeke said, writing the name and road on a slip of paper. "I am going to talk to the judge, though. This guy needs to know that this every-man-for-himself style of living went out of business about two hundred years ago."

"I wouldn't cross him if I were you," Dan warned.

"I'm not going to cross him. I'm going to put the law on him." Zeke put the paper and pen in his coat pocket, slid off the bar stool, and walked out the door.

While Zeke was walking to his pickup, bartender Willard called Howard.

"Howie, this is Danny."

"What's the matter? Didn't I pay for my liquor?" Howard asked with a chuckle.

"No, nothing like that. Listen, some guy in the bar overheard you talking about killing that buck. He's says he's going to put the law on you!"

"Thanks for the heads up. By the way, who is he?" Howard asked, now serious.

"I never seen the guy before. He's a bow hunter, and I think he's pissed about you taking the buck. None of my business, Howie, but I'd lay low. I can see the guy out the window now, talking on a cell phone. He's driving a blue Ford pickup. You could get a visit from the cops yet this afternoon."

"Like I say, thanks for the heads-up. Gotta set up."

Just as Howard and Dan finished their call, Zeke connected by cell phone with Judge Patterson of the 91st District Court based in Mancelona. Zeke knew of the judge from his father-in-law who practiced law in Bad Axe.

"Judge, this is Zeke Simons from Mason."

"Simons, huh? Your name sounds familiar. Are you related to Bill Beekins?" the judge asked.

"He's my father-in-law. Matter of fact, I grew up in Bad Axe, and he was the one who convinced me to go to law school. I've always looked up to him. He's told me of his high regard for you."

"Fine man, Judge Beekins. So, what can I do for you?"

"Well, I'm over in Trout City bow hunting. I come up here every year looking to bag a nice trophy. A few minutes ago, in Mickey's Bar, I heard an old man bragging about shooting a 12-point buck. I hardly believe anyone would be so dumb as to admit it, but he was drunk and talking loud and bragging when he said it."

"That was probably Howard Richards," Judge Patterson replied. "Sounds like something he would do."

"Yes, that's the man. I talked to the bartender, who told me he'd set up a rig that killed a couple of kids. Guess a shotgun was positioned in a tree branch over the road, in a direct line with road traffic."

"Yeah, he's a character all right."

"Well, character or not, I'm calling to report the poaching. I don't know where the 12-point buck is, but it's not roaming the land, fair game for bow hunters, I'm sure of that."

"I'll pass the word on to the Cherry County sheriff, Zeke."

"I'd appreciate it, Judge."

When Howard Richards finished talking with Danny Willard, he walked to his barn. As he opened the door; dust particles from hay and the scurrying of critters danced in the rays of light. Howard's eyes followed the light to the shadowy form of the gutted buck hanging from the rafter. Howard admired his buck, and then took a few minutes to set up in anticipation of the law officials. Afterward, he left the barn, stepped up on his porch, and sat in his rocker. As the wood floor creaked beneath the rhythmic movement of the chair, he mentally rehearsed what he would say to the officer. At his feet, Rudy, his German shepherd, waited, seemingly eager to protect him from the commotion that was soon to ensue.

Zeke asked for directions to Peavine Road at a Trout City gas station and then went looking for a sign on a mailbox. After going two-and-a-half miles west on Peavine, he spotted the mailbox and painted in black letters was H. Richards, 16893 Peavine. A small American flag was taped to the silver mailbox with a magnetic "Support our Troops" ribbon attached to the flag. Across from the Richards' home was a large grove of trees.

A couple hundred yards past the mailbox, Zeke pulled into the muddy entrance to a field and parked. He left his pickup and walked through the woods across the road and parallel to Howard's house and barn. He positioned himself so that he could get a good look at how the police would handle this poacher. Zeke was naïve enough to believe that Howard would not notice his truck, nor see him making his way through the woods. Howard spotted both.

13

About fifteen minutes later, a sheriff's vehicle approached. Howard stepped down from his porch and walked toward the vehicle. Two officers got out of the squad car, and the three men talked for about a minute. It appeared that one of the officers was giving Howard quite a talking-to, gesturing forcefully. Then Howard took his wallet out of his back pocket, opened it, and gave some money to one of the officers. Abruptly the three shook hands and the officers got in their squad car and left.

"I'll be!" Zeke whispered. "Richards is paying them off." He took out his cell phone and once again called Judge Patterson.

When the judge answered, Zeke explained what he had seen. "The deputies came, gave him a talking to, and then this Howard guy gave them what looked to be some bills, which was probably 'hush money.' The cops shook his hand and left."

"Hmmm, that's strange. I wouldn't expect that from the sheriff's deputies," replied the judge.

"The bartender told me this was sort of the County of Howard Richards, and I guess he was right," Zeke said, becoming very agitated. "If this is what happens when a hunter reports poaching, there's no law in this county."

"That's not true, Zeke," the judge replied. "There is law and it is enforced."

"Not according to what I just saw," Zeke sputtered. "Looks like I need to take the law into my own hands."

"I wouldn't advise that, Zeke," the judge said sternly. "Count to ten, and try to relax a bit. Leave it to me; I'll see that justice is done. I'll tell the prosecutor to handle this."

"They didn't even look in his truck or his barn," Zeke hissed, getting more upset. "They made no effort whatsoever to find the dead deer!"

"There must be an explanation, Zeke," the judge replied, trying to sound reassuring. "Whatever you do, don't get involved. Leave it to me. OK?"

Zeke was seeing red by now and wasn't talking or thinking clearly. "I'm calling the DNR. Maybe they'll take me seriously."

"I'm telling you; don't try to do anything about this, Zeke. You're angry and justifiably so, but let it go, or at least get out of the area until you simmer down."

Zeke hung up on the judge, put his cell phone in his pocket and returned to his truck where he looked up the toll-free number to report poaching. When he called he got a recording and left his message: "A guy by the name of Howard Richards, who lives on Peavine Road west of Trout City, shot a buck this morning with a .22 rifle. He was bragging about it in Mickey's Bar around noon today. Deputies came to his house, but they didn't search or arrest him. They did nothing. I'm a taxpaying citizen, and I want this handled immediately!"

About a minute after Zeke snapped his phone shut, it rang.

"Mr. Simons?"

"Speaking."

"This is Officer Cobb of the DNR poaching hotline. We have your message and an officer is on his way to the Richards' home. Thanks for your call."

"Thank you."

"You're welcome, and we appreciate your reporting of the poaching activity. We'll contact you with the results of our investigation."

"Thank you, sir," Zeke said with respect.

Taking his rifle this time, Zeke walked back to his hiding place to watch for the inspection and observe the arrest that was sure to follow.

This was not the first time Michigan Department of Natural Resources Conservation Officer Tim Turner had paid Howard a visit. Officer Turner expected Howard to be home, to be calm, and to be unemotional, at least during any initial dialogue. After he pulled the dark green pickup with the DNR decal on the driver's door into the driveway, Officer Turner wrote in his log book, "1:37, arrived at Howard Richards' residence to investigate poaching."

At the same time Officer Turner pulled onto Richards' property, a DNR dispatcher in Lansing noted that the GPS-equipped vehicle had stopped just off Peavine Road outside of Trout City.

As the DNR truck stopped, Rudy rose from his place on the porch and barked as he bounded toward the vehicle. Using the bull horn without exiting, Officer Turner commanded, "Call him off, Howie. I'm here to talk to you."

"Rudy, come here, boy. Come here," Howard bellowed, as he stepped off the porch. "Nothing to get upset about, boy." Rudy had learned that not to obey meant punishment, so he cowered a bit and walked around, quiet, but ready to attack if he heard the command, "Rudy, sic'em."

Once Rudy backed off, Officer Turner got out of his vehicle. Howie Richards appeared to present a physical threat to no one. He was fat and slow, and while he looked strong, he was weak, old, and wore a dirty shirt under blue denim overalls.

"You don't often stop by just to say hello," Howard said, shielding his eyes from the bright sun. "There must be something on your mind."

"I need to look in your barn, Howie," Tim said with authority. Rudy started to bark again.

"Shut-up!" Howard shouted as if the dog was deaf. Howard turned back to the Officer and asked, "Look in my barn? Why's that?"

"Word has it you were drinking at Mickey's and started bragging about your kill. I'm here to follow up on a complaint."

"I done nothing wrong," Howard exclaimed as the two walked to the front of the barn, about one hundred feet from the farmhouse.

"I'll be the judge of that. Open the barn, Howie," Officer Turner demanded.

As Howard slowly opened the door, the rusty hinges gave off a high-pitched sound, causing several mice and an owl to scatter.

Officer Turner looked straight ahead, and from the rafters, tied with thick rope, hung a gutted 12-point buck.

From across the road, Zeke Simons, using binoculars, also saw the buck.

"There's no tag on this deer. I need to see your tag," Officer Turner demanded.

"Aw, come on," Howard complained. "You know I got it."

"Procedures, Howie. I've got to cover the bases. You know that."

"It's inside," Howard said, pointing toward his old, run-down farmhouse.

"Get it. I'll wait," Officer Turner replied.

As Howard turned and slowly walked out of the barn toward his house, his six-year old grandson Taylor stood at the dining room window, looking out at the officer. The cool air outside and the warm air from his lungs formed condensation so that Taylor saw the officer through the fogged glass, as someone with cataracts would see him. This was not the first time that Taylor had been frightened when he saw the police. The last time the police had come to the farm, the officer took his grandpa away, not knowing a young boy was in the farmhouse. Taylor had been there alone till early the next morning, when his father, on his way home from his four-to-midnight shift, stopped to pick him up.

Taylor was a good boy — shy, intelligent, a good reader, but sometimes a discipline problem. This stemmed more from his desire to control his environment so he could have his way than blatant disrespect for elders. Taylor was about as normal a six-year-old as one could find. Everybody liked Taylor. He was, as a neighbor lady called him, a sweet kid.

Howard suddenly realized that the pickup he noticed was still parked in the tractor entry path to his south woods. He quickly scanned the area across the road and caught a glimpse of a man holding a rifle trying to hide behind some trees.

Howard entered the house through the back door, took his tag out of his hunting jacket in the entry, and then walked into the living room. Taylor had moved away from the window and was pretending to watch TV. Drawing the curtain back, Howard saw a man leaning on a huge tree due south of his barn. He didn't recognize the man, but Howard figured the guy wasn't there to help matters. Howard retrieved his rifle from a closet off the kitchen and went back outside. With his rifle in one hand and a small white envelope in the other, he sauntered toward the barn.

When Zeke saw the white envelope he said to himself, "There's another payoff. This guy buys his crimes!"

Howard walked into the barn. Zeke couldn't see Howard, the buck, and Officer Turner who was inspecting the buck. From across the road Zeke imagined the two to be in a heated conversation.

"I'm going to have to arrest you, Howard," Officer Turner said with authority.

"Oh, no you won't," Howard responded, grasping his rifle with both hands and aiming it at the officer.

"Put that thing down. Now listen, this buck has been shot with a rifle, and it's hanging in your barn. It doesn't look good for you, Howard. We all know your track record on breaking the law."

Howard lowered his rifle slightly. "I hit the deer with my truck. I didn't poach and you can't prove I did!"

"You've gotten away with this sort of thing for too long."

"Well, I'm going to get away with it again. Get off my property!" Howard demanded, as his rifle rose again and he walked backward to the opening of the barn.

"I'm not leaving without you, Howard. You're under arrest for poaching."

Zeke, now out of control, placed his rifle onto his shoulder sighted in on Howard Richards' back. He fired one shot, but Richards didn't fall. Zeke was so emotionally over-wrought, his heart racing, blood pressure sky-high, and feeling disoriented, that he had a sense of being in a dream state.

Suddenly, unseen by Zeke, Officer Turner stepped back, spun to his left and fell onto the dusty barn floor. Howard Richards hurried out of the barn and went to Officer Turner's vehicle. Howard then went to his house, put his tag back in his hunting jacket pocket and placed it on the hook behind his dining room door. Taylor was still watching television and apparently hadn't heard the gunshot.

19

Howard called for him and Rudy to get into his sedan, then sped east toward town.

Zeke was in another world emotionally; it seemed that he had temporarily blacked out. In laymen's terms, he had lost it mentally, and was troubled with irrational thoughts. In psychiatrist's terms, he may have been temporarily insane.

Zeke remained hidden until Howard and his grandson were out of sight. He then ran up to the barn, rifle in hand, and entered. Seeing his prize buck hanging from the rafter, and Officer Turner prone on the floor, he panicked and ran out of the barn to his pick-up. He started his vehicle, backed onto Peavine Road and drove off. He was scared and mentally out of control.

At a remote spot on the way to town, Howard stopped beside the road, and when no one was looking, he removed the silencer and discarded the rifle, throwing it into thick brush by the creek where he was sure no one would find it. Taylor watched the whole thing, but his fear of the leather belt meant he would never tell a soul what his grandfather Richards had just done.

Zeke slowly came to his senses, with little memory of what had happened in the last half hour. He drove to the Wilds' home and found neither of them back from their day's journey. He lay on the couch, but couldn't relax, and all he did was play back in his mind the events of the past few hours. He couldn't accept that he had killed a conservation officer, the very man who was working to investigate the poaching claim.

On the way to Harriett Gunderson's home, Howard had a man-to-man talk with his grandson. "Did you see the officer back at the house?"

"Yeah."

"Did you hear a gunshot?"

"No." Taylor had learned to lie, or to tell the truth based on what his grandpa wanted to hear, because not to do so brought painful consequences. He and Rudy had quickly learned that you do what you can to survive and to be comfortable. His grandpa's belt was representative of a few generations back, when fear of the leather strap helped keep children in line with expected behavior.

Howard ordered Taylor to stay in the car while he went into Harriett's home. Her door was always open, and he found her asleep on the couch in her living room. He went quietly into the kitchen and moved the hands on the kitchen wall clock up to 5:15. Then he went back to Harriett. "Hey, Harriett, get up old gal. It's coming up to dinnertime."

Harriett slowly came to, moaned, coughed, and sat up on the couch. "Can't quit drinking, Howie."

"I know. It's a problem," Howard replied. "You'll lick it someday." Harriett just shook her head, reached for a couple of Tylenol, and downed them with some bottled water.

"Come on, I'll take you to dinner."

"Lunch or dinner?" Harriett asked.

"Lunch? It's almost dinner time," Howard replied. "Let's go to the café in town."

Harriett stood up and got her bearings. She went into the bathroom, splashed water on her face, ran a comb through her hair, and came to the kitchen. She looked at the clock and shook her head. "Naps are getting longer and longer. Sometimes, I don't even know where I am, what day it is, what time it is…" Her voice trailed off, and she started to cry.

"Come on out in the fresh air, Harriett. Taylor and I are going to take you to the café. You need to get out. Come on." The two closed the door behind them and walked to the car. Howard motioned for Taylor to get in the back seat so Harriett could sit up front.

"Hi, Miss Harriett," Taylor said.

"Hi, honey," she replied with a slight nod. "Shouldn't you be in school?"

Before Taylor could answer, Howard spoke up. "He's been to school, Harriett. I told you, it's practically time for dinner."

Taylor didn't understand what his grandpa was saying, but he knew enough to keep quiet.

While Harriett, Howard, and Taylor were in the Fish Hook Café, Lillian Adams, a neighbor, came to Harriett's home for a visit. She knocked on the side door, not really expecting Harriett to answer. Lillian knew she was probably asleep, or at least groggy, but, to be courteous, she knocked and looked in the door window. She glanced toward the kitchen and didn't see anyone, so she walked in and noticed the clock; it was set ahead by almost two hours. She knew the electricity had not gone off in the neighborhood. Further, she knew that the power was on in Harriett's house and that the clock on the wall was not battery-powered, because a chord dangled from it to a wall socket below.

As Lillian walked into the living room to see if Harriett was there, she saw that the digital clock in the VCR was on time. She called out thinking Harriett might be somewhere else in the house, but there was no response. She made a quick run-through, hoping not to find her friend unconscious on the floor. Harriett was not in the house, so Lillian left.

After Howard, Taylor, and Harriett finished their meal, the three took a long drive, Howard suggesting they needed to see the beauty of nature on this sunny fall day. After a color tour of sorts, Howard drove Harriett home. While she was hanging up her coat in the hall, Howard turned the kitchen clock back to 4:40. Harriett came into the kitchen as he was putting the clock back on the wall.

"What are you doing?" Harriett asked.

"Your clock was off by a few minutes, is all," Howard replied. "Just don't want you to be cheated out of living for a few minutes."

"That clock has always been on time," Harriett replied. "I can't imagine why it would slow a bit." She thanked Howard for her meal, saw him to the door, and returned to her almost-empty bottle of gin. She turned on the television and watched a bit of "Dr. Phil." Ironically, he was counseling an alcoholic.

The fact that Officer Turner had not called in all afternoon wasn't unusual. He may have been cruising, checking out hunters, or visiting weigh-in sites, and the dispatcher had had no reason to contact him. However, when Officer Turner didn't return at the end of the shift, the base operator got on the radio and tried to reach him. Hearing no response, she ordered another officer to check Turner's last known place of assignment — the home of Howard Richards on Peavine Road.

When Conservation Officer Virginia Faccio arrived at the Richards farm, she thought it odd that the DNR vehicle door stood open when no one was around. She was familiar with the area, the owner, and his dog, so it was eerie that nothing was moving. The area was deserted except for the dark green pickup with the open door.

Ginny knocked on the house door, expecting no one to be home. When no one answered, she walked to the barn, discovered the body of her fellow officer motionless on the barn floor, and realized she was at a crime scene. Trained to act on her instincts, she first felt for a pulse in his neck. Finding none, she returned to her vehicle to call in the suspicious death of Officer Turner and to request emergency vehicles. She did not go back to the barn; there was nothing she could do, and the last thing she wanted to do was disturb evidence. Her job for the moment was to await emergency personnel and to guide them to the body of Officer Turner. Presently, she heard sirens in the distance; it would be only a matter of minutes before Howard Richards' farm would be a flurry of activity.

Ginny Faccio would be the Conservation Officer who would take over the case following the death of Tim Turner. Howard was a marked man in the eyes of the Department of Natural Resources. He was well known to DNR detectives, who had first encountered

Howard when he lived in the western Upper Peninsula. Twenty years before, he had been the leader of the North Shore Bear Houndsman Association. Then he had been arrested for poaching, and the judge told him that if he was ever arrested for poaching again, he would lose all hunting privileges. Losing the right to hunt would be devastating to Howard. Not only did he enjoy the kill, but he ate what he killed, or so the DNR officials believed. As a result, the call from Zeke Simons regarding Howard's poaching was seen as an opportunity to get one step ahead of a criminal, to end his flaunting of game laws.

At 4:45 in the afternoon, Howard Richards' house, yard, and barn resembled a circus midway. Emergency vehicles were everywhere, lights flashed, and reporters and television crews set up wherever the police would allow. Everyone present had a responsibility and followed through with precision.

A state police detective was stringing yellow tape while a second collected evidence. A police photographer snapped shots one after another. Two emergency medical technicians checked for signs of life in the victim. Finding none, they stepped away, for the body needed to remain where it was found in order for the crime scene investigators to do their work. Officer Turner lay on his back, as if he had been pushed backward. It was as if someone had simply slammed a fist into his chest, and he had fallen down. Ironically, had he been alive, he would have appeared to be looking up at the 12-point buck hanging from the rafter.

Immediately after the body of Tim Turner was inspected by the medical examiner, the body was removed and taken to the county morgue for autopsy. Unfortunately, the movements of the officers and medical personnel in the barn hindered discovery of key evidence on the barn floor. The first EMT to arrive at the body mentioned to Officer Faccio that he noticed what appeared to be letters formed in the dirt of the barn floor: what he saw looked like two Os and a P by the officer's right hand. There were other shapes that also looked like letters, but the EMT dismissed them as random hand movements made by the victim prior to death. The markings, if any existed were brushed out as other authorities inspected the body and prepared it for removal. Although the markings were obscured, the EMT vividly recalled what she had seen.

One of the investigating officers found two rifle bullets, drew a chalk circle around them behind and to the left of the officer's body, and carefully lifted them into an evidence bag. The bullets appeared clean, which meant that if they were from the rifle that killed the officer, there would probably be no bullet fragments in the body to compare to a rifle through a bore analysis.

All of Officer Turner's clothes and personal effects were tagged as evidence. His truck was impounded and eventually hauled away, with everything in it left as it had been found when the authorities arrived.

About 5 p.m., Howard Richards pulled into his driveway with Taylor still in the back seat. Deputy Peggy Sell walked over to the sedan and introduced herself to Taylor, then drove him away in her unmarked car.

Once Taylor was out of sight, a Sheriff's Deputy read Howard Richards his rights and arrested him for murder. Howard resisted the arrest over and over saying, "I didn't shoot anyone. I wasn't here!"

"A DNR Officer was shot on your property, in sight of a gutted buck in your barn, and you claim you weren't here?" the deputy asked.

"I was here till about three-thirty or so, and then Taylor and I went to visit my friend Harriett. I took Taylor and Harriett out to dinner."

"Harriett?"

"Harriett Gunderson, from town."

"Where did you take her to dinner?" asked the deputy.

"The Fish Hook Café — where else is there to go for dinner?" Howard responded sarcastically.

"Can anyone at the Fish Hook vouch that you were there?"

"Betty was the waitress. I guess she could."

At 5:30 p.m., a deputy in a squad car pulled up in front of Harriett's home. Several knocks on the door brought no response. The officer had turned to leave when he heard, "You want something?"

He turned back to the door. "Are you Harriett Gunderson?"

"Yes."

"I'm Officer Gerald Jones, and I'd like to talk to you for a few minutes. May I come in?"

"Guess so." Harriett opened the screen door and the officer entered. She asked if he wanted a beer or something, but he declined. She sagged onto the coach, and he sat in a chair.

"Miss Gunderson, did you talk with Howard Richards this afternoon?"

"Yes. I went with him and his grandson to have dinner."

"How long ago was that?" Officer Jones asked, writing her responses on his notepad.

"About two hours ago, maybe."

"So, you went to dinner around three o'clock. A little early for dinner, wasn't it?"

"Well, you know, I thought so, but Howard said it was time for dinner."

"I see. Where did you go to eat?" Officer Jones asked.

"The Fish Hook Café."

"Can anyone vouch for you?"

"What does 'vouch' mean?" Harriett asked looking confused.

"Was there anyone at the café who saw you, Howard, and his grandson, who would swear they saw you there?"

"The waitress, for sure."

"Did Howard say anything about an officer stopping at his farm earlier this afternoon?" the Deputy asked.

"No. Is he in trouble again?" Harriett asked.

"We don't know yet. But a DNR officer was shot in his barn."

"Shot? Was he killed?" Harriett asked, greatly concerned.

"Yes, ma'am."

"Howard didn't do it," Harriett quickly responded. "He's an old man, and he makes some stupid mistakes, but he wouldn't kill anyone."

"You seem pretty sure of yourself," Officer Jones replied.

"Fifth Commandment," Harriett said. "Howard's big on the commandments. He was raised in a fundamentalist church and those commandments were branded into his mind at a young age. I can see why he's feared, and he's not a nice guy, but he wouldn't kill anyone."

"He supposedly killed those kids who were hitting mailboxes," Officer Jones reminded Harriett.

"No, he didn't. That shotgun was rigged to damage the car. You know, you damage my property, and I'll damage yours. But he never meant any harm to those boys."

"I appreciate your answering my questions," Officer Jones said as he rose to leave.

While the crime scene officers finished up their work, Officer Faccio officially took custody of the deer carcass, assigning it a DNR case number and completing the initial paperwork. Howard gave Ginny the same story he had given Officer Turner. He didn't shoot the buck, but he hit it with his truck, and he'd waited for the hunter who did shoot it to happen by and claim it. Officer Faccio explained that, in not calling the authorities for permission to tag the deer, he had violated the law.

When Ginny called her supervisor to report what she knew of the situation, simply hearing the name Howard Richards in connection with suspicion of poaching was enough for him to prioritize the case. He instructed Ginny to personally transport the deer to the DNR lab on the MSU Campus in East Lansing.

Before leaving for East Lansing, Ginny called the director of the Department of Natural Resources and asked that their top specialist be assigned the responsibility for the necropsy on the deer and to do it as soon as possible. The Director knew about Howard Richards too.

"I want this guy, Ginny. I want him real bad. We're sure he's poaching a variety of animals, and with this poached deer, I think we can put him away for a while. I've given the go-ahead for priority work, so please proceed as soon as you can."

The director assigned Dr. Tatroe of the DNR Wildlife Division to do the necropsy immediately. Dr. Tatroe was an excellent veterinary specialist, Doctor of Veterinary Medicine, with a PhD. in Epidemiology. He had been with the department for twelve years, and part of his job was providing expert testimony on high-level state and national cases.

Late in the afternoon, Zeke called his wife. Angie heard a note of satisfaction in Zeke's voice as he said, "Finally got him."

"Whatever are you talking about?" Angie asked.

"Every year, I sit in my blind. Every year I watch for a big buck to come into view. Every year I play by the rules, buy my tag, obey every rule of the DNR. And this year, this old man shoots my buck with a firearm!"

"But, it's not rifle season," Angie replied, shocked that someone would boldly shoot a buck during bow season.

"When you're a poacher, there is no season," Zeke snarled.

"But what do you mean, you 'got him,' Zeke?" Angie asked.

"I saw this guy downing shots of whiskey and bragging in Mickey's Bar about bagging a huge buck. He said it was down by the creek on Tommy's land. That's where I was, and I heard the shot; I just didn't think he was picking off my buck."

"Ok, Zeke, but what do you mean you 'got him'?" Angie persisted, fearing a response that might change her life forever.

"I looked out the window of the bar when he left, saw him get into a pickup, took down the license number, and called the cops. Actually, I called Judge Patterson. I've had it with these poachers. Not only are they criminals, but they steal the sport from us bow guys."

"That's all you did — call the judge?" Angie asked.

"Yeah, what did you think I meant? I would have liked to put an arrow between his eyes, but I'll let the law do that. That's what they're paid to do."

"Did you give the judge your name?"

"Yeah. I've got nothing to hide."

Angie paused, took a deep breath and said, "Honey, the county sheriff called looking for you. They got your name from the DNR."

"Probably wanted to tell me they arrested the poacher."

"Not quite. They want you to contact them as soon as you can. A conservation officer was found dead in a farmer's barn in Cherry County. They want to talk to you."

Once again, Zeke felt the adrenaline flow into his stomach. He felt a little light headed, like he had years before during anxiety attacks. After a telling pause, he said, "I'll call and then let you know what happens. I may have lost it, honey. I could be in a lot of trouble."

Angie was afraid Zeke's temper would be his downfall; she just didn't know when or where. She had pleaded with him to get professional help, but he wouldn't hear of it.

Lou Searing was 64, had male-patterned baldness, was slightly overweight after retiring from almost 30 years of jogging and competing in hundreds of road races, biathlons and triathlons. Lou had a moderate-to-severe hearing loss as a result of having measles as a two-year-old, so he wore two hearing aids. He went to public schools, graduating from Grand Haven High School, attended Alma College, and then earned BA and MA degrees from Western Michigan University and a doctorate from the University of Kansas. In 1997 he had retired from the position of State Director of Special Education.

In the mid-1990s, Lou developed an interest in criminal investigations. While he and a good friend had been on a cross-country motorcycle ride, his buddy was stabbed to death at a campground in Tennessee. Lou was determined to find who murdered his friend. Eventually he solved the crime, and since then he had accepted other opportunities to solve difficult murder cases, mainly in Michigan.

Lou lived with his wife Carol, also retired from a distinguished career in special education, in their dream home on the shore of Lake Michigan south of Grand Haven. They would walk along the Lake Michigan beach nearly every evening in the summer, and often in spring and fall when weather permitted. They were familiar figures to most of the cottage owners up and down the shore.

"Ready to walk on the beach?" Carol asked.

"Be right there!" Lou replied.

As soon as Samm, the Searing's golden retriever, heard the word "beach," she got all excited. Chasing sticks had been a joyful activity before Samm had intercepted a murderer's bullet meant for Lou a couple of years ago. Now, Samm had an artificial leg, so she preferred dry-land walks, not having much interest in walking in the sand.

On occasion, Samm would hobble down to a Red-Flyer wagon Lou and Carol left down on the shore, and ride along the shoreline. She would have loved to chase seagulls and retrieve sticks but she seemed resigned to that reality. On this evening in early October, Samm rested on the sun porch, ready to watch Lou and Carol walk down the beach, hand-in-hand, letting the cooling waters of Lake Michigan wash over their feet and ankles.

While Lou was taking off his shoes for the walk and Carol was in the house getting a hat and jacket, Lou's cell phone rang. He took it from his pocket and answered, "Lou Searing."

"Mr. Searing, this is Zeke Simons. I'm an attorney from Mason, Michigan, and I'm up in the Trout City area, hunting. I've a lot of respect for you."

"Nice of you to say," Lou replied. "What's on your mind?"

"I'm calling to see if you would be willing to investigate a murder up in Trout City."

"Sorry, Zeke, but I retired from murder investigations last year. I write books from my imagination now."

"I understand, but I'm in a real jam up here," Zeke replied.

"How's that?" Lou asked.

"I'll probably be accused of killing a conservation officer. Because of the circumstances, I'm very much a suspect."

"That's too bad," Lou said. "Did the officer have a family?"

"Yes he did, a wife and a son. The son is disabled and is well-known in Special Olympics."

"That touches me, Zeke. I served on the Special Olympics Michigan Board of Directors for six years. Let me think about this for a while. I'll see if I can help."

"Thank you very much."

"What do you know about the murder?" Lou asked.

"A conservation officer was shot while investigating my complaint of poaching. I called Judge Patterson in Mancelona, but that didn't help."

"I see. Judge Patterson is highly-respected. Are there any suspects besides you?"

"Yeah, the poacher!" Zeke said with emphasis.

"What's his name?"

"Howard Richards. I've learned that he pretty much does what he wants, with little or no regard for the law."

"I see. That can be dangerous."

"Exactly."

"Now, I have to ask: did you kill the officer?" Lou inquired.

"I was a bit out of control, Mr. Searing. I let my anger build up for a long time, and I didn't count to ten or take a walk. I think I'm in big trouble, and I need you, sir."

"With all due respect, you didn't answer my question," Lou replied. "Did you kill anyone?"

"As I said, I was out of control. I fired a shot in the direction of the barn where the officer was investigating the poaching, but I don't think I hit him. I need help, Mr. Searing."

"What on earth did you fire a shot for?" Lou asked.

"I was so upset with that poacher and his paying off the authorities, I just lost it. I wanted to scare him is all, or I think that's what I wanted to do."

"But your bullet may have struck the officer?"

"Maybe, I don't know."

"Did you hear any other shot?" Lou asked.

"I don't recall hearing any. This is like a dream. I'm not sure what I did or saw or heard."

"Let me talk to my wife. If I agree to take the case, I can be there tomorrow," Lou replied.

"Ok, thanks. I really appreciate it."

"Zeke, between now and when I get there, don't talk to anybody. Don't say a word."

"My wife said the sheriff wants me to call him."

"Not a word, Zeke. It's probably a good idea to contact him, but I mean it, name, rank, and serial number — that's it."

"But that will make me look guilty," Zeke protested.

"Anyone you tell your story to can take those words and hang you from a tree on the way out of Dodge."

"Ok, I understand." The two men finished their conversation and Lou put his phone on his belt clip.

Carol emerged from the house, took Lou's hand, and they began their walk along the shore. After about ten minutes of quiet, Carol asked, "Who was on the phone?"

"An attorney from Mason," Lou replied thoughtfully.

"What did he want?" Carol asked.

"He's in trouble. He thinks he's a suspect in the murder of a conservation officer up north."

"What happened?" Carol asked.

"I'm not quite sure, but it has to do with poaching and as I said, the murder of a conservation officer."

"I guess it'll take these people a long time to understand that you've retired from investigating murders," Carol said.

"Yeah, it will."

"It's always something, isn't it?" Carol asked, shaking her head.

"Yeah, this conservation officer had a disabled son who is active in Special Olympics. I would like to try and help, but..."

"Then go help," Carol said.

"But I agreed to retire from this stuff," Lou replied, shocked that Carol would support another investigation. "It is a promise I made to you last year."

"Yes, and I love you for it, but solving these murders is what you do, Lou. It's what makes you happy and gives meaning to your life. I was selfish in asking you to stop what you love to do. Tell you what: I'll go to Kansas and visit my friend Mary Lou and spend some time with my brother and his family. You can call every day and let me know you're okay. I'll worry, but at least I won't be here thinking about the danger all the time and missing our walks on the beach."

"You're sure?" Lou asked, surprised that the door was still open to investigative work.

"I'm sure," Carol replied, giving Lou's hand a squeeze.

Samm barked in the distance from the porch.

"So, where did this murder happen?" Carol asked.

"Near Trout City, up in Cherry County. By the way, who will take care of Samm and the cats when I go up north?" Lou asked.

"Sue from next door will help, I'm sure. Sue thinks Luba and Millie are her cats as much as they're ours."

"Then I guess I'll start on the case," Lou said, glad to be getting involved once again.

"And I'll get a reservation for a flight to Kansas City," Carol replied.

"Tell you what; I'll leave the Harley home and drive the car. That'll put your mind at ease a bit."

"Sounds good."

Lou and Carol walked back to their home, talking about this and that and watching the sun sink toward Wisconsin, creating a marvelous pastel watercolor painting on water and sky. Before going up to the back door, they stopped, faced the glorious sunset, and gave each other a hug. It was a most meaningful ritual. Their love was deep, the envy of many couples their age. They had been through a lot together, and they valued each day that was theirs to share.

Samm wagged her tail to say that she was happy to see them. Lou and Carol petted her and gave her a good brushing.

After talking with Lou, Zeke dialed the Cherry County Sheriff.

"Cherry County Sheriff's Office, Deputy Wallace speaking."

"May I please speak to the Sheriff?" Zeke asked nervously.

"Who's calling?"

"Zeke Simons."

"Is he expecting your call?"

"Yes, he is."

Within a minute, Sheriff Larry Sherman was on the line. "Mr. Simons?"

"Yes. I called home and my wife said you wanted to talk to me."

"That's right. I understand you reported a poaching to Judge Patterson?"

"That's right."

"You accused Howard Richards of shooting a buck, correct?" the sheriff asked.

"That's right. He was bragging about it, standing drunk in Mickey's Bar around noon."

"A conservation officer was shot and killed on his farm when he went out to investigate," Sheriff Sherman replied.

"I'm sorry to hear that, Sheriff," Zeke said, sounding remorseful.

"We need you to come in and talk with us, Mr. Simons."

"Come in for what?" Zeke asked, becoming defensive. "All I did was report a poaching."

"That's the way it appears, but we need to ask you a few questions," the sheriff replied.

"I've talked to a friend, and he advises me not to say anything."

"Not say anything about what?" the sheriff asked. "Thought all you did was report a poaching. He doesn't want you to say you reported a poaching?"

"I'm just telling you what he advised."

"Sounds like you're hiding something, and that only makes me real curious. Understand?" Zeke didn't respond. "You need to come in for more questions, Mr. Simons," the sheriff stated again.

"Not going to do it."

"Not going to do what?" the sheriff asked.

"I'm not coming in."

"Well, that's interesting. You've got something to tell me that you're holding back, and now you're not cooperating. Before you dig your hole any deeper, I suggest you tell us where you are and either ride in with us or voluntarily drive here."

"Have you arrested Howard Richards yet?" Zeke asked.

"Now you're a reporter?" the sheriff replied sarcastically.

"He shot a deer. I'm sorry the conservation officer was killed, but the law is the law, and Richards should have been arrested by now!"

"It seems to me you don't have the roles straight, Mr. Simons. I'm the sheriff. I'm responsible for law and order in this county. I don't need a lecture on what I can or can't do. I'm telling you to get in here, or I'll get a warrant for your arrest. For now, you've got a choice. If you keep this up, I'm coming for you."

Zeke had a flashback to a Michigan State football game the previous year. He had stepped outside Spartan Stadium to get some fresh air and walk a bit because people were all bunched together under the stands smoking. He had not seen the sign that said he couldn't be readmitted without a ticket; a stub didn't count — he needed to have a fresh, unused ticket. When he tried to get back in, he was refused, and he went berserk. He wasn't arrested, but he came close to it, drawing the attention of campus police and stadium security. Now, again, he found himself cornered by someone in authority.

"Sheriff, I'll be there as soon as I can."

The sheriff gave him directions, hung up the phone, and waited for Zeke to show up.

A half-hour later, Zeke pulled up outside the Cherry County Sheriff's Office. The sheriff's name appeared beside the front door in bold letters: Lawrence C. Sherman. Zeke took a deep breath and walked in. The reception area presented a thick glass divider between visitors and the deputy on duty.

"Help you?" The Deputy asked.

"I'm Zeke Simons. Sheriff Sherman asked me to come in and talk to him."

"Have a seat. I'll tell him you're here." The deputy disappeared into an inner office.

"Thank you."

In a matter of seconds the deputy reappeared and escorted Zeke into a small conference room. "The sheriff will be right with you." A minute or two later, the sheriff and a plainclothes deputy entered the room. Sheriff Sherman was relatively short, sported a trimmed moustache, and his brown hair was meticulously combed. He had a thick waist, but he was muscular, and anyone would think twice about crossing him. After some introductions, the sheriff began his questions.

"So we can be sure of your identification, please give us your name and address."

"Zeke Simons, 1436 Apple Blossom Lane, Mason, Michigan."

"Mr. Simons, as I understand it, you overheard Howard Richards talking about shooting a deer."

"That's right. He was drinking and bragging about shooting a 12-point buck. I called to report the poaching."

"You called Judge Patterson? You didn't call my office or the DNR?" Sheriff Sherman asked.

"That's right."

"You got a problem with going through channels, Mr. Simons?" the sheriff asked, upset that he had been turfed.

"No, but as an attorney, I know that sometimes going to the top gets action quicker than going through channels."

"It's America. You can call anyone you want, but around here we follow protocol, understand? You got a problem with the law being broken, you go to those responsible for law enforcement. Understand?" Sheriff Sherman looked Zeke in the eye, pointing a stubby finger into his face.

"Sure."

"So my men responded and talked to Mr. Richards."

"Yeah, but did they look in his truck, or in his barn?" Zeke asked.

"Are you suggesting that my men don't know how to investigate poaching?" Larry asked.

"It seems like your officers would look for the deer, not just talk to the man."

"How do you know they didn't look for it?" the sheriff asked.

Zeke remembered the advice from Lou: name, rank, and serial number.

"I need to talk to an attorney," Zeke said.

"There you go again. You said you wouldn't come in for questioning, and now you won't answer my questions. It seems to me that if you call in a poaching, you leave the problem in legal hands and go about your business. You're not acting like an honest man, Mr. Simons."

"Do your men take bribes, Sheriff?" Zeke asked suddenly.

"What do you mean by that?" the sheriff fired back, taken by surprise.

"I mean, do your men take money to look the other way, or not to look in the first place?"

"Those are pretty strong accusations, Mr. Simons," Sheriff Sherman said sternly. "Do you have any evidence of these claims?"

"Richards gave one of your men some money," Zeke replied.

"According to whom?"

"According to me."

"You were there, is that it?" Sheriff Sherman asked, incredulous. "You were at the scene of the incident?"

"I'm not talking anymore. I want a lawyer."

"Of course you do," Sheriff Sherman said, noting Zeke's response. "You'll need a lawyer, because I'm arresting you for the murder of Officer Turner. You can make a call right after we finish booking you."

"Wait a minute. You can't…"

"Look, if you want to make these decisions, run for sheriff in your own county. Up here, I call the shots, and I make the decisions. Get used to it!" Sheriff Sherman stalked out of the room and went to talk to Howard Richards.

Zeke didn't realize that Howard Richards was in the conference room on the other side of the hall. Sheriff Sherman's interrogation of Howard resembled a couple of good old boys having a beer in a bar.

The Sheriff took out a cigarette, lit it, and drew the smoke into his lungs. He had a murder on his hands, and not a lot of experience in solving one, but he would do his best. He knew how to get votes, and most of his votes came from friends and relatives of Howard Richards. Far from being just an old and cantankerous drunk, Howard Richards was a powerful man in Cherry County.

"What's this about you doing some poaching?" Sheriff Sherman asked.

"Sure, I took the buck. It was a beauty," Howard admitted.

"You shouldn't be doing that Howard," the sheriff stated calmly. Then he bellowed, "But if you're going to do it, at least go home to drink, and brag about it to a relative! Don't go shooting your mouth off in a bar!"

Howard looked at the floor. "I take it somebody heard me?" he asked, knowing that was true from Danny's call.

"Somebody? Well, yeah, an attorney who knows the judge, and, by the way, an attorney who expects action."

"Yeah, yeah, they all do. When you letting me out of here?" Howard asked, becoming a bit impatient.

"We're not. The judge is making sure the law is followed."

"What's that supposed to mean?" Howard asked, knowing full well what the sheriff meant.

"It means this report will be investigated and charges brought against you if we think there is reason to believe the accusation."

"You don't appreciate the tickets for the Policemen's Ball?" Howard asked, winking his left eye.

"You know we do, Howard."

"You also know I don't dance," replied Howard with a smile. "I just pay for the band. You understand?"

"Understood."

"Is somebody taking care of my buck?" Howard asked.

"The DNR has taken it," Sheriff Sherman replied.

"Am I getting the meat?"

"Don't think so. That buck will be gone over with a fine-tooth comb."

"What's that mean?"

"Means a vet with the DNR is going to perform a bunch of tests. They'll know if you shot it with a rifle, or with a bow and arrow, or hit it with your truck. They'll know how it was killed. Trust me, in today's world they'll know more about that deer than you'd ever think they could know."

"All I want to know is, am I getting out of here tonight, Sheriff?" Howard asked.

"Don't think so. We've got a dead conservation officer on your property, and a deer confiscated from your barn. The judge isn't going to want you walking the streets."

"Listen, I didn't shoot the officer," Howard said, raising his voice as he became upset. "I have no high regard for the law, but I don't kill people. You know it and I know it. Do what you need to do — I understand that, but get me Max Bell so he can spring me outta here."

"Bell's your attorney?" Sheriff Sherman asked, surprised.

"Yeah."

"Thought he was retired," the sheriff replied. "He's so old, I'm not sure he can zip up his pants after peein'."

"He's retired, but he still knows how to beat the system. He's got so many judges owing him favors, I'm sure he can cash one in to get me out of here."

"You get a call," replied Sheriff Sherman. "On second thought, why go through procedures? Get outta here. Do your drinking at home, and don't go shooting off your mouth around strangers!" The sheriff pointed to the door.

"Thanks, Sheriff. If you need more tickets sold to the Policemen's Ball, let me know." Howard stood up, put on his hat, and walked out of the sheriff's office, smiling.

Through the bars in his cell, Zeke watched Howard get into his pickup and drive away. Zeke was furious. Here he was, spending the night in a jail cell, while a poacher and a murderer walked out a free man.

Zeke got permission from the sheriff to call Angie. She would be upset, but she would know how to proceed.

"It's me, honey," Zeke said.

"Oh, thank God! I have been so worried."

"Yeah, I know. Well, this mess is turning real ugly."

"What does that mean?"

"They've arrested me on suspicion of murder."

"Oh, my God!" Angie exclaimed. "Are you going to be okay?"

"Oh, yeah, procedures, is all. I called Lou Searing in Grand Haven. I'm hoping he'll come up and investigate this thing, so I'll have an excellent investigator working for me. I have Judge Patterson on my side, and I can't do better than that. I'm in a jam — my own doing, as you can imagine — but…"

"I've a horse show in Cincinnati, but I'm coming up there," Angie interrupted.

"Okay, but there isn't anything you can do. Go to your show. I'll probably be home before you are."

"I'd rather be with you to offer support."

"Okay, but this area is strange, honey. I mean, if you thought living in rural mid-Michigan was a little backward, get ready to go back in time to Dodge City, because these folks don't know they're in the twenty-first century."

"I'll drive up tomorrow."

"This is the only call they will allow me, so please call Tommy and Jane Wilds and explain the situation. They'll be wondering where I am."

"OK, sure."

"I suppose you can find Judge Patterson when you arrive. He's in the courthouse in Mancelona. His secretary will tell you where I am."

"Ok. I love you."

"I love you, too. We'll get through this."

"See you tomorrow."

After calling the Wilds and explaining the dilemma, Angie called her best friend, Tricia Wilson, who came right over to offer support.

"I just know we've got a mess on our hands," Angie moaned. "And we'll probably never recover."

"I'm sure it will all work out in time. Zeke's a smart man," Tricia assured her.

"Smart, yes; mature, no," Angie replied. "I've been worried that his temper would bring him down some day."

"So, he's a suspect in that conservation officer's murder?" Tricia asked.

"Yes."

"He reported poaching, and instead of leaving things up to the law, he decided to get involved. Typical Zeke, always needing to do the work assigned to others."

"That's his nature."

"Yeah, but it was something Zeke said. When he called he said, 'I got him.' He was upset, and he sounded like he wasn't in control."

The two continued talking into the evening. Tricia prepared to leave only after making sure that Angie would call if she needed a shoulder to cry on, or just wanted moral support. The two hugged, and Tricia went home.

OCTOBER 2

Around 9 a.m. Officer Faccio drove into the parking lot of the DNR lab in East Lansing with the deer carcass and the documentation needed to authorize the necropsy. Dr. Tatroe talked briefly with Ginny, accepted the carcass and the paperwork transferring the deer from Officer Faccio to the lab. He already had clearance to make this a top priority.

A case number was assigned, and Dr. Tatroe wasted no time in starting the necropsy. He first did a thorough visual examination of the carcass. He noted the entrance wound on the buck; since it was round and not triangular, he was quite certain the buck had been shot. He also found the exit wound from the bullet. It was relatively small, so he knew the caliber of the rifle was probably .22, rather than a more powerful weapon.

Because Officer Faccio's report noted that the suspect claimed he had hit the deer with his truck, Dr. Tatroe looked for bruises, abrasions, obvious broken bones, or dislocated joints, but he found none. Based on the line of the bullet from entrance to exit, he was able to determine the cause of death: damage to the heart. The deer had probably dropped practically where it was hit, and most likely it had not been able to walk or run more than a few feet. That finding added credibility to his opinion that this deer was not struck by a vehicle.

Dr. Tatroe did note an entry wound caused by an arrow, but that wound wasn't sufficient to bring down the deer. He was quite certain that the arrow had struck the deer after it had died, probably after it had been gutted, because there was little blood at the arrow site in the muscular right chest area. He surmised that either the arrow was a cover-up attempt by the poacher, or the deer might have been hit by a bow hunter. The arrow had done nothing more than puncture the skin of the buck.

Following the visual examination, Dr. Tatroe did a radiological evaluation, which, for practical purposes, allowed him to "look" inside the carcass. Because he knew the route of the missile that killed the deer, he concentrated first on X-rays of the route through the body, looking for any bullet fragments. He knew that the design of modern bullets cause a mushroom effect after the bullet hits its target; the bullet explodes rather than tears a straight path through the deer. But this bullet had been a small caliber, which ripped open the heart, leaving no explosion residue typical of larger-caliber rifles. Dr. Tatroe found no fragments as he looked through the light-encased X-ray viewing device.

Dr. Tatroe completed his necropsy of the deer and began to write up his report. He cited the case number, followed by a detailed report noting substantial anatomical detail, describing what he had observed in his visual inspection of the carcass as well as what he had seen on the X-rays and what procedures he had followed in the necropsy.

His report would initially go to Officer Faccio, and additional copies would be sent to various people within the Department of Natural Resources, as well as to the prosecutor in the jurisdiction where the alleged poaching had been committed. No bullet fragments were found, so there was nothing to send to the state police crime lab.

Dr. Tatroe called his supervisor to report his findings. Following the briefing, the supervisor authorized a call to Officer Faccio. Once she learned the rifle was probably a .22 caliber, Ginny sought a search warrant from the judge.

Finally, Dr. Tatroe sent the DNR Director a short memo, informing him that his directive to handle this case immediately had been followed. Now all that awaited him was a court appearance to testify to his necropsy and subsequent report.

At mid-morning, Lou Searing pulled into Trout City. He got a cup of hot coffee at the Café, along with directions to the Cherry County Sheriff's office. He drove into the small parking lot and went inside.

"Help you?" the deputy on duty asked.

"I'm here to see the sheriff."

"Name, please."

"Lou Searing."

"Is he expecting you?"

"No."

"Have a seat."

In a couple of minutes the deputy returned. "He can see you in about fifteen minutes. Can you wait?"

"Yes, thanks." Beside Lou, on a small lamp table, was the local newspaper with the lead article about the killing of a local conservation officer. He picked it up and began reading:

Conservation Officer Killed In Cherry County

Timothy Turner, a 10-year award-winning conservation officer with the Michigan Department of Natural Resources, was gunned down on the property of Howard Richards yesterday afternoon. Turner was responding to a possible poaching incident when he was shot. There were no witnesses, but police are talking with two men about the incident. Both men are suspects, and one has been charged with murder.

Lou expected that Zeke was the one who had been arrested, but he would confirm this as soon as the sheriff was free. He heard a phone ring. The deputy answered and said to Lou, "Come in. Sheriff Sherman will see you now."

Lou walked into the sheriff's office. The sheriff didn't get up, but simply pointed to the wooden chair across from his desk and said, "Have a seat."

"Thank you. Here's my card; the information will serve as an introduction. You may wish to keep it for future reference." The sheriff took Lou's card and read:

Louis Searing, Private Investigator
Once I accept your case, your problem is mine.
In short order, neither of us will have a problem.
616-555-7612.

"Well, Mr. Searing, we don't get many private investigators up in these parts. What is it that you plan to investigate?" the sheriff asked.

"Seems a conservation officer was killed in the line of duty, and I..."

"Listen, Private Eye, I don't need any help," Sheriff Sherman snapped. "I've the help of my staff, the state police, and the FBI. I got more help than any sheriff could ever hope for."

"You misunderstand. I'm not here to give you any help. My client gets my help."

"Your client?" the sheriff asked.

"Zeke Simons."

"I see. Are you his attorney?"

"Do you see 'Attorney' written on my card?" Lou asked.

"No."

"Well then, guess you should believe what you read."

"It is my understanding that Mr. Simons needs an attorney," the sheriff replied.

"He might, and he probably does," Lou said. "But he also needs me, and I'd like to talk to him."

"Not possible."

"So you do have him in custody?" Lou asked.

"That's right."

"Charged with what?"

"Suspicion of murder."

"Your evidence?" Lou asked.

"He was at the scene of the crime."

"That's it — at the scene of the crime?"

"That's all I need," the sheriff replied. "We have other evidence, but I'm not at liberty to talk about it. Now, if you will excuse me."

Lou took out his cell phone and dialed the number for an Cherry County Judge. "May I speak to Judge Patterson please?" Presently a voice said, "This is Judge Patterson."

"My name is Lou Searing, and I'm sitting in the office of the Cherry County Sheriff. Seems he has jailed a client of mine, Zeke

Simons. I'm a private investigator, not an attorney, but, as I recall, a sheriff needs a bit more evidence than someone's presence at the scene of a crime to arrest a man for murder. Furthermore, I understand there was no arraignment and no communication with your office." There was a pause while Lou listened and Sheriff Sherman moved nervously in his leather chair.

"I see. Well, in the first place, my client needs a good attorney, and secondly, he needs to be released. And if any bond needs to be posted, I have arranged for that as well." There was another pause. Then Lou dropped a bombshell when he said, "Your Honor, doesn't it seem fair that, if Howard Richards was released when the poached deer was hanging from a rafter in his barn, and the conservation officer was shot on Richards' property, that my client should enjoy the same treatment and freedom from incarceration that Mr. Richards now enjoys?" There was another telling pause.

"I'm coming over to get Zeke out of jail," the judge replied. "I don't want you there when this happens. But, I do want to see you and Zeke in my Mancelona office once he is free. I'll see you soon."

"I understand. Thank you, Your Honor." Lou closed his cell phone.

"He's coming over here, I take it," the sheriff said.

"Good listening, and, as you might surmise, he isn't a very happy man."

The Sheriff picked up his phone and said to a member of his staff, "Bring Mr. Simons to the conference room." He put the phone down, picked up Lou's business card, crumpled it up and tossed it into a wastebasket across the room.

"Apparently you down-state folks don't know how we do business up here," the sheriff said sarcastically.

"And apparently you up-north folks don't know much about the Constitution, criminal law, or common sense," Lou fired back. "I'm finished for now, but I'm sure we'll meet again." Lou stood up and left. He had gotten Zeke out of jail, but that was the easy part. Now, he needed to solve the crime.

Judge Patterson drove to the sheriff's office to free Zeke. He knew that if the case came to his court, he would have to excuse himself because he knew Zeke's father-in-law, Judge Beekins. And now he would become an obvious player in the drama.

Sheriff Sherman went out to greet his visitor, "Good morning, Judge."

"Hello, Sheriff."

"What brings Your Honor to my office? Bringing an early turkey for Thanksgiving?"

"I want Zeke Simons released immediately."

"Well, he's a suspect in the murder of Officer Turner; I don't think that's in the public interest, Judge."

"Forget the public interest," Judge Patterson replied. "I want him released this minute."

"Ok, as long as you're willing to be responsible for the man. If he's proven guilty, it is going to be pretty embarrassing for you, Judge."

"I don't recall asking for your advice," Judge Patterson snapped.

"Yes, sir. I'll get him."

About five minutes later, Zeke, in his street clothes and with his personal belongings returned, appeared with the sheriff. "He's all yours, Judge." There were no greetings between Zeke and the judge. It was obvious that Judge Patterson was in no mood for pleasantries.

As Judge Patterson and Zeke walked out of the building, the judge said to Zeke, "Drive your car or truck to my office in Mancelona. It's about a 15-minute drive. I'll meet you there."

"Thank you," Zeke said. As the two vehicles left, Sheriff Sherman shook his head and went immediately to his office to record exactly what had happened and what had been said. He was afraid he would need it in court someday. Sheriff Sherman fully expected Lou Searing to pay off the judge to get Zeke released.

Instead of driving directly to Mancelona, Zeke headed for Peavine Road. He had business to take care of, and seeing the judge could wait, even if he did owe him his freedom.

Wanting to take matters into his own hands, and furious that Howard Richards was released while he was jailed, Zeke was looking for a confrontation. While one voice in his head suggested he calm down, a more powerful voice shrieked that the buck had been denied justice, the conservation officer had been denied his life, and Zeke himself had been denied his freedom. If the cops in this part of the world were corrupt, at least he was willing to right a wrong.

Zeke sped to Peavine Road and then down to the Richards farm. As he pulled into the driveway, Rudy bounded toward the pickup with yellowish teeth showing. Rudy defied Zeke to open the truck door. Howard stood on the porch, smiling at the stand-off. Zeke knew there was no way he would get out of his truck, and Howard would not call off his dog. Zeke reluctantly put his truck in reverse, silently vowed to be back, and headed off to Mancelona and a meeting with Judge Patterson.

Howard went into his house and called the sheriff.

"Yeah, what do you want now?" Sheriff Sherman asked.

"Well, there are some tire tracks that aren't mine that I noticed in the drive and in the grass beside the driveway. If you're looking for a murderer, you just might want to come out and take some photos or make plaster casts. They may be tracks from emergency vehicles, but you never know. The tracks could have come from whoever killed that conservation officer, maybe even from the guy who called the judge on me."

"Too late, Howard."

"I said to come out and take photos and cast," Howard replied with authority.

"We'll come out and take a look. On second thought, I'll ask the state police to come out and collect the evidence."

"That's more like it."

Zeke drove into Mancelona intending to visit the judge as he was directed. As he pulled up to the courthouse, Lou approached him with a hand extended. "You must be Zeke Simons. I'm Lou Searing."

"Thanks for agreeing to help me, Mr. Searing."

As Zeke headed for the front door of the courthouse, Lou said, "Zeke, I need to talk to you."

"I know, but I need to see the judge. He told me to come to his office when I left the jail."

"I'm coming along," Lou said.

"Fine."

The two followed the signs to the office of Judge Patterson. As Zeke opened the door, the receptionist looked up and managed a smile. "May I help you?"

"Yes. Please tell Judge Patterson that Zeke Simons is here to see him."

"Please have a seat. I'll tell him you're here."

"Thank you."

The two men sat on a solid oak bench. Before Lou could ask a question of Zeke, the receptionist approached. "Judge Patterson will see you now."

The men rose and followed her into the judge's office. Once the three greeted each other, the receptionist left, closing the door behind her.

"I was concerned," Judge Patterson began, looking Zeke in the eye. "I asked you to come right to my office, but it took you much more time to drive here than it should have. Did you get your directions confused?"

"No, I knew what I was doing. I just wanted to be alone for a few minutes. I got some gas and drove around for a bit to try and relax, is all. Sorry to cause you concern." The judge looked at Lou which tipped Zeke that an introduction was in order. "Judge Patterson, this is a friend of mine and a very good investigator, Lou Searing."

The two men shook hands, "Pleased to meet you, Lou. Your name is familiar. Didn't you solve the Marina Murders?" the judge asked.

"Yes, my partner and I got lucky on that one," Lou replied humbly.

"I doubt that. Solving any crime is never easy, nor lucky for that matter. At any rate, I'm pleased to meet you."

"The pleasure is mine, Your Honor."

"Is your partner working with you?" the judge asked.

"No, Maggie's not going to be on this case," Lou replied. "She and her husband adopted a boy from Korea, and she's not taking any chances with criminals who might not have her best interests in mind."

"That makes sense. As I recall, she was an important member of your team."

"Most certainly. But, she's only a phone call away."

"I see. Well, welcome to northern Michigan. I'm glad you'll be working on this case."

"Thank you."

"Can I get you gentlemen some coffee?" the judge asked.

"No thanks," both replied simultaneously.

"Well, Zeke, first of all, let me reiterate the respect I have for your father-in-law. He'll be here shortly. He's quite concerned with these developments. He has a great deal of respect and love for you."

"Yes. Judge Beekins is very special to me."

"So — what is going on here, Zeke?" the judge asked.

"Well, like I said on the phone, I heard this guy bragging about taking a buck with a rifle, and I wanted some justice. I called you, and things just sort of escalated."

"Things? What things?"

"I found out where Richards lived and drove out there. I hid in the woods across the road to watch the arrest. Two deputies approached Richards, talked for a minute or two, and then Richards gave them what looked to be money, and they shook hands and left."

"Then what happened?"

"I called you. Then I called the DNR, and they sent an officer out to investigate my poaching claim. At least this guy went to the barn, but Richards went to the house and came out with another envelope and a rifle. He handed the envelope to the officer, and that was the second payoff. I was really upset at this point. A few minutes later Howard calmly walked out of the barn, carrying the same rifle and went to the officer's vehicle for a moment, went into his house, and then came out with a boy and drove away. I went across the road and up to barn, saw the officer lying on the floor and, thinking I had been framed, I ran to my truck and left the area."

"Did you call the sheriff?"

"No."

"No? Was the officer dead or alive when you entered the barn?"

"There was no movement as I recall. I assumed he was dead."

"You didn't fire your rifle, right?"

"I think I did. I wanted to scare Richards but I didn't think I hit anyone. But, I remember firing a shot from across the road. I get so angry about something that I sort of forget, guess my memory just leaves me."

"He was wounded or dead, and you didn't do anything to get emergency personnel and law enforcement on the scene?" the judge asked.

"No, I didn't. Everything was sort of swirling around in my head — sort of like I was living a nightmare."

"Any chance that you might have killed the officer?" the judge asked.

"Of course not! Why would you ask such a thing?" Zeke replied indignantly.

"I got a call from the State Police Crime Lab. The video camera was on in Officer Turner's vehicle, and you were recorded going into the barn and coming out carrying a rifle."

Lou was taking in the first account he'd heard of the incident. He didn't comment or ask questions. He would have time with his client later, but this time belonged to the judge.

"Did you tell anyone what you saw at the Richards farm?" the judge asked.

"No." Zeke was lying, but he remembered Lou's advice to say nothing, and he had said a lot more than that.

"Are you sure?"

"I'm sure."

"Good. Because if the sheriff knows you were at the scene, he can twist and turn that fact, and we've got some bad actors in the county who can squeeze a guilty verdict out of an innocent man. The people sort of bond up here: they take care of their own, and sometimes it gets in the way of the truth."

Zeke felt a rush of adrenaline, and his heart quickened. "What's going to happen now?" Zeke asked.

"What did they arrest you for, Zeke?" the judge asked, though he already knew, having talked to the sheriff and the prosecutor.

"It's all fuzzy, and I didn't have an attorney present, but I guess it was suspicion of murder."

"I see, and they base that on what, Zeke? I thought you called in a possible poaching, and you just said no one knew you were at the Richards' when the shot was fired."

"Judge, this is all like a nightmare. I don't know what is going on. Nothing is making sense to me."

"Zeke, listen to me. You lied to me," the judge replied angrily.

"I..."

"Zeke, you admitted to the sheriff that you saw Howard Richards give an envelope to his men," Judge Patterson explained. "You told the sheriff that you were at the scene, but you just told me that no one knew you were in the vicinity of the Richards home."

Zeke felt a wave of nausea come over him. "I need to get to a bathroom. I'm going to be sick."

"Bathroom's across the hall," Judge Patterson replied. Zeke got up and hurried from the room. The judge picked up his phone. "Security? Don't let anyone leave the courthouse till I contact you."

With Zeke out of the room, Lou felt he could speak. "Looks like a mess, Judge."

"Yeah, I think so. I don't know what to make of it. From what I know of Zeke, all of this is out of character. Is that your perception?"

"I don't know Zeke," Lou began. "But he appears to have a temper. My guess is he isn't the most mature man I've ever met. He could be way out of his element here. He is sort of in a foreign land, away from family, job, people who know him."

"Yes."

"Would this Richards guy have a motive to kill the officer?" Lou asked.

"I don't think so, but I don't know. He has paid some people to get what he wants in the past, although I haven't heard of him paying off police officers. But, he pretty much gets what he wants around these parts. He's got a lot of friends, and a lot of people owe him favors."

"I see."

"I can't say what happened in that barn yesterday afternoon," the judge admitted. "There could have been an argument. The officer may have told him he would be arrested. Richards may have told him to get off his property, but he wouldn't. Lots of things could have happened."

"Is Richards capable of murder?" Lou asked.

"I suppose he is, but so is Zeke."

Zeke returned to the judge's office looking pale. The judge called Security and told them that people were free to move in and out of the courthouse.

"You okay, Zeke?" the judge asked as he hung up the phone.

"I don't know. I'm in a spiral. I feel like I'm trapped. I can't think clearly. I lied to you. I told the police things I shouldn't have. I've been arrested for murder. I'm out of control."

"Two things are going to happen now, Zeke," the judge replied. "First, I'll take you to the mental health center to get you some medication and some counseling."

"No way, absolutely not!" Zeke responded.

"Zeke, you're not yourself," Judge Patterson explained. "I'm concerned for you."

"Once I walk into a mental health place, my political aspirations are over!"

"You don't think being arrested for murder is going to damage your political career?" the judge asked.

"Yes, but I will be proven innocent, and people can accept my being falsely accused better than they can my possibly being mentally ill."

"I'll do what I can to get records of your admission to the mental health clinic sealed."

"Judge, if I might make a suggestion?" said Lou.

"Go ahead."

"Zeke, you didn't take my advice when I talked to you before; I ask you to do it now. Go to the clinic. You need attention. You need to trust me and the judge. We're in a better position to think clearly on your behalf than you are."

Zeke sat quietly with his head down and his hands folded. After about ten seconds of silence, he said weakly, "All right."

"Thank you," replied Judge Patterson. "The second thing is that I will arrange for an excellent attorney to represent you." When Zeke simply nodded, the judge continued.

"Her name is Audrey Moylan. She's from Grand Rapids, and she's one of the finest trial attorneys I've ever met."

While the three were planning their next steps, the crime scene team from the state police worked at the Richards' farm making casts from the tire marks left by Zeke's truck. Rain was forecast, so the investigators worked quickly to get a good sample for comparison with Zeke's truck tires. The lead detective had asked the officers to look around while the team was on-site, because one can never get enough information in a murder investigation. One of the officers decided to walk around inside the barn, on the off-chance that he might see something new. He stood at the spot where Officer Turner had undoubtedly been when he was hit with the rifle bullet; he looked all around, but what he saw appeared normal. He inspected the floor, but he found nothing of note.

After the casts were made, the officers gathered their materials and headed back to the lab to compare the casts to Zeke's tires. Their timing was perfect, for rain was beginning to fall.

Howard watched them through his window with a smile on his face. Now there would be no question that this hot-shot attorney had been on his property. It would appear obvious that the stranger from downstate had killed the conservation officer, and once that notion got around, many local people would want a posse to take the attorney out of town and hang him from the nearest oak tree. In Howard's mind, the case had been won, the stranger's plan to frame him had failed, and presently he would be home free.

While Zeke, Lou, and Judge Patterson were en route to the county mental health clinic, Zeke's father-in-law, Judge William "Bill" Beekins, was driving into town. Judge Patterson had called him and explained where they would be and how to get there. As the three waited in the reception area, Judge Beekins entered the clinic.

Zeke looked up, saw Judge Beekins, and immediately realized that the judge had come all the way from the middle of Michigan's Thumb to be with him. Zeke stood to greet him, hugged him, and teared from the emotion. Judge Beekins held tight and repeated, "It's okay, my boy, it's okay."

Judge William Beekins was seventy-seven years old, tall and exceptionally handsome, with a full head of white hair. He always dressed in a suit and tie with shined shoes and a red rose in his lapel, a tradition he had adopted when he won his first case as a prosecutor in Bad Axe. While not a superstitious man, he often said that the flower brought him good luck in his tough cases. Eventually, the flower became a part of the man, and Judge Beekins seen without a flower in his lapel became akin to a puppy without a wagging tail.

Presently Zeke released his hold, stood back, and looked his father figure in the eyes. "Thanks for coming."

"Not a problem, my boy. That's what families are for." He used the word "family," because he had been considerable more of a father to Zeke than Lucky Simons, who had enjoyed a successful professional hockey career. Zeke had always expected to follow in his father's footsteps and become a professional athlete, so his participation in youth hockey had been assumed. Zeke had also felt strong pressure to perform well and to lead a disciplined life in order to reach his father's athletic goals.

But the boy did not share his father's dreams, and this led to Lucky's disappointment, frustration, anger, and eventually disrespect and alienation. In a rebellious state of mind, Zeke got into trouble with a destructive gang of kids, his grades dropped, and he often thought about running away to some place warm and more exciting than Michigan's Thumb.

At the time, Judge Beekins was an assistant county prosecutor. Always perceptive of people, he recognized the father-son conflict and stepped in to give Zeke an adult role model. Zeke and "Bill" took up hunting together, and it was during those hunting trips that Zeke enjoyed an adult companion who understood his wanting to do better in school and his compassion for those less fortunate. Both loved communing with nature while pheasant hunting, deer hunting in a northern Michigan woods, or waiting to pull a prize bass from icy waters in a shanty on a Michigan lake in the dead of winter. In a matter of months, Zeke began to look to Judge Beekins as a role model, a relationship which had continued to the present.

Zeke's mother supported Judge Beekins' intervention, seeing him as a godsend. Lucky Simons eventually accepted Zeke's desire not to follow in his footsteps but the years of trying to make his son a clone of himself had taken its toll. While they could co-exist in the same house, there was little respect or affection between the two. Lucky had taken a young up-and-coming hockey player under his wing and showered him with attention and affection. Ironically, Lucky had become to a neighbor boy what Judge Beekins had become to Zeke.

Angie awoke alone in her bed. She had been up half the night with anxiety so it was almost ten-thirty. It took a few seconds to realize that Zeke was up north, in jail, and a suspect in a murder. When she looked through the front window, at least four cars were parked at the curb. She suspected they were reporters, so she kept the curtains pulled. She wanted to be protected in her own shell.

Angie answered the phone's ring.

"Mrs. Simons?"

"Yes."

"This is your father's secretary, Ann."

"Hi, Ann."

"The judge asked me to call you to let you know that he is on his way to Trout City. Apparently Zeke is now out of jail and is threatening someone. Judge Beekins said to tell you that he is sure it'll turn out okay, but he wants to get up there and try to keep Zeke calm."

"Thanks for calling."

"You're welcome."

This was good news and bad. The man Zeke respected most was on his way to settle the problem, but it appeared that Zeke had broken the law, and there would be a price to pay.

Angie realized that the situation had disaster written all over it. The local newspaper was sure to print a story about Zeke being in trouble up north. Potential clients would be skeptical about doing business with a man out of control, and Zeke's aspirations of becoming a judge or running for office might well be history.

Angie showered and began packing, wondering how she would get out of the driveway without being harassed. On the other hand, maybe she should face the reporters, answer their questions and get rid of them. She'd tell them the truth, which was that she didn't know anything. She was going to his side. Sorry she couldn't be more helpful. That would be it, three sentences, and only three sentences — nothing more, and nothing less.

Officer Turner's family was devastated. Tim and his wife, Marie, were the parents of Philip, a child that the couple had been told might not be born, and if he was, he would be disabled for life. Philip beat the odds, was born and did have a disability; but, if ever a child took on life and gave new meaning to courage, tenacity, and enthusiasm, it was Philip. At age ten his smile and personality and his enjoyment of life made him the poster boy for Special Olympics in which Philip competed in track and swimming.

Marie was grief-stricken. Philip worshipped his father; she didn't know how to tell him that his father was dead. Philip looked up to Tim, and did everything he could to please him. Tim had gone to every Special Olympics event that his son entered at the area, district, and state level. In fact, he became a fixture at the events, and he was such a tremendous supporter and fund-raiser that Lois Arnold, the Executive Director of Special Olympics Michigan, had tried to convince him to run for the Board of Directors. She believed he could offer positive suggestions for fund-raising, while also serving as a model parent to hundreds of families.

Marie realized that a ten-year-old-boy might not truly understand the consequences of a father's death. She immediately summoned help for herself and Philip from their pastor, Reverend Evans, of the Hope Methodist Church in Trout City.

It was Reverend Evans who told Philip about his father's death. Phil couldn't understand his mother's uncontrollable sobbing, which had a great emotional effect on him. Though he felt sad, Phil didn't completely believe the news, which was probably a psychological defense mechanism. He packed the knowledge away in the recesses of his mind, but his mother's constant sobbing was real, and that touched him greatly. Nothing affected the boy more than to see his mother in pain.

Jerry Tomlinson, age 54, sat in a trailer outside of Dansville, Michigan, with an open beer bottle and a lit cigarette. As he read a paper he had taken from McDonald's, his heartbeat accelerated at the headline:

Mason Attorney, Anthony 'Zeke' Simons Arrested in Cherry County — Suspected of Murder

Zeke Simons, prominent attorney from Mason, Michigan, was arrested yesterday afternoon in the town of Trout City in the northwest part of Michigan. According to authorities, Mr. Simons had reported a poaching incident and was in the area while a DNR officer, Tim Turner, was investigating. The officer subsequently died of a gunshot wound. The prosecutor for Cherry County, Wil Purcell, indicated in a phone interview that there is no direct evidence that Mr. Simons killed the officer; but since he was at the scene when the death occurred, there was sufficient reason to arrest Simons. Officer Turner is survived by his wife Marie, and his ten-year-old son, Philip.

"That's the guy that put me away for five years!" Jerry said aloud. Zeke was working for the Ingham County Prosecuting Attorney at the time and worked to achieve a guilty verdict from the jury. Suddenly Jerry was filled with a mission; he could envision what Jack Ruby must have thought when he heard that President Kennedy had been murdered.

That attorney took the life of a kid's father, thought Jerry. He flashed back to his sentencing when Zeke had responded to his glare with a smile. And now he's probably going to hire some corrupt attorney to get him the freedom that he denied me, Jerry thought. Taking a drink of beer and a long draw on his cigarette, Jerry planned a trip up north to inject his form of justice into the mix.

When Angie arrived at the mental health clinic, she was as happy to see Zeke as he was to see her, but he was embarrassed to have put them both in this situation. They embraced and shed a few tears. Angie met Lou and Judge Patterson and gave her father an affectionate hug. Angie had expected to be a "hunting widow" for a few days, and quite frankly that was to have been a nice break for her. But what was to have been a fun few days up north for Zeke, relaxing and hunting the elusive trophy buck, had turned into a nightmare.

Howard's attorney, Max Bell, pulled into the driveway. Rudy knew better than to greet Max in his typical manner. Besides, it was raining, and Rudy had enough sense not to risk a shower when he didn't need one. Max got out of the car, opened his umbrella, walked to the door, knocked, and was admitted.

"Thanks for coming over, Max," Howard began. "Want some coffee or a drink?"

"No thanks. I hardly have time to sit down. Just want to talk to you about what we need to do. It looks like you really need some help, my friend."

"Yeah, some attorney downstate is trying to pin poaching and murder on me."

"Is he right?" Max asked.

"Yeah, he's right about the poaching, but man, it's what I do."

"It's against the law, Howie. You know that."

"Don't mean nothing to me," Howard replied. "I gotta eat, it's deer season, and who cares what weapon I use? I got a tag."

"A bow-hunting tag?"

"Yeah, I get both kinds, every tag I need. I gotta have something legal to show the authorities. But even though the thing's in my pocket, it don't mean nothing."

"What happened, Howie?" Max asked.

"I was in Mickey's telling friends about bagging a 12-point buck, and yeah, I said I used my rifle. Some hot-shot lawyer from downstate overheard me, and he didn't like me taking his prize buck, so he called Judge Patterson."

"It's his right to report poaching, Howie."

"Yeah, but in the end, that'll be his mistake," Howard said, shaking his head. "People do stupid things."

"So, then what happened?" Max asked.

"I got a call from Danny telling me the lawyer was asking questions and would probably be calling the cops. So I waited, and sure enough, a couple of deputies pulled up. I told them I hit the deer with my car, and since it was a fresh hit, laying there on the road, I gutted it and took it home and hung it from the rafter in my barn."

"Did the cops inspect?"

"Nope. They believed me. They told me that investigating poaching was the responsibility of the DNR, and an officer would probably be out. Since they were there, I gave them the money I had collected from selling some Policemen's Ball tickets. We shook hands, and they were on their way."

"Is that really what happened in the poaching claim? I need to know so I can represent you. I need the truth."

Howard was growing angry. "No, that's not what happened, but that's what I'm telling people, including the judge and jury. And that's what I expect you to say in court!"

"So, what really happened?" Max asked.

"I went out hunting, saw the buck, and shot it with my .22. Then I stuck an arrow into the wound so it would look like the deer was killed by an arrow. Then I shot another arrow into it from a few feet so it would look like he'd been hit twice. I gutted it, took it home, strung it up, and went to Mickey's for some drinking with my friends."

"Is the front of your truck damaged in any way? You'll need to have some proof. After all, you're claiming to have hit a heavy animal, you know."

"It's not damaged now, but I'll take care of it."

"You'd better get some deer hair stuck on the grill or someplace. If you're going to create an alibi, you need to dress it up pretty well. I don't like it, Howie, but I'll do my best to defend this, if that's what you want. But I'm sure I'll meet my match in court because it looks like their lawyer has money."

"Probably does. You'll do just fine, Max. I can't pay you much, but whatever I can do in any other way, you let me know."

"One thing you can do is stick to your story. Whatever we decide, you gotta stick to it like glue. Don't go shooting off your mouth, you hear? I'll try to control things with my questions and challenging the prosecutor, but you gotta do as I say. This will probably be my toughest case, and I'm 80 years old, you know."

"You'll do a good job," Howard replied. "And, I'll see to it that it won't be a tough case. It's going to be a piece of cake."

"Now, for the murder of the conservation officer. Guess I need to ask the sixty-four-thousand-dollar question: Did you kill Officer Turner?"

"Am I going to have to take one of those lie-detector tests?" Howard asked.

"Probably."

"What do you want me to say?" Howie asked.

"That depends. Answer my question first. Did you kill that officer?"

"No, I didn't shoot him. I did the poaching, but I didn't kill that officer."

"The poaching I can handle. But if you didn't kill that officer, it's the best news I've heard in a long time."

"Glad I could make your day."

POACHING MAN AND BEAST

"You got any idea who did kill the guy?" Max asked.

"Yeah, I do."

"And that would be…"

"The guy who called the cops on me for poaching," Howard replied with anger. "He wanted to set me up, but the laugh will be on him. With your help, I'll give him what he deserves for framing me and killing a man with a family."

"Tell me what happened."

"I was gone. I guess the officer came to my place, went into my barn looking for the deer, and then this hot-shot lawyer killed him to frame me. But I can prove I wasn't home, and I am sure the sheriff can find enough evidence that Zeke whatever-his-name-is, is guilty."

"Your evidence for not being home?" Max asked, pen in hand to take down Howard's alibi.

"I took Harriett to the Fish Hook. People saw us there."

"Good. We should win this one easily, too," Attorney Bell said, slapping Howard on the back.

That evening, the sheriff called Judge Patterson to inform him that they had sufficient evidence to arrest Zeke for the murder of Officer Turner. They had reviewed the video from the DNR vehicle; it showed Zeke coming out of the Richards barn with a rifle, looking upset. A bullet they suspected came from Zeke's rifle had been found at the scene and they were awaiting a lab test to determine a match to the bore of Zeke's confiscated rifle. Zeke's truck tire marks had been found on the Richards property.

"I know you want this man free, but the evidence doesn't support you, Judge. He is the prime suspect, Your Honor."

"Thanks for the call. OK, pick him up, but I will be watching all the proceedings from a distance, and I want the law followed to a tee. Understand?"

"Yes, Your Honor."

A half-hour later, Zeke was once again arrested for the murder of Officer Turner. Zeke listened as his rights were read understanding that the procedure was being followed only after Judge Patterson had been briefed.

OCTOBER 3

Early the next morning, Lou Searing paid Zeke a visit in the county jail. The psychiatrist reported that Zeke was doing fine. He had taken some Valium the night before, slept well, and had eaten breakfast. Since he seemed stable, interviewing him was acceptable.

"Good morning, Zeke," Lou said, extending his hand to his client, who sat across from him in a guarded conference room of the jail.

Zeke took the offered hand. "I got myself in a mess this time, Mr. Searing."

"Yeah, looks like you did."

"Thanks for coming up," Zeke said. "Guess I didn't take the time to say that yesterday."

"Well, you had a lot on your mind, and you weren't exactly yourself. Just be thankful you had Judge Patterson to take over for you, and that your father-in-law showed up. If this had happened in some dark corner of the world, you'd have been up a creek, big time."

"Yeah."

"Well, if you'll talk a bit, I want to start investigating. I really don't have a minute to lose. I heard everything you told us last evening. I don't need to know what you told the sheriff that led to the arrest. That's for your attorney to hear, and I understand that she's asked the partners in her law firm to take a few cases so she can help you out."

"I hadn't heard that," Zeke replied.

"Judge Patterson told me that last evening. Apparently he's getting you the best trial lawyer in the state."

"I don't suppose that's necessary, but I'm thankful."

"Why don't you think it's necessary?" Lou asked.

"I'm sure I didn't kill the conservation officer. All I did was report poaching."

"Believe me, you need the best legal advice you can get. Just be thankful the judge has this connection."

"I am, believe me, I am."

"Now, answer a few questions, so I can get to work," Lou requested. "I need to know the exact spot where you were positioned to see Mr. Richards and the conservation officer."

"If you were to walk straight out of Howard Richards' barn and go across the road, cross the gully, and walk to the biggest tree, you'd be right where I was."

"OK. So you heard the shot and saw the officer fall?"

"I don't remember any of it. Whatever happened is just a blur. I fired a shot to scare Richards; I remember that, but not much of anything else."

"Did you see this Howard shoot the officer?"

"No."

"No? Who did you see shoot the officer?"

"I think I saw Howard carrying a rifle when he took his bribe into the barn."

"Did he have the rifle when he came out?"

"I don't think so. I was so angry, I don't remember very well, but I don't think he had a rifle."

"You fired a shot from across the road, right?" Lou asked.

"It is all like a nightmare. But yeah, I fired one shot in the direction of the barn. I was really out of control."

"Why were you carrying a rifle?" Lou asked. "Isn't that illegal during bow season?"

"I always have my rifle with me. I never know what I might meet."

"Where is your rifle now?"

"The police took it."

Jerry Tomlinson sat alone in his trailer, plotting how he could become a hero to the folks up north and also get revenge against this lawyer who messed up his life. He went to the Internet to get as much information as he could about the Trout City area. Jerry was intelligent; his problem was his inability to direct his intellect in appropriate ways. His lack of good judgment as a boy remained a part of his personality in his adult life.

Wil Purcell, the Cherry Country Prosecutor had spent a few hours interviewing Howard and inspecting the evidence collected at the scene. He needed as much information as possible to prepare his case for the preliminary hearing and eventually, for the trial.

The carcass of the deer was found on Howard Richards' property, and two rifle bullets were found at the scene. Because one bullet was believed to have come from Zeke's deer rifle, it was important to get Howard's rifle to determine if the second bullet was shot from that weapon. After Howard refused to turn his rifle over to the authorities voluntarily, Officer Faccio obtained a search warrant to look for the rifle on Howard's property. If the second bullet came from Howard's rifle, it would provide the authorities with another possible murder suspect.

A county judge approved the search warrant request, and warrant in hand, Officer Faccio went to Howard Richards' home. The warrant authorized her gaining entrance and searching for the rifle in the house, in any building on the property, or in his vehicles.

When she arrived, Howard was napping on the couch in his living room. Awakened by a series of loud knocks, he got up, limped to the window on his arthritic hip joints, and looked through the curtains to see the DNR vehicle in his drive.

Howard moved to the door and opened it. "Yeah, you need something?"

Officer Faccio spoke politely but firmly. "Mr. Richards, I have a warrant to conduct a search of your home for evidence regarding the death of Officer Turner."

"I don't care what you got — you're not coming into this house! And if you don't get off my property right now, my dog will have you for dinner!" Howard stepped back to slam the door, but Ginny slipped her foot in the doorway.

"Mr. Richards, don't fight this thing, okay? I've a backup officer within viewing distance of here. This microphone is hot, recording every word you and I say. Any difficulty I have serving this warrant may be used as evidence in court, and I can assure you that the penalties for interfering with this order will be considerably more serious than the allowable penalty for poaching. Cooperate with me, Mr. Richards."

"You're on my property without my consent. Now get out!" Howie bellowed. He pushed Officer Faccio onto the porch and slammed the door.

Ginny returned to her pickup and called for backup. "Mr. Richards is not cooperating. Approach with caution. He is undoubtedly armed and dangerous. He's like a cornered tiger."

The dispatcher responded, "Leave the property. We'll work with the sheriff to secure backup."

"I'd rather have the state police," Ginny replied. "I don't trust the sheriff."

"It's his jurisdiction."

"I understand that, but I don't believe the sheriff or his deputies would treat Mr. Richards as a hostile suspect. Richards seems to be practically an honorary member of their force. Do what you need to do, but my preference is either the FBI or the state police."

"The FBI?"

"They're familiar with this man from their investigation of the gray wolf killings," Officer Faccio said.

"OK. Leave the area, Officer, and wait for a directive from the supervisor."

"Thank you."

Ginny backed her pickup onto Peavine Road and drove away, frustrated in her failed attempt to conduct the search. She knew that if Howard Richards had any sense, he would destroy whatever evidence was in his home or on his property, primarily his 30-30 Remington hunting rifle.

Within a half-hour, four state police cruisers and a county SWAT team descended on Howard Richards' home. The SWAT team dispersed, taking positions in all directions, using buildings on the farm, trees, and their vehicles as protection, should Howard decide to relive Butch Cassidy and the Sundance Kid.

The on-site commanding officer, with bullhorn in hand as well as a cell phone, attempted to get Howard's attention. At first he thought the house was empty, but then he saw a curtain move slightly in what was probably a dining room. Suddenly he recalled that Howard's grandson often stayed with him when he wasn't in school. I don't want a kid to witness this, he thought.

The commanding officer asked a trooper to call the elementary school in town and ask if Taylor Richards was there. A few minutes later the response was that Taylor was in school. "Thank God for that," he sighed.

The officer dialed Howard's home phone number. On the fifth ring Howard answered. "What!"

"This is State Police Trooper Loren Watkins. Come out of the front door with your hands up. Don't try anything. Do you understand me?"

The phone went dead, obviously slammed down. Trooper Watkins wanted Howard alive and he desperately wanted the rifle. Within a few minutes, one of the troopers noticed that smoke had started rising from the chimney, which had not been the case when they arrived.

While Trooper Watkins continued to reach Howard on the bullhorn and by telephone, another trooper approached with a rifle and calmly said, "I think this is what you're looking for."

"Where did you find this?"

"On the floor of the back seat of that old Ford beside the barn."

"Good work."

"Well, you had the search warrant, so I started to search. I can see another rifle through the window of a red pickup, but the truck is locked, or you'd have two pieces of evidence."

"Thanks. Good work. But the gun used for the poaching could be in the house, and maybe its stock is going up in smoke at this minute."

"Yeah, but it isn't the stock we need, and the fire won't melt the barrel. The guy is simply digging himself deeper into a hole by resisting."

"From what I've heard, he has no experience in resisting the law because he has always been in control of the law."

"That's in our favor, then. On the other hand, he just might be suicidal. If he's halfway intelligent, he knows his life from today on might be spent in the slammer, so he could get pretty desperate."

"I hope not. That man has a lot of information about gray wolf poaching, and I want him giving testimony for that. Poaching deer is enough, but it's the gray wolf poaching that the entire department wants him for."

Howard realized that, if he didn't walk out as directed, not only would his problems multiply, but the media would get wind of the standoff. Attention on him from outside his kingdom, so to speak, would lessen his chances of controlling his fate. In addition, there was no incriminating evidence in his house. It was just that legal authorities would be in his home, and that was against his wishes. Besides, special attention to his poaching would anger and incite environmental groups seeking public sympathy for the wolves. He struggled to make the best decision for himself.

Howard Richards opened the front door and, waving a white handkerchief, went down the four steps of his front porch, one at a time, with short winces of pain in each step. The troopers approached him carefully with weapons drawn because given his history, he might have placed an explosive device on his body, intending to kill himself and take some troopers with him.

The police did a quick body search, put handcuffs on him, and led him to an awaiting state police cruiser. All of this time, Howard mumbled profanities and claimed his innocence of any wrong-doing.

Trooper Watkins walked over to Officer Faccio and said, "The place is yours. Hope you find what you're looking for."

"Thanks for your help. I am glad it ended peacefully."

Max Bell was the first to meet with Howard at the state police post. "Everything is going to be okay, Howard," Max said in a reassuring tone. "I'm glad you surrendered at your home. If you hadn't done that, I would have had to fight a wave of public opinion, not necessarily from our county, but from environmental groups across the state, and maybe the nation. God forbid this draw the attention of those news shows on the major networks. So, thanks for getting out of there without a lot of fanfare. Best decision you've made in a long time."

"I didn't want to give in. I hate not being in control," Howard said, with clenched fists.

"I know, but sometimes you have to give up a little control to gain a lot of control," Max replied.

"Are we going to court on this poaching thing, or do we simply pay off some people?" Howard asked, hoping for a positive response to the latter.

"I think we need to go to court," Max replied. "I'd rather have this matter settled legally with a record of your innocence. That verdict will help us in the future, in case any problems surface."

"So, we'll win the court case, right?" Howard asked.

"Oh, for sure. We haven't lost yet, have we?"

"No."

"Well, then, we aren't going to lose now," Max replied confidently. "We're only talking about poaching a deer. Most people who get caught just pay a fine, but we're doing the right thing by keeping your record clean, just like we did with those two kids. Picking off mailboxes like mosquitoes on a hot summer night — those kids just flew into one of those zappers, didn't they? Howard, you get credit on that one — very ingenious of you."

By now, the residents in the county had become involved. Newspaper and television stories had been written and distributed, but the reporting was not objective: The officer had been a family man with a disabled son who not only worshipped his dad, but who was also a celebrity in Special Olympics, and the pieces generally put a negative slant on Zeke, the slick downstate attorney, who was in their back yard.

Nothing brought this stark reality home more than the eggs thrown at Angie's car or the hateful words sprayed on Lou's windshield. Lou was used to people being upset with him, but usually it was the criminals, not the general public.

Lou's experience had been that messages on windows were often followed by telephone threats, and then slashed tires. But Lou understood what was happening, for hatred up close and personal was familiar to him. He'd gut it out, but he knew all of this would be frightening to Angie Simons. This behavior was not the norm in Mason and she would take it very personally and be most upset.

Lou recommended that Angie ask for a police escort to the county line, go back to Mason, and stay in touch with Zeke by phone. She agreed that was the best course of action. She told Zeke she loved him and to call daily if he could and that she'd be in the courtroom, if and when this came to trial.

Lou quickly figured out that if he was going to solve this case, he would find everything he needed in the evidence collected by the sheriff. The basics of the case were obvious: the officer was killed by either Zeke or Howard. If Howard was the murderer, it was probably because he was about to be arrested for poaching. On the other hand, if Zeke was the murderer, it was either a tragic accident caused by an immature man or a case of temporary insanity.

Obtaining the evidence was a matter of asking Audrey Moylan for it, for court procedures require the defense to have access to the evidence that will be used to prove guilt. Lou had already talked to Zeke and formed an understanding of what may have transpired that ugly afternoon. It remained to ask attorney Moylan for ballistic reports, the pathologist's autopsy report on Officer Turner, including supporting photos and X-rays, the video recording taken from Officer Turner's DNR vehicle, and the officer's log book noting the call purpose and time. Lou was convinced that his efforts would revolve around these four items.

This should be the safest case he had investigated to date. There would be no dodging bullets, no confrontations in back alleys. This would be a somewhat boring job of solving a crime from what was on paper, but he looked forward to the analysis and to helping Audrey defend Zeke.

Audrey Moylan was 37 years old. She was six feet tall, thin, and smartly dressed in professional attire. She wore her light-brown hair long, and wore little makeup. She exuded confidence, professionalism, and projected a no-nonsense attitude toward doing nothing less than a complete job.

Audrey's decision to take on this case was a result of an internship with Judge Patterson in 1996. The top student in her class at the Detroit School of Law, on the campus of Michigan State University, she had wanted to work for a judge in a rural area. She was committed to defending people who did not have the resources to obtain legal services.

Ironically, she was about to represent not someone unable to afford legal assistance, but a colleague, and a wealthy one at that. But it was Judge Patterson and a chance to give back to him for all he had given to her that caused her to get involved.

She would say later, of the work with Judge Patterson, "I learned more about the practice of law from him than from any textbook or course. His compassion for the people and his commitment to justice provided me with attitudes and skills that will allow me to be an attorney worthy of the title. I am forever indebted to Judge Patterson." When the judge called and asked for her help, she didn't even think about it, her reaction was immediate.

As soon as Audrey arrived in Trout City, she prepared for Zeke's arraignment. This was the prosecutor's opportunity to convince the judge that sufficient evidence existed to charge Zeke with murder and to bring him to trial. Audrey met with Zeke alone and asked him a lot of questions, each one geared to finding either ammunition to support her position or facts to use in his defense. After about an hour of questioning, Audrey checked her notes and said, "From what you have told me, I expect the judge will remand you to jail and order a jury trial in circuit court. As you know, the judge will not be Judge Patterson. He excused himself from the case because of his personal involvement in your situation. The trial, and there probably will be one, will be before Judge Judith Johnson, who is a fair, thorough, and no-nonsense judge.

"I will ask for your release on bail, but I doubt I'll win, and I'm okay with that. To be honest, I really don't think your staying in jail is a bad option, because it will keep you safe from people in the area who have jumped to conclusions and want you found guilty. So, my recommendation is that we simply go before the judge and listen to the prosecutor's case. I will do what I can to defend you, if anything crazy comes up."

"Why do you think the trial is a given?" Zeke asked.

"You admitted you were at the scene or in the vicinity of the crime, you were seen on the conservation officer's video, one of the bullets found in the barn probably came from your rifle, and a man is dead."

"Yeah, but what about Richards?"

"There is no evidence he shot a rifle, or that he was even at the crime scene, except for your witnessing it, and your word isn't worth a lot up here. So, while the evidence against you is not solid, the judge will have no choice but to jail you and bind you over for trial, which, as I said, is fine with me."

"Thank you."

"We're going to be quite challenged, Zeke. They got a search warrant to look through all your belongings in the Wilds' home. The sheriff has impounded your truck, your hunting equipment, bow and arrow, rifle, and hunting clothes. The prosecutor has already sent an associate to Mason to research you. He certainly already knows more about you than I do, and more than most of your friends know."

"But, we'll win the case in the courtroom?" Zeke asked.

"I fully expect to, yes," Audrey replied assuredly. "There is detective work to do, but yes, I expect we'll win the case. The only thing that might work against us is the jury, because the trial will be held in Mancelona. To be honest, I think my job is more to pick an objective jury than to gather material for your defense. I have already talked with Mr. Searing and I expect him to analyze the evidence and give me the facts with which I can establish a reasonable doubt that you killed Officer Turner."

"Thanks for your help."

"You're welcome," Audrey replied. "I'm fully aware that you are an attorney, and I expect you to talk to me about your thoughts and experiences. I know you are emotionally involved in this, but don't hesitate to tell me if you disagree, or agree for that matter, with my advice or direction."

"I will. I do have something on my mind."

"What's that?"

"Are you going to have me testify?" Zeke asked.

"Right now, I expect I will," Audrey replied. "Of course, the risk is that the prosecutor would also have the opportunity to question you. All we need to do is prove that there is reasonable doubt that you killed Officer Turner. I expect to be able to do that, so we'll make the decision whether you'll testify after we're into trial. But if I think your testimony will help, with your permission, I'll call you to the stand. If I don't, the jury may see you as guilty, thinking, if you didn't do it, why don't you get up on the stand and tell your story?

"Remember, I believe that even if I do an excellent job of choosing jurors, some will be convinced that you shot the officer. But that's often the case in any court proceeding."

"I'm thankful you're here," Zeke said sincerely.

"We'll talk again soon."

OCTOBER 4

Three people stood before Judge Dilbert O'Rieley at 9 a.m. in the chambers of the 91st District Court for Zeke's arraignment: County Prosecutor, Wil Purcell, Defense Attorney, Audrey Moylan, and the defendant, Zeke Simons.

Judge O'Rieley opened the proceedings. "Mr. Purcell, what charge and evidence do you present against the defendant?"

"Your Honor, we are bringing a charge of second degree murder. It is our contention that Mr. Simons fired a bullet unintentionally striking Conservation Officer Timothy Turner and killing him. A bullet found in the Howard Richards' barn matches a rifle owned by the defendant. By the defendant's own admission, he was at or near the Richards' barn while Officer Turner was investigating a poaching claim, he fired a rifle, and on the recording from Officer Turner's vehicle, the defendant is seen exiting the Richards' barn with a rifle."

"Defense Attorney Moylan, your response."

"Thank you, Your Honor. We admit that my client was in the vicinity of the crime, but he is not guilty of murder."

Judge O'Rieley informed Mr. Simons of his constitutional rights and with practically no thought, offered a decision. "We have a victim, Mr. Turner; a possible motive, intense anger involving poaching; and compelling evidence to suggest that the defendant may have intentionally or accidentally killed Mr. Turner. I hereby find sufficient justification for moving to a preliminary hearing."

"Your Honor, my client wishes to waive his right to a preliminary hearing."

"Request granted. The defendant is hereby bound over for trial in circuit court.

"Your Honor, I recommend that my client be free on bail," Audrey moved.

"I am going to rule that he remain in the county jail without bail. Mr. Simons likely is a threat to society."

OCTOBER 5

Lou began in earnest to investigate the murder of Officer Turner. The poaching matter was important to his client, but obtaining evidence in the murder was of a higher priority. He would leave the poaching matter to the DNR and assist if asked, but otherwise he would concentrate on the murder investigation.

Lou had met with Officer Faccio and the two had hit it off. Each respected the other and believed that working together would be in their best interests. Ginny promised to make available to Lou all reports she received related to both the poaching charge and the murder of Officer Turner.

Once Lou seriously reviewed the available information, he was struck by two things. The first was the video recording in Officer Turner's vehicle. It was perplexing that the video began approximately three minutes before Zeke entered the barn with a rifle.

At home in Grand Haven, Lou put the disk into his DVD. While viewing the DNR on board video he was struck by a key question, Who had turned it on? The video initially showed Officer Turner stopping a vehicle on a country road — pulling over a pickup and talking with the driver. The entire episode was recorded. Then there was no other recording until the camera came on and showed a partially-opened barn door. Then Zeke Simons comes into view with a rifle; he first looked into the barn and then entered. Within a minute he reappeared looking very disturbed, and began to run out and away from the barn.

After viewing the piece, Lou called Officer Faccio. "I have a few questions for you, if you don't mind."

"I'll help if I can, Lou," replied Officer Faccio.

"How is the camera in a DNR vehicle turned on? Does the officer have to throw a switch in the cab? Can it be activated by an officer at a distance from the truck? Can it be set to automatically go on at a certain time? Does it automatically record sound as well as picture?"

"The officer has to throw a switch," Officer Faccio explained. "There is no activation from outside the truck, no programming to begin recording at a certain time. And no, the camera — at least the one in Officer Turner's vehicle — does not record sound."

"Thanks. This switch that activates the camera, what kind of a switch is it?"

"It's a toggle switch on the camera itself," Ginny replied.

"Up-and-down movement or side-to-side?"

"Up-and-down."

"Ok, thanks."

Armed with this information Lou asked himself the key question: if Officer Turner is in the barn and can't activate the camera, who turned it on? Was it Zeke on his way toward the barn? No way, Lou reasoned. He doubted Zeke even knew a camera was on board, let alone how to activate it. And, even if he did, why would he record himself wandering into a potential crime scene?

Lou was certain that Howard had to have activated the switch. This was consistent with Zeke's assertion that Howard went over to the DNR vehicle before going into his house. Why? Lou surmised that Howard hoped the video would capture Zeke going into the barn, with any observer concluding that Zeke shot Officer Turner in the barn and then left. However, Lou remembered Howard's comment in his interrogation that he wasn't home when the officer was shot.

Before leaving for Grand Haven, Lou and Attorney Moylan agreed that Audrey would talk to townspeople. Lou had been associated with Zeke Simons and most in the community of Trout City thought Zeke was guilty. Audrey, on the other hand, had the title of attorney, that carried some respect, and perhaps she could get more information.

Lou went home to Grand Haven and would work quickly and thoroughly once he had the requested evidence.

Audrey began with the people in the bar when Howard made his bold statement, but she found them reluctant to talk about Howard Richards. Howard's son declined comment, and he refused her request to talk with Taylor. People who lived on Peavine Road wouldn't talk. At first she thought their reactions were simply apathy, but she came to believe the reason for their lack of response was fear. Howard was not only disliked, he was also feared.

The only person willing to answer her questions was Ron Otto, the editor of the daily newspaper, The Trout City Herald Times.

"Thanks for talking to me, Ron," Audrey began.

"Sure. Howard knows that I print whatever I want. I don't accept his money, and I don't do favors for people. I print what I think is newsworthy, and I don't answer to anyone, not even the advertisers. If you like what I say, you buy my paper. But if you don't like me or what I say, save your money."

"I like your attitude, Ron," Audrey replied.

Ron sighed. "I learned very early in my career that Abe Lincoln was right — you can't make everyone happy all the time. So I finally decided that the only person I was going to make happy was myself, and that's what I do. Now, what did you want to ask me?"

"What can you tell me about Howard Richards?"

"He's a no-good, lying SOB."

"That didn't take much thought."

"Nope. I don't respect the man, and I don't like him. And I don't believe anything he says. He's a poor excuse for a human being."

"Who do you think killed Officer Turner?" Audrey asked.

"Richards is capable of it. If someone is in his way, look out."

"The police report quoted a female friend of his that he couldn't kill anyone because of his religious upbringing and his adherence to the Ten Commandments."

"That's crazy! The only commandment he lives by is the eleventh: Thou shall do unto others before they do unto you!"

"Are you the Lone Ranger here, or do others think of him this way?" Audrey asked.

"I'm not alone. He's got his friends, and he's got his enemies. There are people who tolerate him, and those who just plain stay out of his way."

"I see. So what you're saying is that, when I look at my jury profiles, it might be a good idea to find out how Howard Richards rates in their minds."

"I would do that, yes. If you can't get a change in venue from Judge Johnson, you're going to have a hard time finding people who don't know Howard or haven't interacted with him in some way.

The guy has lived here for a long time — came down from the western U.P. twenty or so years ago. He still has a lot of friends up there. My guess is they're undesirables, but that's just my opinion. Howard's held every office a citizen can hold in Trout City. He's been on the school board, the library board, and the county board. He's been Grand Marshal of the Trout City Festival Parade. He's active in his church, though many of the members are embarrassed by him. The guy is well-known."

"But you hold him in such disdain."

"I sure do."

"Why, exactly?" Audrey asked, pen in hand, ready to record a response.

"You probably haven't been up here long enough to hear the phrase, the County of Howard."

"No."

"I didn't think so," Ron replied. "Well, the man is a control freak. Everything has to be on his terms, the way he wants it. He has to be in charge and no law, no policy, no rule, nothing of a regulatory nature has any credibility for him. If something isn't the way Howard Richards wants it, he bends it so that it is. As far as I'm concerned, someone like that is not a rational human being. I don't like cheaters or unlawful people, and he's both."

"I see. Does he know right from wrong?" Audrey asked. "Does he have a conscience?"

"Oh yeah, he knows right from wrong," Ron replied. "That's not the issue. The point is, is it right for Howard? However he answers that question is how he acts. This poaching is a perfect example — doesn't surprise me a bit. He goes hunting with his rifle when he wants to — seasons don't mean anything to him. If hunting is what Howard wants to do, he hunts. If shooting a buck is what he wants to do, he shoots the buck. If killing kids for busting his mailbox sounds right, he does that. And he'll do whatever it takes to make whatever problem he created for himself go away — bribe, lie, cheat, frame someone, it doesn't matter."

"I'm getting an earful. Nobody will talk to me all day, and then you give me a dissertation on the guy."

"You asked."

"So you believe he was poaching," Audrey stated.

"Sure. He was bragging about it in the bar."

"You believe him when he says he didn't fire a rifle at the officer?"

"No."

"Why?"

"Because, as I just said, Howard only does what is right for Howard. Here's where his lying comes in: if he shot him, and if admitting it would be right for Howard, he'd admit to it. But like now, if it's not right for Howard, as in putting him in jail for the rest of his life, he won't admit it. And furthermore, he'll figure out a way to frame someone else, and that's probably what's happening."

"But maybe Zeke really did shoot Officer Turner," Audrey said, to solicit a reaction. "I've heard that Zeke did this to frame Howard. Remember, he wasn't himself, maybe even temporarily insane."

"That's always possible, but when you're dealing with Howard, you never know what to believe — never."

"Is there anybody else I can talk to who would give me a different take on this man?"

"The sheriff."

"Really?" Audrey asked.

"Yup. Howard has the guy wrapped around his finger."

"Is there anyone else who likes or at least tolerates Howard?"

"Yeah, Harriet Gunderson does," Ron replied, smiling and shaking his head. "That's a perfect example of birds of a feather flying together. They're both crazy."

"Harriett lives in town, I take it," Audrey assumed.

"Right. She's an alcoholic, with a lot of memory problems. You've got to take everything she says with a grain of salt too. People don't know if she's living in a fantasy world and just talks about life as she creates it, or if there is any truth to what she says. I tend to think the former is more likely the case, but I'm not a physician, so what do I know?"

"Thanks, Ron. You've been most helpful."

"I'll do what I can to be unbiased in my reporting. It's going to be hard, because I hope Howard spends the rest of his life in the slammer, whether he's guilty of this crime or not. Sorry to feel this way, but I'm being honest with you."

OCTOBER 6

Lou's second piece of evidence, Officer Turner's log book, was obtained through Audrey Moylan. Lou had already made contact with the State Police Crime Lab in Grayling to examine the log book for any possible clues.

Lou was sitting in a Kiwanis Meeting in Grand Haven when his cell phone vibrated on his right hip. He excused himself and answered the phone. The call was from a technician at the Lab.

"Mr. Searing?"

"Yes."

"We have some information for you. We've done some tests on Officer Turner's log book and it is our contention that the numeral 1 in the time of arrival, 1:37, was altered to a 4, making the time of arrival look like 4:37."

"Interesting."

"Yes. The one was changed to a four; and we know this because of the pressure of the pen. The pen was the same, but the depth of indentation is vastly different from the rest of the time noted. The 1:37 is clear to seven ply, while the altered 1 is only to two ply.

This is highly unusual; when someone writes a numeral, the pressure applied to the entire number is routinely equal."

"Very good. Have you put your findings in writing?" Lou asked.

"Yes. The report has already been written."

"Thank you very much," Lou said

As Lou returned to his Kiwanis Meeting, he figuratively put a missing piece of the puzzle into place. He knew, from DNR dispatch records, that Officer Turner was sent to the Richards farm at 1:19 p.m. And, the DNR tracking system in East Lansing showed the vehicle on Peavine Road from 1:36 until it was removed at 6:28 p.m. Finally, he trusted Zeke's account of Howard's whereabouts, given Howard's comments in Mickey's Bar.

So, Lou thought, Howard turned on the video camera in the cab of the truck and altered the arrival time from 1:37 to 4:37. This was undoubtedly done in a naïve attempt to support his claim that he was not at the scene of the crime when it occurred. Attorney Moylan would have no problem convincing jurors that Howard Richards was lying in his claim that he wasn't around when Officer Turner was killed.

Lou thought, when it rains, it pours, when he received one more piece of information later in the day. Lou had arranged for the autopsy report to be reviewed by a friend from his days at Alma College. Dr. Bill Dillon was a noted pathologist at Grand Rapids' Spectrum Hospital. Bill was pleased to work with Lou and turned on a dime to review and comment on Officer Turner's autopsy report.

Lou was watching a Golf Channel report on Tiger Woods' career when his fax machine began to spit out a five-page report. Lou turned off the TV, and sat at the kitchen table with the report and a fresh cup of hot coffee. What he read was as chilling as the whitecaps crashing on the shore outside his Lake Michigan home.

Dr. Dillon claimed that the radiology plates were the equivalent of mixing apples and oranges. X-rays showing the path of the bullet through the body were two different bodies. Upper-body organs were different sizes, and their positions were not exactly identified. Most significant was that in consistent plates of Officer Turner, the visuals clearly showed the trajectory of the bullet going into and out of the body at a steep angle, assuming the victim was upright when hit by the missile from the rifle. The angle was 60 degrees downward.

The rest of the report was detailed medical jargon, most of which was over Lou's head, but a sentence in the summary packed the most punch. Dr. Dillon had written: "Victim was killed instantly by the passage of a bullet discharged from a 30-30 rifle positioned at an angle of 60 degrees."

Again, if Lou believed Zeke, and he did, a bullet fired from Zeke's 30-06 rifle at forty to fifty yards would have very little if any trajectory angle; at that distance the bullet would still be almost parallel to the ground. For the bullet that entered and exited Officer Turner's body to have an angle of 60 degrees at forty to fifty yards would mean that Zeke would have had to fire the weapon from above the tree line.

This was the best news of all; in Lou's opinion, it was sufficient and credible evidence that Zeke was innocent. The next logical question was, who shot the officer? The wound couldn't have been self-inflicted. Unless Howard got up on the top of a ladder to shoot Turner, he wasn't the one who fired the shot either. But Lou's job was to find evidence that Audrey Moylan could use to defend Zeke and to create reasonable doubt in the jurors' minds.

Lou called Audrey and told her of his findings and conclusions. She took notes but asked Lou to send her a report so she could plan her defense around Lou's analysis of the evidence.

OCTOBER 11

At the 9 a.m. Mass at St. Patrick's in Grand Haven, he sat next to his friends Tom and Fran Hogan. Before the service, they quietly chatted about a number of things, including when Carol was coming home from Kansas City.

"I pick her up in Grand Rapids this afternoon. It'll be good to have her home."

"Say hello for us. Maybe we can get together soon," Tom replied.

"That would be great."

The lector welcomed everyone to St. Pat's and announced the opening hymn, The Church's One Foundation on page 216. All rose, and the service proceeded.

In the Nazarene Baptist Church in Trout City was Taylor Richards and his father Eric. Eric attended the adult Sunday school, and Taylor sat on a kid-sized chair in the Sunday school listening to the lesson for the week. Normally he was a difficult kid to handle, paying attention to anything but the teacher. He was often punching someone, pulling hair, needing a drink of water, or wanting to go to the bathroom, but today, he was different, almost angelic. He sat still and actually paid attention to what the teacher was saying.

The lesson concerned the sin of bearing false witness. The teacher, Mary Fees, brought this rather complex idea down to the level of second- and third-graders when she said, "It is a sin to lie. God does not like it when we lie. Whenever we lie, we upset God, and that is not good."

Mrs. Fees figured that every child in class had a concept of God, and also an understanding of telling a lie. And they knew what it meant to be upset, so she hoped she was effective in explaining the sin of lying.

"What does God do to you when you lie?" one of the girls asked, looking concerned.

"Well, Jesus says that if we don't follow the Commandments, we will not go to Heaven and live with God for eternity," Mrs. Fees said, gently.

"That means you don't go to Heaven, right?" a kid in the back of the class asked, leaning back and balancing his chair on its hind legs.

"Yes, I guess so. If we sin, God is unhappy with us. But, if you are truly sorry for your sin and ask God to forgive you, Jesus says He will forgive. You then are sort of back to the batter's box with a new turn at bat, kind of."

Looking over at Taylor, Mary saw tears rolling down his cheeks. He reached up to wipe the tears away, but it didn't seem that anyone saw his emotions. She didn't want to embarrass him by drawing attention to it.

After Mrs. Fees ended the class with a prayer, the other kids scurried for the door, while Taylor stayed back. Within a minute, he and the teacher were alone in the room.

"Is something bothering you, Taylor?" Mrs. Fees asked. "Something you want to talk about?"

"I lie a lot," Taylor began.

"I can see that it bothers you," Mrs. Fees replied. "I'm sorry if what I said made you cry."

"But, if I don't lie, my grandfather hurts me."

"Hurts you, Taylor?"

"Yeah, I know God doesn't like me when I lie, but if I don't lie, it hurts."

"What hurts, Taylor?" Mrs. Fees asked, concerned at the turn the conversation was taking.

"The belt."

"The belt? Your grandfather hits you with a belt?" Mrs. Fees asked, reaching to give Taylor a hug.

"Yeah."

"Why, that's terrible."

"Don't say anything, okay?" Taylor pleaded. "If my grandpa found out I said something, I'd really get it."

"But this is wrong. This is much worse than telling a lie."

"I gotta go," Taylor said, pulling away from Mrs. Fees' embrace. "My grandpa and dad are waiting. Bye."

"Bye, Taylor. I'll be thinking of you. See you next week."

"Maybe." He walked through the door and was gone.

Mrs. Fees had had no training in reporting abuse, nor had she training as a teacher. She was merely a mother who had agreed to teach Sunday School. She knew nothing of the laws regarding confidentiality, but Taylor had asked her not to say anything, and she decided she would honor that request. If what Taylor said was true, that he would "really get it," then she didn't want to be the cause of that.

On the way home from church, Mrs. Fees realized that Taylor had wanted to tell somebody about this, or he wouldn't have stayed afterward. Maybe this was a sign from God that she was to do something. She decided she would pray to learn what she should do with the information. For now, and until God answered her prayer, she would be silent and hope that Taylor would ask God to forgive him for his lies. Perhaps God would work a miracle to stop Taylor's grandfather from harming the youngster.

Zeke was going out of his mind sitting in the county jail. He had never been confined to anything except his deer blind, but that was by choice and only for a few hours. This was a totally different situation.

For whatever reason, the men in the cells on each side and across from him didn't like him. Maybe word had gotten around that he was a trial lawyer, reminding these guys of the attorneys who convinced a jury of their guilt. So, not only did Zeke have no privacy, but there was no conversation between the cells, or even in the common area where the men ate meals and were free to exercise.

Finally, the man most dominating in size and demeanor asked Zeke, "What you in here for, little guy?"

"Rather not say," Zeke replied, staring at the floor.

"You'd rather not say? Listen! When I ask a question, it gets answered, understand?"

"And if I don't answer?" Zeke asked.

"You don't want to know. Now, answer my question: Why you in here? Me and the others want to know."

"DUI."

"Don't lie to me, a-hole. We know you're in here for killing that conservation officer. He has a kid with a disability. Did you know that before you killed him? You're a despicable human being."

"I didn't think an animal like you would know what that fancy word meant," Zeke fired back.

"Human being? It's a concept you wouldn't know anything about."

"No, despicable," Zeke replied. "Guess it does take an S.O.B. like you to know what the word means."

While other inmates began yelling to get the attention of the guard, the big dude punched Zeke in the gut. "From now on, your name is 'A-hole,' and you answer my questions truthfully, because if you don't, the next punch is going to require a lot of stitches. We don't like papa-killers, especially papas who got handicapped kids. Understand?"

Lou was a half-hour early at the Gerald R. Ford International Airport, anxiously awaiting Carol's flight from Kansas City. There was a half-hour delay, but finally arrive she did, stepping into Lou's waiting arms. The two smiled from the moment they saw each other, embraced, kissed, and walked arm-in-arm to the luggage area. There was a lot of news to share from Kansas City, as well as an update on the case in Trout City.

All seemed back to normal as the couple pulled up to their home on the shore of Lake Michigan. The final welcome was delivered by Samm who wagged her tail for a good five minutes. The cats seemed to welcome Carol about as enthusiastically as if she had just returned from a day's shopping.

OCTOBER 12

The crowd in Mickey's Bar was predictable on a cold night with snow flurries gently falling outside and NFL football on huge screens inside. There was only one guy in the place that most of the others didn't know, and as far as they were concerned, he was just some guy passing through town, or maybe a hunter, tired of hunting camp and wanting some companionship and a wide screen television for some ESPN football.

As usual, Howard Richards was front and center, slapping people on the back, paying for drinks, and drinking those bought by others. For some reason, the men thought the stranger could be trusted, so they didn't restrict their comments.

"Looks like the rich lawyer from downstate is going to pay big-time for shooting off his mouth about you bagging that buck, huh, Howie?" A bearded man with a large protruding belly slapped Howard's shoulder.

"No question about it," Howie bellowed. "He's got a cell waiting for him in Marquette. The workshop up there might as well be putting his name on a cage."

"Stupid lawyer," Danny, the bartender, said. "Everybody knows people don't mess with you, Howie."

"Well, not everybody," another man mumbled over a scotch and water.

"I warned him when he talked to me," Danny added. "I knew he was playing with fire, but he wouldn't listen. Can you imagine one buck being worth a guy's career, his freedom for life? Sad, but you gotta play the cards dealt to ya. Right, guys?"

The stranger walked closer to the men at the bar. "I'm passing through. What are you guys talking about? You got me curious."

"Howie here bagged a 12-point buck a couple days ago. Some hotshot attorney from downstate overheard him bragging and called the cops to investigate. For some reason, the lawyer killed the conservation officer when he came out to investigate the poaching claim."

"Uh-huh. Going to be a trial, is there?" the stranger asked.

"Reckon so. Gotta follow protocol, they tell me," Howard said, making fun of the waste of time before a judge and jury.

"Howie's got friends around these parts," Danny said. "There isn't a man or woman for that matter, in his right mind that would return a guilty verdict on Howie, even if he was guilty."

"Is that lawyer's name Zeke Simons, by any chance?" the stranger asked.

"Yeah, I think that's his name. That's his name, ain't it, Howie?" Danny asked.

"Simons? Yeah, that's him," Howard replied.

"Can someone answer a question for me?" the stranger asked.

"We'll try," Danny laughed. "We try to answer all questions from our paying customers."

"Do they have those metal detecting machines that court visitors have to go through to get to the courtroom in this county?"

"Nah, that's big-city stuff," Howard replied. "We don't need any of that up here. Nobody cares about the few cases that get to court, so why spend money on that new-fangled stuff? Everybody knows everybody, and, well, we just don't take all that stuff seriously. Besides, word is you can get cancer from walking through them things."

"Thanks," the stranger replied and then turning toward Howie, said, "Hope you win your case. Sometimes them hot-shot lawyers need to know how the little guy feels."

Howard nodded his thanks and shook the man's hand. The stranger finished his glass of beer, left a good tip on the bar, and walked out.

His cheerful manner disappearing, Howard said to Danny, "Get his license number and a description of his vehicle. He's a new guy. I can't trust him. He could have been sent here by the attorney, or maybe Judge Patterson. I don't trust the judge any more either. Patterson better have some retirement plans, because he won't get elected next year. I'll see to it."

Before the stranger had gotten out of the parking lot, Howard was talking to the sheriff. "Do a check on a red Ford Escort, license Michigan JJJ-655."

"OK. You going to hang on, or do you want me to call you?" the sheriff asked.

"I'll hang on."

About a minute later, Howard heard, "Got it."

"Good. What do you got?"

"Car's registered to Jerry Tomlinson from Dansville. He's done time for breaking and entering and armed robbery."

"Where's this Dansville? Isn't there a Dansville, Illinois?" Howard asked.

"Yeah," the sheriff replied.

"Ok, thanks."

"Anything else you need?" the sheriff asked. "You want him pulled over?"

"No, not if he's from Illinois. Guess he was just a curious Joe."

"How do you mean, Howie?" the sheriff asked.

"Well, he asked if this county has metal detectors at the courthouse."

"Wonder what brought that to mind?" the sheriff asked.

"I can't help you, Sheriff. Like I said, guess he's just curious, is all."

Heading south, Jerry began the long drive back to Dansville, Michigan. He'd learned what he wanted to know, and once he learned the date of the trial, he'd be back.

OCTOBER 13

Mrs. Fees, the Sunday School teacher, was bothered by Taylor's admission. She decided to talk privately with the minister. When Reverend Evans could see her, she drove to the church and was invited into his office.

"One of my students in Sunday school, Taylor Richards, told me that he has been abused by his grandfather. Can I do something about that?"

"Would that be Howard Richards?" Reverend Evans asked.

"Yes. Taylor's Dad is Eric, and Eric's father is Howard."

Reverend Evans looked uncomfortable. "Judging others is so easy, and it's such a sin, Mrs. Fees, we must be very careful. And further-more, I really don't think it is the church's function to become in-volved in the affairs of our members. I have enough trouble keeping us in the black and downplaying the petty interactions and hostilities of the congregation. If we start accusing members of abuse, any kind of abuse, it sets us up to be a party to a lot of domestic issues. Once we get involved with one issue, why wouldn't we get involved with another? And I'll tell you this: after twenty-seven years in this job, I'm sure there is hardly a home that doesn't have something askew about it. So, if Taylor has told you he is being abused, it's good that he shared it, but we're not going to get involved. Let him tell a school teacher, or a doctor, or a relative, or a neighbor. There are lots of people he can talk to who are in a position to help him. He didn't ask for your help, did he?"

"No, in fact he asked me not to say anything about it, because if I did, he might get hit more and more."

"There you go — he doesn't even want our help."

"But I think I should do something! I think Taylor is reaching out for help."

"Well, like I said, let him reach out to someone outside the church. And I'll tell you this: if you do get involved, which I hope you don't, you will not be involved as a member of this church. And you did not talk to me. Am I clear?"

"Yes, Reverend."

Given the brush-off she received, Mary Fees knew that Reverend Evans simply didn't want to have a potential problem dropped in his lap, even by a devout and loyal member of his following. When she accepted the responsibility to teach the class, she had vowed to do the best she could. And, while she had no training to be a teacher, she had unlimited love and compassion for the children. For her to be aware of Taylor's pain and not to act was unconscionable to her.

One of Mary's neighbors, Laura Lindsay, was a teacher so that afternoon when Laura had come home from school, she asked Laura for some advice. Mary explained what Taylor had said, and what the Reverend had said, and asked what she should do.

"Did you see any evidence of abuse — a wound, a burn, a bruise on this boy's body?" Laura asked.

"No. He told me his grandpa hit him with a belt, but I didn't see any welts or bruises or anything."

"I imagine you didn't record this conversation," Laura said.

"Oh no, we were just chatting after class. I knew something was bothering him because of his tears."

"Well, the first thing I would do is write everything down as you recall it," Laura advised. "Play back the conversation in your mind, and write down exactly what was said. Include any of Taylor's emotions or actions that would signal fear or pain or whatever. Then you should inform Protective Services."

"Where do I find them?" Mrs. Fees asked.

"They would be in the phone book under County Government."

"But Taylor said not to tell anyone, and I don't want to violate his confidence."

"Yes, that is a dilemma, but it's your call. If the danger to Taylor escalates, and you didn't act, you'll feel even guiltier. If you do report it, your confidentially will be honored, and Protective Services will look into this without divulging the source of their information."

"I see."

"If I were you, I would talk face-to-face with the social worker, or whoever is willing to see you in Protective Services," Laura advised. "Explain what this boy said, and tell the person about his not wanting you to tell anyone. They get this sort of thing all the time. They'll know what they can do and how best to handle it."

"Ok. Thanks, Laura. I knew you would know what to do."

"You're welcome."

OCTOBER 20

The poaching trial of Howard Richards was held in Mancelona, in the courtroom of the Honorable Judge Lester Cothran. The prosecuting attorney for Cherry County, Wil Purcell, was not going to personally prosecute the case on behalf of the people. Instead he assigned Assistant Prosecutor Harrison Corbett, who would be presenting his first case. Everybody needs to begin sometime, Prosecutor Purcell thought, and this trial would be a good beginning for Corbett.

Neither Howard's attorney, Max Bell, nor Harrison Corbett was concerned with the members of the jury. Both attorneys were satisfied with the jury pool, and the jury selection was routine. Prosecutor Corbett challenged one seated juror for cause when she indicated that she was against hunting, considering those who hunt to be inhumane. In addition, she also was a member of the Sierra Club. Her replacement met with the approval of both attorneys. Judge Cothran released the remaining pool of jurors and got right down to business, asking the prosecutor and the defense attorney to give opening statements.

"Prosecutor Corbett, your opening statement, please."

"Thank you, Your Honor. Members of the jury, once you hear the facts, I believe you will find that the defendant is guilty of poaching on October 1st. This is all I have to say, Your Honor. Thank you."

"Mr. Bell, your opening statement."

"Ladies and gentlemen of the jury, thank you for serving on this jury," Max began. "As you know, my client has been accused of poaching a deer. The accusation is that he shot a 12-point buck out of season. The alleged shooting occurred on October 1st, which is opening day of bow season for white-tailed deer in the Lower Peninsula. Mr. Richards did hit the deer with his pickup truck, and in that sense he played a role in its death. But I will show that the deer must have been shot by another person, the one truly guilty of the poaching. Thank you."

"Thank you. Mr. Corbett, your first witness."

"The People call Mr. Zeke Simons."

Zeke took the stand, took the oath, and sat down.

"Mr. Simons, for the record, please state your name, address, and occupation."

"Anthony Simons, 1436 Apple Blossom Lane, Mason, Michigan. I'm an attorney."

"You are the person who reported the poaching, correct?" Harrison asked.

"Yes, I am."

"Tell us about that."

"I was in Mickey's Bar on October first having lunch, and the defendant was there telling people he had shot a 12-point buck that morning."

"So, by his own admission, he was poaching, correct?"

"Absolutely."

"Did he say anything about hitting the deer with his truck?"

"No."

"No more questions, Your Honor."

"Mr. Bell, your witness," the judge said.

Max Bell stood and walked toward Zeke. "You're a bow hunter, correct?"

"Yes."

"Mr. Simons, as a rule, bow hunters don't seem to like firearm hunters. Would you agree with that?"

"Not necessarily. We just don't like them when they shoot our game out of season."

"Did you see the defendant shoot a deer?"

"No."

"So, the only thing you were acting on in reporting poaching is my client's alleged comment that he shot a deer."

"Yes."

"Is it possible that my client was telling a story about someone else poaching a deer, and you mistakenly thought he killed the deer?" Max asked.

"No, that is not possible."

"So, you seem to be taking one sentence, 'I shot a 12-point buck' out of context, without hearing any conversation prior to the statement that you reacted to. Am I right?"

Zeke persisted. "He said, 'I shot a 12-point buck this morning.' Those were his exact words."

"His exact words, as you think you heard them?"

"They were his exact words," Zeke replied.

"May I suggest that you heard, 'I got a 12-point buck this morning?' If Mr. Richards got a buck, it could have been by hitting the buck, or having it given to him, for instance. There are many ways Mr. Richards could have gotten the buck. Do you agree that my client could have said, 'I got a buck,' and not, 'I shot a buck?'"

Zeke continued to hold firm. "I was sure he said, 'I shot a buck.'"

"That wasn't my question. My question was, could my client have said, 'I got a buck,' and you misunderstood? All I'm asking, Mr. Simons, is whether that's possible?

"I suppose so."

"No more questions, Your Honor."

"Mr. Corbett, your next witness."

"The people call Dr. Dan Tatroe."

Dr. Tatroe took the stand, swore to tell the truth, and sat down, awaiting questioning.

Mr. Corbett began. "Doctor, you were the person who performed the necropsy on the 12-point buck, correct?"

"Yes, I was."

"What did you find?"

"The deer was shot by a firearm, probably with a .22 caliber rifle, suffering a direct hit into the heart. The buck was not hit by a vehicle. The skin was abraded by movement of the carcass along the ground, and into a vehicle, or into a transferring device."

"You're certain of your findings?" Mr. Corbett asked. "The deer was not shot with an arrow?"

"No, it was not," Dr. Tatroe replied emphatically. "The poacher tried to make it appear that way, but one arrow entry wound wasn't sufficient to kill the animal, and the second arrow was simply jammed into the entrance wound made by the bullet piercing the deer's hide."

"Thank you, Doctor. No more questions."

"Your witness, Mr. Bell."

"Doctor, we are familiar with your reputation as a veterinary technician with the DNR. In general we do not question your findings. But I must ask, in doing your work is it possible for you to tell who shot the buck?"

"No."

"So, the shot from a .22 caliber rifle could have come from anyone, correct?"

"Yes."

"And, it is your experience that the abrasions on the deer are not related to being struck or even hit by a glancing blow by a vehicle."

"Yes, it is."

"But, will you admit that it is possible for the deer to have been clipped by a vehicle so that, in its weakened state, it wouldn't take much for a vehicle to knock the buck off balance and have it die near or in the road?"

"That's possible, but I don't believe that is what happened," Doctor Tatroe replied.

"I understand you don't, but I am only asking if it is possible."

"Yes, I suppose it's possible, but highly unlikely."

"Thank you, Doctor. No more questions, Your Honor."

"Mr. Corbett, your next witness."

"We have no more witnesses, Your Honor. We rest our case."

"Mr. Bell, your first witness."

"I would like to call Mr. Stuart Rollins."

Mr. Rollins took the stand and swore to tell the truth.

Mr. Bell, holding a yellow legal pad, approached a small podium and began his questioning. "Mr. Rollins, you are an insurance adjuster for AutoInsure. Is that correct?"

"Yes."

"And, in that capacity, you inspect car-deer accidents to determine if a client is due payment on a policy with your company. Is that correct?"

"Yes."

"Mr. Rollins, please explain to the jury your experience in responding to your customers who have hit a deer."

"I would say the majority of such vehicle-damage claims are animal-related, damage to the car either from the animal, or from the driver hitting a tree or embankment while trying to avoid the animal."

"Mr. Rollins, with all due respect, I didn't ask you to account for the means in which autos are damaged, although it is interesting. I asked you to explain your experience in responding to customers with auto damage as a result of hitting a deer."

"Yes, you did. I apologize. This is my first time testifying in a trial, and I'm a little nervous. People are nervous when they talk to me about their accidents and so I guess the cards are in a different hand in this trial. I'm sorry. What was your question?"

The judge interrupted. "Mr. Rollins, please relax and try just to answer the questions that the attorneys ask. Okay?"

"Yes, sure. Sorry."

"Mr. Bell wants you to tell the jury what experience you have had in responding to damage claims from your customers," Judge Cothran explained.

"Yes, I've responded to every one of them. We believe in service and in quick service, so whenever I get a call, I immediately go to the vehicle. People are usually upset, nervous like I am now, and so they want someone to get right to work on the claim. They are usually busy people who need a car for their jobs."

Mr. Bell and Judge Cothran locked eyes and Mr. Bell simply shook his head, as if to say, I don't know what more I can do.

Once again the judge interrupted. "Mr. Rollins, how many years have you been investigating vehicle damage?"

"I investigate every claim, and…"

"Mr. Rollins, how many years? That is all I want to know," Judge Cothran stated patiently.

"Uh, three."

"Thank you. That is how I want you to respond to every question asked of you. Answer briefly and accurately. Understand?"

"Yes, sir."

"Mr. Bell, please continue."

"Thank you, Your Honor. Did you investigate Mr. Richards' claim that his auto was damaged by hitting a deer?"

"Yes." Mr. Rollins looked at Judge Cothran, who nodded and smiled.

"Did your investigation determine that, in fact, Mr. Richards did hit the deer?"

"Yes, it did." Again, Stuart looked at the judge, who nodded again and looked away.

"So, you would conclude that, if my client hit the deer, it probably was running from the woods, and ran into the path of the pickup."

"Yes."

"Thank you. No more questions, Your Honor."

"Prosecutor Corbett, your witness."

Prosecutor Corbett smiled briefly, stood and approached Mr. Rollins. "When you investigate a car-deer accident, can you be certain that the vehicle struck a deer?"

"Yes."

"I mean, it couldn't have struck a fox, or a moose, or a cow, or a horse?"

"We know when the vehicle strikes a deer because of the tell-tale damage to the vehicle and the hair or fur that is almost always found on the vehicle."

"I see. So you have no evidence whether the deer was poached or killed legally, nor do you know who killed the deer, correct? I mean you can't be sure who was driving the vehicle that struck the deer. Right?"

"The person who is filing a claim hit the deer," Stuart replied

"Oh, really. You have access to video coverage?"

"Of course not, but why would someone other than the vehicle owner use the vehicle involved in the accident?"

"So, you assume that the owner of the vehicle and your policy holder are always the same person."

"Sure."

"No more questions, Your Honor."

"You may step down, Mr. Rollins," Judge Cothran said, thankful the witness had completed his testimony. "Thank you."

"That's it?" Stuart asked.

"That's it," Judge Cothran replied. "You are dismissed."

"Thank you."

The judge tried to move the testimony along. "Your next witness, Mr. Bell."

"The defense calls Dan Willard."

After being sworn in, Danny took his seat, appearing a bit nervous on the stand.

"Mr. Willard, you are a bartender at Mickey's in Trout City?"

"Yes, I am."

"Do you know Mr. Richards?"

"Yes, I do."

"Did he tell people in your bar that he shot the buck on October 1st?"

"He was telling a story about a deer being killed, but I don't recall him saying that he actually killed the buck."

"He is alleged to have said to others that he shot the buck down by the Cherry County line. In fact, Mr. Simons testified that my client used the words, 'I shot a 12-point buck this morning.' Did you hear him say that?"

"I can't testify to those exact words. It has been a few weeks, and there's always noise in the bar, plus I've got some hearing loss. But, I don't recall him saying that he actually shot it, but he was talking about a deer being shot."

"Did anyone in the bar tell you that he had said, 'I shot a 12-point buck this morning'?"

"No."

"No one said anything about killing a buck?"

"Yeah, Howard talked about the killing of a buck, but I don't recall him saying flat out, 'I killed a buck,'" Danny testified.

"So, if Mr. Richards had been bragging about killing a deer on October 1st, you would have known about it, correct?" Max asked.

"Most definitely. A barber and a bartender hear whatever is going on in town. My bar walls hear more secrets than any other four walls in the county."

"Did you call Mr. Richards any time after he left the bar?"

"Yes."

"Why did you call him?"

"The bow hunter was pretty upset about what he thought he heard, and Howard is a good customer. I feared for him, to be honest. I called him to tell him to be careful."

"No more questions, Your Honor."

"Mr. Corbett, your witness."

"Let me try to understand. It is your testimony that Mr. Richards said that a buck was shot on October 1st, right?"

"Yes."

"And, it is your testimony that you called Mr. Richards to tell him that Mr. Simons had overheard him say, 'I shot a 12-point buck this morning'?"

"No. I testified that a bow hunter was 'upset about what he thought he heard.'"

"And you interpret what he heard to be that Mr. Richards shot the buck."

POACHING MAN AND BEAST

"Yes."

"If you didn't think Howard said he shot a 12-point buck, you didn't try to set Mr. Simons straight, did you?"

"No, I did not."

"So as far as you were concerned, Howard Richards had said he shot the buck."

Danny took a few seconds before responding, and even then he softly said, 'Yeah," as he nodded his head in agreement.

"I have no further questions, Your Honor," Corbett stated.

Judge Cothran dismissed Mr. Wilkins.

"Your next witness, Mr. Bell."

"I have no further witnesses, Your Honor."

"We will take a break before closing arguments. The jury will now retire to the jury room. The bailiff will instruct you on lunch procedures. We are in recess until one o'clock."

Sitting in the second row, Lou couldn't believe what he was seeing and hearing. The prosecuting attorney had missed key opportunities to put conclusive evidence before the jury. Maybe this guy skipped a trial procedure class at law school, Lou thought. Or maybe he didn't get high grades in investigating and preparing a case. What he had just seen was unprofessional and upsetting.

During the noon-hour break, Conservation Officer Faccio stood outside the courthouse calling Judge Patterson on her cell phone. "I simply can't believe it."

"Believe what?"

"I'm in Mancelona, at Howard Richards' trial for poaching, and the prosecutor, Mr. Corbett, not Mr. Purcell, simply sat down and conceded to the defense. He only had one witness besides Zeke, and Corbett didn't protect him when he testified! This prosecutor had no evidence against Howard, and he had practically no questions for the defense witnesses. About all he did was make a fool of the insurance adjuster."

"Hmm, not like him as far as I know," Judge Patterson replied.

"Well, I can't speak to that, but I've never witnessed such a travesty in all my years investigating poaching." Officer Faccio was quiet, disturbed by what she had witnessed.

"There isn't much I can do, Officer. One judge doesn't interfere with the trials of another judge," Judge Patterson replied.

"I don't know what the jury thinks, but based on evidence and testimony of the few witnesses, Howard is innocent, with little if any evidence to indicate he shot the deer out-of-season."

"Try to relax a bit," Judge Patterson advised. "In the long run, the truth will prevail."

"That's nice to hear, but this case renders everything conservation officers do to protect the hunting laws of this state absolutely meaningless."

When court reconvened after lunch, both attorneys presented short closing statements. After the judge instructed them, the jury retired to the jury room. In half an hour, they returned with the expected verdict of "Not Guilty." The judge thanked the jurors and released them, and Howard Richards went free with a clear record.

Had it not been for Officer Faccio's comments to the President of Justice for Wildlife, the case might have been buried in the archives of court proceedings in Cherry County. Letters to the editor, protests to the city council, and ads in the paper admonishing Prosecutor Purcell for the horrendous prosecution of a known poacher started a chain reaction of protest. Every leader in Trout City was outraged at the decision in favor of Howard Richards.

While the public had felt sympathy for Howard in the mailbox case, they had an opposite reaction to the poaching. Not everyone believed him to be a murderer, but they did believe him to be a poacher, and for him to get away with this activity touched an open wound in the community.

Justice for Wildlife pulled all the stops in using this matter to benefit their cause. They protested daily outside the DNR branch office, and also outside the courthouse, where Mr. Purcell's office was located.

Max Bell, Prosecutor Purcell, and even Howard Richards hadn't expected a reaction like this. In all previous incidents involving Howard, a few people were upset, but this case produced an effect like lighting a cigarette while filling a gas tank.

OCTOBER 22

One consequence of this outcry affected the student body at Trout City High School. Janet Abs, president of the student council, saw it as an opportunity to work toward a change in the community. She met with Vince Porter, president of the school chapter of Future Farmers of America, and Josh Bacon, the president of the Key Club, a youth organization sponsored by the Trout City Kiwanis Club. The three agreed to meet at McDonald's on the edge of town after school.

Janet, a born leader, was bright, articulate, and an all-around good student. She was on the volleyball team, in the senior play, and active in her church youth fellowship group. She had been accepted with a full academic scholarship at Alma College and would start classes next fall.

Vince, the eldest of four sons was also a leader. He planned to follow his father in farming and would attend Michigan State University the following summer to major in animal husbandry.

Finally, Josh Bacon was more of a follower than a leader. As an all-state basketball player, he had earned a scholarship to play at Ohio State. As president of the Key Club, a nod to his popularity, he

POACHING MAN AND BEAST

proudly added this leadership experience to his college application. Josh had been dating Janet for two years and supported her idea to make a difference at Trout City High.

Once comfortable in a booth, each ordered a Pepsi, and Janet began, "Thanks for meeting with me, guys."

"Sure, Jan," Vince replied. "What's up?"

"I've been thinking about our town, and the rumors of how corrupt it may be, and that's been bothering me. I wanted to talk with you guys and share some thoughts."

"Ok, shoot," Josh said, having served as her sounding board on several occasions.

"I think kids think this isn't a 'cool' town to live in, and most seniors who get into college look forward to getting out of town, with little expectation of coming back. Do you agree?"

"No question about it," Vince replied. "But, that is probably true of seniors from most small towns."

"I agree," Josh added.

"Well, it shouldn't be that way," Janet replied. "I think we can do something about it and make our town an upstanding community."

"What do you have in mind, Jan?" Josh asked.

"I have an idea or two, and, I'm sure you guys can come up with even better ones."

Vince said, "Ok, let's start there. What is your idea?"

"Please don't laugh now," Janet began. "I thought the Student Council could sponsor an essay contest for all the kids in school."

"And the title would be, 'Why Living in Trout City is Not Cool'?" Vince asked, laughing.

"Come on guys, get serious," Janet bristled.

"Okay. I couldn't help it."

"I was thinking more of something like, 'Trout City Is a Great City Because'," Janet said.

"That would be OK, but Trout City is not a great city," Vince said, shaking his head.

"At least this idea is positive, which is more than any of us can say now," Janet replied. "Anyway, a second idea is to have a famous person come in, give a speech, and then have people break up into groups and discuss the topic."

"What topic are you thinking of?" Josh asked, to be supportive.

"Something like 'Effective Citizenship in Today's Society'," Janet replied.

Vince pointed his index finger into his mouth, signaling barfing. "Sorry, Janet, but that's about as boring as you can get. We'd surely draw about a half-dozen people, and we'd be half the group."

"Maybe, but those are my ideas. They aren't much, but I wanted to tell you about them."

"I like what Janet is trying to do. Maybe our clubs could sponsor a couple of activities leading to something positive," Vince added.

"Exactly," Janet replied.

"I assume that you are thinking about this because of the murder trial coming up at the courthouse," Josh said.

"Yes, but that's the tip of the iceberg," Janet reminded her friends. "People here don't vote because they think the town is controlled by certain individuals and their vote doesn't count. Some people around here just laugh at the hunting rules. Few people participate in city government. Most of the committees never meet and practically nobody volunteers to serve. A school millage hasn't passed since — I think my parents said it was back in the 1980s. Our crime rate is much above communities our size, and most of the time nothing gets done. I mean, we're a pretty poor example of people living together in a community."

"You certainly don't think we can turn all of this around, do you?" Josh asked.

"No, but I think we can do something," Janet answered. "After all, for those of us planning to stay in the area, something has to be done to give us a future."

"Listen, I've got basketball practice," Josh said, sliding out of the booth. "But I'll think about this. Let's meet again."

"I need to go too," Vince added. "I agree with Josh; we should meet again after giving this some thought."

"Okay, but before you go, how about exploring the possibility of a 'Trout City Youth in Government Day'?" suggested Janet. "Students could spend a day with the sheriff, the mayor, and other officials. Afterward we can all come together and discuss what we experienced, good and bad. Maybe something positive could come from that."

"Bingo! I think that's it!" Vince replied, genuinely enthused.

"I agree. Good idea. Let's think about that and meet again," Josh proposed.

"Thanks, guys," said Janet as the two young men, both wearing varsity jackets with a huge trout mascot on the back, walked out of McDonald's.

Meanwhile, unbeknownst to Janet, Vince, and Josh, Scott Anderson, a law student at the University of Michigan, had learned about the mailbox-smashing/shotgun-blast incident and decided to analyze this event. The "Introduction to Criminal Law" class taught by Professor Lyn Beekman required students to search the Internet for an activity that seemed illogical or indicated a grave injustice. Each member of the class was to research an event and provide a detailed legal analysis of the circumstances and/or legal action. They were expected to cite previous litigation that would serve as precedent or violations of federal or state law inherent in the matter. Finally, each student needed to present a detailed plan that might address justice in the situation.

Scott learned of this injustice because a ninth grade Trout City student had written about the mailbox-smashing incident and put it on her Internet web site. This was akin to tossing a note in a bottle into the sea, hoping someone would find it, open the bottle and act on the note. But Scott Anderson found the story and adopted it for his project.

NOVEMBER 6

Scott Anderson decided to take a one-day trip to Trout City. As part of his report, he wanted to interview some key players in the "Mailbox Murders" as he now titled his project. Scott first planned to visit the newspaper editor. Then he would go to the high school to try to interview at least one of the survivors of the accident. Finally, he wanted to talk to the prosecutor.

The editor of the paper, Ron Otto, was in his office along with the beat writer who covered the accident and its investigation. Ron began, "The murder of those two boys was one of the biggest tragedies ever to hit this community. I wrote a couple of editorials urging justice in the matter, and the mail and phone calls were threatening. I was shocked at the hate mail I received after our story said that Howard Richards was wrong in doing what he did. Seriously, I guess people had been, in a sense, terrorized by kids doing destructive things in the community: smashing mailboxes, smashing pumpkins, egging cars, breaking into garages, you name it. All of this is illegal and wrong, and I asked for the legal process to work. But Howard Richards took the problem personally and decided to act outside the system. He ended up becoming a folk hero for taking on the kids and showing them that he'd had it with the petty crimes."

"Were you treated the same way?" Scott asked the reporter.

"No, I didn't have any problems. I simply reported the facts. But, I will say this: I believe things happen in back rooms, if you know what I mean. It wasn't through any quirk of fate that this thing never came to trial. I don't know where you live, but around here, the image of justice is sometimes drawn with dollar bills or promises to help in the future."

"This issue divided your readers, then?" Scott asked.

"You bet," Ron replied. "I have never been scared of anything in my life, and I have a reputation of putting out a respectable paper. But I've got a family, two kids in school, and a wife who had just about had it with the phone calls. I decided to stop editorializing about the case and to concentrate on supporting the prosecutor's opponent in the next election."

Scott thanked Mr. Otto and his reporter and drove to the high school. The principal, Pat Sagala, agreed he might talk with one of the students who survived the shotgun blast that killed two friends, and she called Bobby Acton from study hall. Scott and Bobby met in a conference room.

Scott introduced himself as a law student who had chosen the mailbox murders as a class project. He explained that he wanted to research the case and examine why justice hadn't been served, if that was in fact the conclusion.

"It was a terrible night — the worst night of my life. I've never seen such a mess as I did that night." Bobby looked down and shook his head as memories flashed through his mind.

"Will you talk about it?" Scott asked sympathetically.

"Oh yeah, time heals. I think about it almost every day, but yeah, I can talk about it now. We were out driving around, and we'd had some beer. Teddy and I were in the back of the pickup, Chuck was driving, and Leon was in the passenger seat. Chuck would speed up, and then, as he approached the box that was to get it, he would slow down. Teddy and I took turns. Teddy would kneel and hold my legs and I would reach out with a bat and slam it into the mailbox. It made a horrendous sound!

"But that night at Richards' mailbox, when I hit the box, the shotgun went off, and Chuck and Leon didn't have a chance. It was hanging from the tree, parallel to the road, so the pellets came through the windshield like darts and killed them instantly. The pickup went out of control, and Teddy and I were thrown out of the back. We were able to get up, but we were in a different world. I remember hearing old man Richards laughing and clapping his hands, but we never saw him.

"It was a long time before another car came by and I guess that person had a cell phone and called 911. Then there were police and EMS crews all around. I can still see Chuck and Leon lying in the front seat, and all those lights flashing and swirling. It was terrible."

"Richards had set up a system to ambush you?" Scott asked.

"Yeah, it was no secret. He bragged about it and people thought of him as a hero."

"Your parents took this to court, right?" Scott asked.

"No, the pressure from the community was intense. I know we were wrong, but people said our parents were bad parents, and I think it was easier to just bury the guys and try to get on with our lives. Besides, our parents didn't have money to pay a lawyer. Teddy needed some medical procedures, and that cost a lot of money. His parents didn't have any insurance."

"So, there was no court case, nobody sued this man, there were no tickets or fines or anything?" Scott asked, astounded that the prosecutor didn't act on behalf of the people.

"Not that I know of."

"Does this upset you?" Scott asked.

"Does what upset me?" Bobby asked.

"That no trial was held, that there was no punishment for killing your friends?"

"I guess we were doing terrible things, breaking the law. Nearly everyone said we got what we deserved, and we heard it so much that I guess we sort of believed it after a while. It was weeks before people talked to me and Teddy. Even today, we're bad kids. Though that scared us so, we could be Sunday school teachers now."

"Thanks for talking with me," Scott said, shaking Bobby's hand. "Guess you had better get back to class."

"Good luck with your report."

"Thanks. I'm sorry about your friends." Bobby went back to class, and Scott thanked Mrs. Sagala for the opportunity to interview Bobby.

Scott left the school and went to City Hall, hoping to see Wil Purcell, the prosecutor. Scott explained Professor Beekman's assignment and what he hoped to learn, and met with resistance. Wil had no interest in talking with him, especially about the mailbox murders, but he thought he might avoid further attention by giving Scott enough to make him go away.

"I'd really like to talk with you," Wil Purcell said. "I remember law school. I know you have projects to work on, and it's all part of learning how to be a lawyer. But I've got things to do, cases to prepare for. If you had made an appointment, I could have given you a little more time, but..."

"I apologize for just popping in here unannounced, and I do appreciate your seeing me. Let me ask quickly, why didn't this case go to trial? Why didn't you prosecute an obvious act of terror on children?"

"Children? These were high school kids damaging personal property. If there needed to be a trial, it should have been prosecuting the kids for destruction of property and drunkenness."

"Perhaps, but why didn't the legal process work? As I understand it, there was no fine, no probation, nothing in regard to the deaths. Am I right?" Scott asked.

"As I recall, I didn't have sufficient evidence to prosecute Mr. Richards, and I'm not going to waste valuable taxpayer money if I don't think a case can be won."

"Two kids were shot dead by a rifle deliberately positioned in a tree in front of a man's home, a man who claimed responsibility, and you didn't think you could win?" Scott asked, shaking his head. He couldn't help judging Purcell, which probably wasn't a good decision.

"Listen, when you graduate, pass the bar, pay your dues, and become a prosecutor, you can make these decisions. You have no idea what information was provided to me by investigating officers. My lesson for you is this: better not rush to judgment until you have all the information you need. I resent your challenging me, and I don't appreciate the immature way you've conducted yourself in my office. Professor Beekman will hear from me!"

With that, Prosecutor Purcell walked out of the room, leaving Scott sitting in a chair holding a cold cup of coffee. Scott gathered up his papers, thanked the secretary for her help, and left the building.

Scott's last goal was to try to interview the almost-mythical Howard Richards. He found the address in the phone book and set out to find Peavine Road. As he approached the Richards farm, he encountered an eerie feeling. He pulled into the driveway, believing no one was home. The curtains were drawn, there were no vehicles in the area, and no pets or farm animals were in sight, but just as Scott put the car into reverse gear, the house door opened, and an elderly man came onto the porch, following a bounding German shepherd. Howard shouted, "Rudy! Stop!" and the dog slowed and obeyed. Howard cautiously approached the vehicle.

"Are you Mr. Richards?" asked Scott.

"Yeah, what do you want?"

"I'm a student at the University of Michigan. You don't have a dislike for Wolverines do you?" Scott asked with a smile.

"Wolverines, Spartans, Broncos, Chips — who cares? It's all a media game to sell millions of dollars of sports stuff. So, what do you want?"

"I hoped to ask you a few questions about the rigging you set up that stopped the kids destroying mailboxes."

"Why would you want that?" Howard asked.

"I heard about your ingenious invention, and I wanted to meet and talk to the inventor," Scott replied.

"Well, you've met him."

"Thanks. I understand you became sort of a local hero for standing up to these punks."

"Yeah, I guess you could say that," Howard began. "I taught them a lesson about respect for the property of others."

"And, not to have a trial — that was quite a relief, I imagine."

"Yeah, it pays to know the prosecutor."

"Did you pay the prosecutor?" Scott asked, surprised at this forthright question.

"Well, sometimes you gotta do what you gotta do. I wasn't going to do time or pay a stupid fee for stopping what the cops couldn't stop."

"Makes sense. What did the payoff cost you?" Scott asked boldly.

"Getting kind of personal, are you?" Howard asked.

"Yeah, guess I am, but I'm just curious what a prosecutor would need to stop this from going to court. It wasn't polite of me to ask. Sorry," Scott said apologetically.

Howard, thinking he could still control the law, bragged to Scott about the payoff. "Five grand."

"Five grand? Where would you find that kind of money?"

"A lot of people in this county owe me, and I figured it was time to cash in some favors."

"Well, thanks for talking with me," Scott said. "I'm on my way back to Ann Arbor. You really figured out a way to curb youth crime. Gotta hand it to you, mister."

"Thanks."

"Have a good day."

"You, too."

Scott drove away chuckling at how he had used ego, pride, and flattery to get information. Guess that's why I got an "A" in my Trial Procedures Class, Scott thought to himself.

"I'm surprised he talked to me, and even more surprised that he told a total stranger what he did. I could have been an FBI agent," Scott thought out loud.

As Scott drove out of town for Ann Arbor, swirling red lights appeared in his rear-view mirror. While his eyes immediately glanced at his speedometer, his mind wondered if this was a random stop. Or was he about to be harassed by the police. He pulled over, his heart beating at a good clip. Law school expenses and a tight budget didn't leave much room for a speeding ticket, but he was speeding by a few miles per hour. So, if it wasn't a warning, it shouldn't be much, he thought.

"You need to get someplace fast, young man?" the officer asked.

"I was moving with the traffic. I didn't think I was speeding."

"Anything over the posted limit is speeding. I need to see your license, registration, and proof of insurance, please."

When Scott gave him the items, the officer saw he was from out of town. "Ann Arbor — you go to the University of Michigan?"

"Yes."

The officer stepped back. "Please get out of the car, put your hands on the car, and spread your feet."

"For speeding?" Scott asked.

"Checking for drugs, Mr. Anderson. It's routine with anyone your age and in college."

"This can't be happening," Scott said. "I don't do drugs, and I wasn't speeding!"

"Do what I say, buddy. Let's not make this difficult."

Scott got out of the car and did as he was told. The officer looked around in his vehicle and then directed Scott to open the trunk. Finding nothing suspicious, he came back to Scott. "Ok, you can get in your car while I write up this ticket."

Scott got back in the car and tried to take a few deep breaths. This was not right, and he was steaming about how he was being treated.

A few minutes later the officer returned to Scott's car, but two other police vehicles had arrived, then several officers taking positions which gave passing motorists the impression that some heavy action was about to ensue.

The officer handed Scott his documents. "I'm doing you a favor, Mr. Anderson. I've cited you for only going 15 over the limit when you were doing 20. This will save you a few bucks. I also decided not to do a drug arrest. You seem like an OK guy."

"Fifteen? No way! I was moving with the traffic and not going more than five miles over the limit."

"You're going to have to tell it to the judge. If I were you, I'd just pay it and be thankful I'm treating you good."

Scott could make a scene, or he could take the ticket, roll up the window and drive away. His introduction to Trout City complete, he bit his tongue and drove toward the expressway.

NOVEMBER 21

Snow was falling outside the county courthouse in Mancelona, but the courtroom was warm and quiet when Zeke Simons, dressed in khaki slacks and a blue blazer, was escorted to his seat at the defense table by an Cherry County Deputy. He glanced behind him and acknowledged Angie and Judge Beekins. He then listened to words from his attorney.

On the other side of the room, Marie Turner and other members of her family appeared sad and quiet, often whispering words of support for the wife of their deceased relative. Officer Turner's father was present, but his mother's health since the murder was such that it was a prudent decision for her to not be in the courtroom. Marie felt it best that Philip not attend the proceedings either, so he had gone to school that morning as usual.

At 9:23, the bailiff announced the arrival of the judge and asked all present to stand. Judge Johnson sat in her huge leather chair and pulled herself up to the bench, arranging papers and preparing for a long day.

All visitors to the courtroom were seated. Angie sat behind Zeke, with her father, Judge Beekins, on her right and her good friend

Tricia on her left. Angie looked tired, scared, and nervous. Lou sat next to Judge Beekins. The Wilds' were in the row behind Angie.

Approximately twenty-five seats were occupied by potential jurors and approximately one hundred seats were available for the media and the general public, but so many people had crowded into the courtroom, it was standing room only.

Judge Johnson began. "This case is the State of Michigan versus Simons. Mr. Simons is accused of the second-degree murder of Conservation Officer Timothy Turner on October 1st of this year.

"At this time, I will ask the bailiff to randomly select the names of jurors present. If you hear your name, please come forward and sit in the jury box."

The bailiff went through thirteen names, twelve of whom would serve on the jury, one of whom would be an alternate. With the initial panel in place, Judge Johnson asked the prosecuting attorney, Wil Purcell to begin his questioning of the jurors. "Prosecutor Purcell, do you have objections to any juror or any questions for the jury."

"No, Your Honor."

Prosecutor Purcell really didn't care who was on the jury, for he felt he would win the case easily. But he definitely wanted juror number eight on the panel. He had instructed the man that if he was chosen to be a juror and survived questioning, he should volunteer to be the foreman. If this were the case, he was certain to guide the others to a guilty verdict for the prosecution.

"Defense Attorney Moylan, you may question the jurors," Judge Johnson said.

"Thank you, Your Honor." Audrey rose, carrying a large notebook of juror profiles to a small podium. Once there, she turned toward the thirteen jurors. "I want to begin by thanking each of you for giving the court your time and attention to this important case. As you may know, my client is an attorney. My first question has to do with the legal profession. Have any of you had a bad experience with an attorney?"

When juror number six raised his hand, she said, "Please explain your experience, sir."

"My attorney didn't do his homework and caused me to lose a lot of money."

"Would you be more specific, please?" Audrey asked.

"I contested my mother's will, and he did practically nothing to represent me. I hate him, and I think all lawyers are liars, cheats, and no-good bums."

Audrey turned to the judge. "Your Honor, I ask to excuse juror number six for cause," Audrey said.

Judge Johnson nodded. "Juror number six, you are dismissed. Thank you."

A replacement juror was chosen, and Audrey continued her questioning. "Officer Turner was killed by a rifle shot. My second question has to do with your beliefs about guns. Do any of you have strong anti-gun feelings or beliefs?" Miss Moylan asked.

Juror number two raised her hand. "Ma'am, your feelings are?" Audrey asked.

"I am pro gun control. Guns in the hands of people with unchecked emotions or no training can, like this man, kill another."

"Your Honor, I wish to dismiss juror number two for cause," Audrey said.

"Juror number two, you are dismissed," replied the judge.

Audrey continued. "Have any of you ever had a family member wounded or killed by gunfire?"

Juror number nine raised his hand. "Your story, sir?" Audrey asked.

"My grandfather died in a hunting accident about forty years ago. It was ruled an accident, but I have my doubts, because the guy who fired the gun never really liked my grandpa."

"Thank you. Your Honor, I would like juror number nine dismissed for cause," Audrey said.

Judge Johnson replied, "Dismissed. Thank you, juror number nine."

Audrey moved closer to the jury. "This is a rather bold question, but I must ask it before we begin. Do any of you believe Mr. Simons is guilty of killing Officer Turner?" Two hands went up; juror number one and juror number eleven.

"Juror number one, you think Mr. Simons is guilty?" Audrey asked.

"Yes. I know Mr. Richards, and he'd never harm anybody, so it had to be him," the juror said, pointing at Zeke Simons sitting behind the defendant's table.

"Juror number eleven, you also think my client is guilty?" Audrey asked.

"Yes."

"Why do you think this, without hearing any of the evidence?" Audrey asked.

"Because he's not from around here. People in our town don't kill other people."

"Thank you. Your Honor, I ask that jurors one and eleven be dismissed for cause."

"Jurors number one and eleven, you are dismissed," replied Judge Johnson.

"Counselor, any other questions?"

"Just one, Your Honor. Do any of you resent hunters coming into your county?" Eight hands went up.

"Even with this resentment, do any of you believe that you cannot listen to the testimony and render a fair verdict?" No one raised a hand.

"If there are no other dismissals for cause, and if neither of you has any more questions, we have a jury, Judge Johnson said, thankful to have this phase of the trial over with a minimum of conflict.

"Your Honor, the defense requests the dismissal of juror number eight," Audrey said.

"Juror number eight, you are dismissed," Judge Johnson ordered. "The bailiff will pull one more name." Prosecutor Purcell was not pleased, but was still highly optimistic he would win.

As the name was pulled, and a woman replaced juror number eight, the judge said, "You have heard all the questions asked of the seated jurors. Do you have any concern about your ability to serve on this jury, given your thoughts on any of the questions?"

"I believe I can serve," the woman replied.

"Thank you. Does either the defense or the prosecution have any objection to this juror?" Before answering, Audrey quickly looked up the profile for this juror and saw, "Valedictorian of the class of 1994; student council president 1992-1993." That was good news; she indicated that the new juror was acceptable to her.

Judge Johnson declared, "This will be the jury for this trial. Potential jurors in the audience may return to your homes or places of employment. You are still in the jury pool, so I suggest you contact the clerk for instructions for the remainder of the week."

The jurors in the gallery picked up their belongings and filed out of the courtroom. On his way out, one of the men glanced to his right and noticed a somewhat familiar face. As he drove away from the courthouse, he had trouble recalling where he had seen the guy, but then he remembered; it was the man in the bar who had asked about the metal detectors. He got a cold chill when he put two and two together. The only reason he would want to know about metal detectors was if he expected to bring something into the courtroom that would be detected, like a gun or a bomb. Should he say something to someone? The question lingered in his mind all the way to Mickey's.

Judge Johnson explained to the seated jurors what would happen in the case, reminding them of their responsibilities. She expected that the case would last a couple of days, and, when away from the courtroom, they were not to talk about the facts or mention any of the testimony, and they were to avoid watching any news coverage or reading newspaper accounts of the trial. She then said, "I want to make it clear to you that it is the prosecutor's role to convince you beyond a reasonable doubt that the defendant is guilty of the crime. It is the defense who will present evidence and testimony in support of there being a reasonable doubt that Mr. Simons murdered the deceased victim. Are you clear on this?" Several jurors nodded.

"We will now have opening statements," the judge said to a hushed crowd. "Prosecutor Purcell, please proceed."

"Thank you, Your Honor. Members of the jury: As you might imagine, uncontrollable anger often leads to tragic consequences. Unfortunately, Mr. Simons, this bright and effective attorney, simply allowed his emotions to overcome his common sense. These out-of-control emotions were based on false information and misperceptions of reality. On October 1st, the defendant, upset — and rightly so — about an alleged poaching, contacted the police through Judge Patterson. Then, instead of allowing the authorities to do the work they are trained to do, and paid with your tax dollars to do, he drove to the vicinity of the Richards home on Peavine Road. He became even more angered when he thought — and I repeat, thought — that the police had taken a bribe from Mr. Richards. He then called the DNR, who sent their own investigator to the scene. Once again, Mr. Simons was on hand to witness the work of Officer Turner. Once again after Mr. Richards had handed his hunting license to the officer, Mr. Simons thought it was a bribe. Then, angry and out of control, he fired a shot at the officer, which action would cause the authorities to charge Mr. Richards with murder. For there was on Howard Richards' property an officer of the DNR. The bullet from Mr. Simons' rifle met its mark and felled Officer Turner. Unfortunately for the defendant, his plan backfired, and his action was discovered through the work of our fine law enforcement officers. During this trial, I will provide evidence that what I have just described happened, and you will have no doubt as to the murderer of Officer Tim Turner and that he died from a direct hit from that man sitting over there, the defendant, Mr. Zeke Simons. Thank you."

"Defense Attorney Moylan, your opening statement."

"Ladies and gentlemen of the jury, thank you for your attention. As you have heard, my client, Mr. Simons, has been accused of murder. It is my intent to offer you facts that will cause you to have no doubt that Mr. Simons is innocent of murder. I will provide evidence that shows my client was not the killer. I will show that the behavior of Mr. Richards following the death of Officer Turner was irrational — behavior associated with a guilty person."

"Objection," Wil Purcell interrupted Audrey.

"Sustained," the judge responded. "Miss Moylan, the court reminds you that the person on trial is Mr. Simons, not Mr. Richards. You are responsible for defending your client, not presenting judgments with regard to Mr. Richards. Am I clear?"

"Yes, Your Honor," Audrey replied, giving a very slight bow to the bench.

Audrey accepted the reprimand, but her strategy was working. She fully intended to plant seeds of doubt by shifting the focus at the scene of the crime from her client to Mr. Richards. Her presentation in an opening statement drew the expected objection from Judge Johnson, but she got her point across.

Audrey continued her opening statement. "I intend to show that my client, Mr. Simons, did not kill Mr. Turner. I believe at the conclusion of this trial that you will clearly have reason to doubt the implication that my client was responsible for this sad and senseless death. Thank you."

"Mr. Purcell, you have how many witnesses to present?" Judge Johnson asked.

Rising from his seat, Prosecutor Purcell stated, "Approximately six, Your Honor."

"Very good. Please call your first witness."

"The prosecution calls Officer Ginny Faccio." Dressed in her fresh green uniform, Officer Faccio approached the witness stand and took the oath.

Prosecutor Purcell walked from the table to the witness box. "Miss Faccio, please state your title."

"I am a conservation officer with the Department of Natural Resources."

"How many years have you held that position?"

"This is my twelfth year."

"You have investigated numerous cases, I presume."

"Yes, many each year."

"On October 1st, about what time did you arrive at the Richards farm?"

"According to my log book, it was 5:04 p.m."

"Was Mr. Richards or his grandson Taylor present?"

"No."

"What did you see when you arrived?"

"I saw Officer Turner's vehicle standing in the driveway with the driver's door open."

"What did you do first?"

"I knocked on the door of the house, and I heard loud barking but no one answered my knock. Then I walked to the barn and discovered Officer Turner dead on the barn floor."

"He was obviously dead when you saw him?"

"Yes."

"What action did you take at that time?"

"I checked for vital signs and found none. I contacted base and explained what I had found, and I was directed to stay at the scene until medical and law enforcement personnel arrived."

"And you did that."

"Yes. I went over to look in Officer Turner's truck, found his logbook, and noted the time of his arrival."

"Which was what?"

"4:37 p.m."

"No more questions, Your Honor. Thank you."

"Miss Moylan, your witness."

"Thank you." Audrey rose and approached the podium with her notes. "Officer Faccio, in the twelve years that you have served as a

CO, have you had any dealings with the owner of the farm where the victim was murdered?"

"Objection! Mr. Richards is not on trial, and I resent Miss Moylan continually making comments about Mr. Richards and his possible involvement in this case."

"Your Honor, a man was shot on the property of Mr. Richards," Audrey began. "I am fully aware that Mr. Richards is not on trial, but I have an obligation to my client and to justice to show reasonable doubt that my client was responsible. To do that, I believe I should have the right to show that the owner of the land where the murder took place is of questionable character."

"Overruled."

"Thank you. As I was saying, Officer Faccio, have you had other occasions to interact with Mr. Richards?"

"Yes, many occasions."

"I see. What were some of those encounters?"

"Objection."

"Overruled."

"Mostly hunting behavior."

"Like what?"

"Poaching, hunting with an expired license, trespassing, illegal firearms."

"So, this man is not what your office would call a model citizen when it comes to abiding by the law?" Audrey asked.

"No, he is not."

"No more questions."

"Mr. Purcell, your next witness."

"The State calls Michigan State University Director of Campus Security, Nick Leon." Mr. Leon approached the bench, took his oath and sat down. He looked up and saw Prosecutor Purcell coming toward him.

"Mr. Leon, do you know Zeke Simons?"

"Yes."

"If he is in the courtroom, can you identify him?"

"Yes," Nick said, as he pointed at Zeke seated at the defense table. "That is him over there."

"How do you know Zeke Simons?"

"We were following security procedures at the Michigan State vs. Rutgers football game a year ago when Mr. Simons left the stadium complex and then tried to reenter without a ticket."

"This upset him, I take it?" Wil asked.

"Definitely."

"Could you explain to the jury just how he expressed his anger at not being allowed back in?"

"Yes. I suppose the best description I could use would be controlled rage. He was verbal, his body language showed much emotion. He was threatening. He was demanding. He was out of control. That's about the best I can do to describe his behavior."

"Would you say he had been drinking?"

"No, I wouldn't say that. He was just mad."

"Was he escorted to campus police facilities?"

"No. I was able to calm him a bit, and after several minutes we talked it through, so I allowed him back into the game."

"Was it scary, seeing a man not in control of himself?" Wil asked.

"Yes, it was."

"Did you fear for your life or the safety of others in the vicinity?"

"Yes. Campus police and other security personnel quickly responded in case he became physically violent."

"But they weren't needed?"

"No, like I say, he eventually calmed down."

"Have you seen this type of behavior at sporting events?"

"On occasion, but it's rare, and usually it's because of alcohol."

"I see. Thank you, Mr. Leon."

"Your witness, Miss Moylan.

"Thank you. Mr. Leon, I don't doubt that my client acted emotionally at that football game. We admit that he has a history of not controlling his emotions. What I am interested in is his state of mind when he is angry. Did you talk to him about what had happened after he had calmed a bit?"

"Yes."

"Did he recall the incident as you witnessed it?" Audrey asked.

"As I recall, he knew he was mad that we wouldn't let him in, but he didn't remember swearing at the ticket taker, and he didn't remember kicking the ticket stand."

"I see. It seems that such behavior would have been sufficient to have him physically removed from the area," Audrey said, wanting to communicate that the episode must not have been too upsetting.

"We came close to that," Leon responded. "I realized he was mad, and I could see his point. He didn't know the policy, and we encounter a few others who get upset with the policy. But nobody has acted like Mr. Simons. I figured that I could calm him down, and I didn't want to aggravate the situation by physically removing him."

"I see."

"When I explained his behavior, he apologized to the ticket taker and promised to reimburse the University for the damage he caused."

"No more questions, Your Honor."

"Counselor Purcell, your next witness."

"The people call Sheriff Lawrence Sherman." Sheriff Sherman was sworn in, took his seat, and provided basic information about himself for the record.

"Sheriff, please tell the jury how you first became aware of the defendant."

"I received a phone call from Judge Patterson."

"What was said?" Wil asked.

"The judge told me he had received a call from a gentleman who believed that Howard had been poaching in Cherry County. I explained that poaching is investigated by the DNR and suggested that he use the Poaching Hotline. He didn't want to do that, and he directed me to look into the matter."

"What action, if any, did you take?"

"I sent two deputies to Howard Richards' farm."

"What did they report to you?" Wil Purcell asked.

"They told me that they had talked to Howard, who claimed that he did not poach the deer, but had hit it with his truck. My officers explained that the jurisdiction for investigating poaching is with the DNR, who would be notified and would undoubtedly be stopping out."

"Did Howard give them an envelope?"

"Yes, he was making a donation to the Police for Kids Program."

"What is that?"

"We have a DARE officer visit the schools, but that is not in our approved budget. We must raise money through a number of fund-raisers. He gave my officer a twenty dollar bill to support our Police for Kids Program. He refers to all of our fund-raisers as 'The Policemen's Ball.'"

"You arrested the defendant later that evening, October 1st. Is that correct?"

"Yes. I had probable cause to arrest Mr. Simons."

"Please explain this to the jury."

"I had a reasonable belief that Mr. Simons had committed a crime."

"You based this on what?" Wil asked.

"I based it on my interview of him. He indicated that he observed Officer Turner in the barn on the property of Howard Richards and that he also saw the 12-point buck. That put him at the scene of the crime. He admitted having a rifle with him and being extremely angry at Mr. Richards. I sought an arrest warrant from authorities and it was granted."

"You didn't suspect Mr. Richards of the crime?"

"I brought Mr. Richards in for questioning, but based on what I learned, I did not have evidence to reasonably believe that he had murdered Mr. Turner."

"So, you released him?"

"Yes. I had reason to arrest him for poaching, but I leave those matters to the DNR."

"No more questions."

"Your witness, Miss Moylan."

"Sheriff Sherman, didn't it occur to you that Mr. Richards had a motive to kill Officer Turner? Didn't it occur to you that an officer of the law was on the property of Mr. Richards, about to arrest him for poaching, and that this was a threat to Howard's freedom?"

"Yes, I considered that."

"And yet you arrest my client?" Audrey asked in frustration.

"The defendant was at the scene of the crime, angry, and with a rifle, which he said he fired in the direction of the victim. A man was shot and killed. I had reason to believe the shot was fired by the defendant, and I acted on that belief."

"What time were your officers at Mr. Richards' home?" Audrey asked.

"I don't have that information with me."

"In general, was it in the middle of the night, dinner time, early in the morning?"

"Early afternoon."

"No more questions."

"This court will adjourn for lunch," Judge Johnson announced. "Jurors, the bailiff will explain our procedures to you in the jury room. We will reconvene at 1:30 this afternoon."

At exactly 1:30 p.m., Judge Johnson entered the courtroom, sat down, summarized the morning events, and explained what would happen in the afternoon. She then looked at Prosecutor Purcell. "Next witness."

"The people call Dr. Elliott."

Dr. Troy Elliott, chief pathologist at Trout City General Hospital, took the stand.

"Dr. Elliott, your report is entered as Exhibit G and is, as to be expected, full of medical jargon with numerous charts and diagrams. The jury is free to study your report, but I would like you, in layman's terms, to explain to the jury what you found."

"During the autopsy, I found that Officer Turner was killed by one bullet that entered his chest, went through the left auricle of the heart, and exited under the scapula or backbone. There were no bullet fragments found in the body, and the bullet, as I noted, was not within the body. Since the bullet passed through the heart, Officer Turner died almost instantly."

"Thank you for that simple explanation. Could a bullet fired from across the road from the Richards' barn follow the path you just described?" Wil asked.

"Yes."

"In other words, fired from approximately 40 yards, a bullet would have enough momentum to travel through the body?"

"The bullet could definitely be fired at that distance and kill a victim in the manner I just described."

"Obviously, the victim was standing when he was shot."

"Correct."

"Furthermore, he was facing the barn door, looking out across the road."

"Based on the trajectory of the missile, yes, he was."

"No more questions."

"Attorney Moylan, your witness."

"Mr. Elliott, I respect your credentials, but I fail to see where you have any expertise in firearm projectiles. You are not a firearms expert, correct?"

"You are correct."

"So, your testimony about the path of a bullet from 40 yards is no more authoritative than that of a four-year-old. Is that a fair statement?" Audrey asked.

"Yes."

"So, the jury may assume credibility with your autopsy report but the path of the bullet to the body is not something you have expertise in determining. Am I correct?"

"Yes." A few jurors smiled as they could appreciate the skill with which Attorney Moylan put the witness in his place.

"Dr. Elliott, did you personally conduct the autopsy and write this report?"

"Yes. It has my signature, doesn't it?"

"Yes, it does."

"Then I wrote the report."

"Did you conduct the radiology tests and assemble the results for your report?" Audrey asked.

"Yes, with assistance from an X-ray technician."

Attorney Moylan held up the file including the X-rays and said one more time, "The record should show that Dr. Elliott is fully responsible for this report, having written it himself, and having assembled supportive information himself. That is your testimony. Correct, Doctor?"

"That is correct."

"No more questions at this time, Your Honor, however, I ask the court to hold Dr. Elliott over so that I can recall him during the defense portion of the trial."

"Your request is granted," Judge Johnson said without hesitation. "Your next witness, Counselor."

"The State calls Dr. Roberts."

Dr. Roberts, a psychiatrist, was sworn in and took the stand.

"Might extreme anger cause a person to fire a rifle in the direction of whatever angers him or her?"

"Yes. People in a state of great anger will often use whatever is available to lash out at whatever is causing the anger. This can include weapons, tools, rocks, or whatever is available in the vicinity of the person."

"Is it common for a person to lash out in some way, although acting this way lacks any common sense?" Wil asked.

"That depends on the psychological makeup of the person, the degree of anger, the seriousness of the consequences of the activity."

"So, if a person is holding a rifle and sees something that causes extreme anger, it is possible, if not probable, that the rifle might be used to resolve that anger?"

"Yes, it could, and most likely, if it was used, the person would have no rational thought in taking this action."

"For example?" Wil asked.

"Well, in your model, it's illegal to fire a rifle in the vicinity of a home, and to do so within earshot of an officer of the law borders on foolishness. What I mean to imply is that when the defendant fired his rifle, he undoubtedly had not thought out the consequences of the action he was about to take."

"No more questions, Your Honor."

"Miss Moylan, your witness."

"I have no questions, Your Honor."

"Your next witness, Mr. Purcell."

"The prosecution rests, Your Honor."

"This seems a good place to end for the day. Court is adjourned until 10 a.m. tomorrow."

NOVEMBER 22

A cold but bright sunny day greeted the citizens of Trout City. There was a lot of talking between those in the packed courtroom. The bailiff announced the arrival of Judge Johnson who took her seat and matter-of-factly got right to business. "We will continue the trial with presentation by the defense. Miss Moylan."

"Thank you, Your Honor. The defense calls Mr. Howard Richards." Howard rose stiffly and ambled up to the witness stand using a cane and wearing his Sunday go-to-meeting clothes. He was clean-shaven and looked quite respectable. He raised his hand and vowed to tell the truth, the whole truth, and nothing but the truth. As he was sworn in, Audrey fully expected "the truth" to be a figure of speech which would not enter into Mr. Richards' mind. She also expected that this case would have to be appealed as the chances the jury would find her client not guilty appeared slim. If and when the case came to appeal, she could easily demonstrate that Howard Richards was guilty of perjury, and one way or another, the old man could spend the rest of his days in a penitentiary.

Howard took his seat and straightened his sport coat. It was uncomfortable on him, and he only wore the jacket for weddings and funerals. Lately, he thought, funerals had outnumbered weddings, five-to-one.

Attorney Moylan rose from the defense table and walked toward the small podium. She put down her notes and looked at Howard Richards. "For the record, please provide your full name and address."

"Howard William Richards. I live at 16893 Peavine Road, outside of Trout City, Michigan."

"Thank you. I will make some statements, and I ask you either to agree that they are facts or to tell the court why you believe they are not true."

"Okay."

"First, you shot a 12-point buck with a rifle on October 1st."

"That is not true. I hit a buck with my truck."

"Just answer my questions, Mr. Richards. I take it from your response that you maintain you did not shoot a 12-point buck on October 1st."

"I did not."

"It is now your testimony that you struck this buck with your truck."

"Yes."

"Please tell the court about that."

"I was driving along Rangeline Road, and, all of a sudden from my right, this big buck came right at me. I didn't see it till about the time I hit it. I stopped the truck and went back to the buck. It was dead — I could tell that. I waited a few minutes to see if a hunter happened by following the blood from the buck. No one came by, so I figured the buck was mine. I gutted it, put it in my pickup, took it to my house, and hung it from the rafter in my barn. Then I went to Mickey's to have some drinks with my friends."

Audrey continued. "Second fact: Officer Turner was shot in the barn on your property on Peavine Road."

"I didn't kill him."

"I didn't say you did," Audrey replied. "I stated a fact and asked you to agree whether it was fact or not. I repeat: Officer Turner was shot in the barn on your property on Peavine Road."

"Yes, that is a fact. He was…"

"Please — just answer my question," Audrey snapped. "Third fact: you received a call from the bartender at Mickey's telling you that the defendant was upset with you, saying you shot the buck out of season."

"Yes, that is a fact."

"Fourth fact. You killed two high school kids who were knocking out mailboxes a couple of years ago."

"Objection! This has nothing to do with this case!" Prosecutor Purcell shouted, rising from his chair.

"Sustained. Counselor, no references are to be made to previous litigations involving the witness."

Audrey faced the judge. "I think it's important to establish Mr. Richards' inappropriate directing of his temper and angry feelings involving people," Audrey replied. "I was simply stating a fact which is a public record."

"The charges against your client are not to involve any past litigation involving Mr. Richards," Judge Johnson stated firmly. "If you wish to determine his reaction to anger, you will have to do that under questioning that relates to the charge against Mr. Simons."

"Yes, Your Honor," Audrey replied.

"Continue."

"Mr. Richards, one more statement for your response. It is a fact that you were neither in your barn nor on your property when Mr. Turner was killed?"

"Yes, that is a fact."

"Thank you. Now, Mr. Richards, I would like you to do some writing for me. While using this stylus which is connected to a computer to give the court the opportunity to see your writing, please write down the numbers one through ten — not the words, the numerals."

"Objection!" Prosecutor Purcell shouted. "This isn't a school. Once again, this has nothing to do with this case."

"Overruled," Judge Johnson said.

Howard took the slate and pencil and wrote the numbers one to ten.

"Thank you. At this time I would like to enter into the proceedings portions of 25 DNR reports written by Officer Tim Turner. His supervisor has verified that this is his writing. Wherever there is a number, I have highlighted the numeral and, you can now see a listing of all the numbers on the screen. Please note that wherever there is the numeral four, not once is there a triangle formed to the left of the vertical line." The jury looked at the pattern of numbers.

"Now, if I may have your attention once again, I would like to ask Mr. Richards a question or two about numbers." Audrey held up a card with a European seven made with a horizontal line through it near the top. "Mr. Richards, do you ever write a seven like this?"

"Naw, too fancy. A seven is only over and down."

"Do you ever make a two like this," Audrey asked, showing a two with no loop, a curve around, stop and a line to the right.

"I don't know, maybe sometimes."

"Well, on your card there is a pretty good loop at the bottom."

"Yeah, but, I mean, I suppose at some time I might make a two like that."

"That's fine. I accept that. Lastly, do you ever make a four like this?" Audrey held up a four with the upper left portion forming a triangle 4.

"Yes. That's how I was taught. Something wrong with my four?" Howard asked sarcastically, without knowing the corner that Audrey had just backed him into.

Audrey continued. "I would like the jury to take a look at the page of Officer Turner's log book. Note how he wrote the time of his arrival at the Richards farm. The numeral four which you didn't see in Mr. Turner's reports suddenly is used, and oddly enough, the four is made in the same way that Mr. Richards makes a four. But it is Mr. Richards' testimony that he was not present when Officer Turner was at his residence." Audrey then let the silence work to her advantage. The jurors stared at the evidence on the screen.

"Finally, in a police report, a friend of yours, by the name of Harriet Gunderson says you took her to dinner, but that it was too early for dinner."

"Well, ma'am, with all due respect, you need to take whatever Harriett says with a grain of salt," Howard said with a smile. "She's been into the sauce a lot." There was chuckling from the visitors.

"Order!" Judge Johnson said, hitting the gavel pad.

"Did you change her clock?" Audrey asked.

"Yeah, I did. I looked at my watch and I saw that it was off about five minutes, so I took it down from the wall and made the correction."

"Five minutes bothers you?" Audrey asked, with a smile.

"Yeah, I like things to be accurate, that's all. I was doing her a favor. She gets all upset over nothing."

"So your testimony is that you did change the clock, but only because it was off by five minutes, not by a few hours."

"Yes. That is true."

"Mr. Richards, did you reach into Officer Turner's vehicle and flip a toggle switch activating the camera?"

"No, I did not."

"Did not what?"

"Did not flip a switch in the truck," Howard said.

"I see. You went to the pickup but didn't flip a camera switch — is that what you are saying?"

"That's right." Watching Howard, Mr. Purcell wiped the sweat away from his upper lip.

Audrey continued. "Mr. Richards, when Officer Turner was on your property, did you notice the defendant standing across the road from your barn?"

"Yes."

"Is the woods across the road from your house and barn your property?"

"No."

"And, did the defendant fire a rifle from across the road?"

"Yup. He fired it right at me."

"You saw the rifle pointed at you?" Audrey asked with emphasis.

"Well, no, but I know he was angry at me." Howard started to fidget in his chair.

"Let me repeat because this is important, Mr. Richards. It is your testimony that you were not at your home when Officer Turner arrived, but that you were home when the two policemen came to your home. If you were not home, you were not in the barn area when a rifle was fired, the bullet from which struck and killed Officer Turner. And finally, you went to Officer Turner's truck but, did not — I repeat, did not — flip the toggle switch to activate the camera. You saw the defendant in the woods across the road from your property, and you say a shot was fired at you. Is everything I've said the truth as you swore to tell it?"

"Yes."

"Thank you. No more questions, Your Honor."

"Mr. Purcell, your witness."

"I have no questions, Your Honor," Wil Purcell said, desperately hoping the jury didn't realize that Howard had perjured himself without even realizing it. He realized how effective Audrey Moylan was as a defense attorney. He had never faced a more competent attorney, and he hoped this trial would soon be over.

Judge Johnson brought the gavel down on her oak bench and announced that court would adjourn until after lunch.

Court reconvened at 1:30. Judge Johnson entered the courtroom while everyone stood, took her seat, arranged her papers, looked at Attorney Moylan, and said, "Your next witness."

"The defense calls Taylor Richards."

Taylor was not in the courtroom. He was being videotaped from a room in the courthouse. He slowly walked to the witness stand, climbed onto the witness chair, and looked directly at Miss Moylan. Taylor could see her on a monitor in his room and the jury and all those in the courtroom could see Taylor on four television monitors set up throughout the room.

"Please tell us your full name."

"My name is Taylor Richards."

"Where do you live, Taylor?"

"1241 First Street."

"How old are you, Taylor?" Audrey asked.

"Six — almost seven." Taylor replied.

"Okay. Thank you. Do you know what this trial is about, Taylor?"

"I think so."

"What is it about?" Audrey asked.

"A man was killed at my grandpa's farm."

"That's right. I would like to ask you some questions about that day. Okay?"

Taylor just looked down and nodded.

"Tell me what you were doing that afternoon," Miss Moylan asked.

"I didn't go to school because I was sick. My dad had to work, so he took me to my grandpa's house."

"Grandpa Richards?"

"Un-huh."

"Were you at your grandpa's house all day?"

"Most of the day, yeah."

"Was your grandfather with you?" Audrey asked.

"Some of the time."

"Some of the time?"

"Yeah, he told me to watch TV and not to answer the door if anyone came. Then he left."

"Do you know where he went?"

"No."

"Was he home for lunch?"

"No."

"Did you eat lunch?"

"Yeah, I ate some cookies and peanut butter."

"So, you were alone most of the day?" Audrey asked.

"Just a few hours, I guess."

"Then your grandpa came home?"

"Yeah. Some policemen came in the afternoon," Taylor added, taking a deep breath.

"Do you know what time that was?" Audrey inquired.

"No."

"But your grandpa was there when the policemen came?"

"Yeah."

"Was he there when another policeman came?"

"I don't know for sure, but Rudy got pretty upset."

"Rudy?"

"He's grandpa's dog."

"Ok, so you don't know what time the second visitor came, but whenever it was, your grandpa was home?"

"I think so. I was watching TV, and Rudy barked. Rudy goes with grandpa, so if Rudy was there, so was grandpa."

"Did you see the visitor?

"No."

"Did you hear a shot from a rifle?"

"No."

"Later, did you leave with your grandpa?"

"Yes."

"Do you know what time that was?"

"No."

"Where did you go?"

"We took Mrs. Harriet to the café for dinner."

"Oh, so it must have been dinnertime, right?"

"I guess so."

"Then you came back to your grandpa's home?"

"Yeah,"

"And, what did you see?" Audrey asked.

"A lot of police cars and ambulances and stuff."

"And that is when you met Officer Sell."

"Un-huh."

"Taylor, let's go back to when you were watching TV and Rudy was barking. What show was on the television?"

"Well, when the policemen came, I was watching Nickelodeon."

"Are you sure?"

"Yes, because there was a cartoon on and there was a policeman in the cartoon."

"Ok. What were you watching when Rudy barked the second time?"

"I don't know. I kept changing the channels."

"Why?"

"All I could find was arguing and kissing and I don't like those shows."

"Were these shows still on when the second policeman came?"

"Yeah."

"Thank you, Taylor. Those are all of my questions, Your Honor."

"Counselor Purcell, your questions."

"I have no questions, Your Honor."

"The defense will present its next witness," Judge Johnson said.

"The defense calls Dan Willard."

Dan took the stand and completed his pre-interrogation questions.

"You are the bartender at Mickey's in Trout City, correct?" Audrey asked.

"Yes."

"You were in Mickey's around noon on October 1st?"

"I'm there every day the place is open," Dan replied.

"I appreciate that, but my question is, were you in Mickey's around the noon hour on October 1st?"

"Sorry. Yes, I was."

"Was the defendant in the bar on that day?"

"Yes, he was."

"During what time would you say he was in the bar?"

"I'd say from around eleven till twelve-thirty."

"Mr. Willard, did Mr. Richards say to you in the hearing of others that he had shot a 12-point buck the morning of October 1st?"

"Yes, he did."

"Did he say he hit the deer with his truck?"

"No, he didn't."

"Is it your opinion that Mr. Richards knew he had broken the law by shooting the buck?"

"Yes." Danny didn't look at Howard. It was easier to look away.

"No more questions, Your Honor."

"Your witness, Counselor," Judge Johnson said.

Wil Purcell stood, stretched his legs a bit, and approached the witness. "Mr. Willard, has Mr. Richards been a regular customer over the years?"

"One of our best customers, yes."

"Has Mr. Richards been known to tell a tale or two?"

Dan laughed. "He tells some real tall tales. Yes, sir, he's a storyteller."

"Is some of what he talks about not true?" Wil asked.

"I hope so, because a lot of what he says is way out there."

"So, sometimes Mr. Richards tells made-up stories and sometimes he tells true stories. Is that your testimony?" asked Prosecutor Purcell.

"Yes. He tells some whoppers."

"On the first of October, were you convinced that Howard Richards was telling the truth when he said he killed a 12-point buck?"

"No, it's hard to tell. You see, he likes attention. He likes to be — what do they call them folks — the life of the party, I guess you'd say."

"So, on that day, Howard could have hit a deer with his truck — a deer that had been shot by someone else — and then come into Mickey's bragging about shooting a 12-point buck?"

"Oh, yeah, that's definitely possible. And, it's probably what happened."

"Objection! The witness is not to make assumptions," Audrey said, rising from her seat.

Judge Johnson replied. "Sustained. Mr. Willard, you are to answer the questions and not draw conclusions. Do you understand?"

"Yes, I'm sorry."

Wil continued, "Did the defendant order anything to drink while he was at your bar on October 1st?"

"Yes."

"What did he order?"

"He had a few beers."

"Few, as in three, or more or less?"

"I can't remember what every customer orders, but I'd say at least three or four."

"Thank you. No more questions."

Judge Johnson dismissed Mr. Willard.

"**Y**our next witness, Miss Moylan."

"We would like to call, Dr. Tatroe," Audrey replied. Dr. Dan Tatroe approached the witness stand, placed his right hand on the Bible, swore to tell the truth, and took his seat. A handsome man of about 35, he was smartly dressed and seemed quite at ease. His demeanor communicated confidence and indicated considerable experience in a courtroom.

"Dr. Tatroe, please state your full name and address for the record," Audrey asked.

"Daniel J. Tatroe. I live at 1695 Berkley Road in Williamston, Michigan."

"Your title is 'Doctor', correct?"

"Yes, I am a Doctor of Veterinary Medicine, employed by the Department of Natural Resources."

"How many years of experience do you have as a veterinarian, Doctor?"

"This is my tenth year since receiving my license."

"So you're knowledgeable when it comes to animal autopsies."

"I would say so, yes."

"You've testified in courts of law before?" Audrey asked.

"Yes, at district, circuit, state, and federal levels."

"Your specialty is what, Doctor?"

"Animal necropsies."

"Thank you. Doctor, did you do a necropsy on the 12-point buck that was killed in Cherry County on October 1st?"

"Yes, I did."

"Would you please tell the jury how that animal died?"

"It is my opinion that the buck was shot in the chest with a .22 caliber shell."

"Did you find any other wounds on the animal?"

"Yes, there was a wound caused by an arrow, which I believe was jammed into the entrance wound from the rifle. There was also another entrance wound caused solely by an arrow."

"How do you know that the arrow didn't kill the deer instead of the rifle bullet?"

"There was no blood at the site of the arrow wound which indicates that the animal was dead at the time the arrow entered its body."

"Was this deer hit by a car or a truck?" Audrey asked.

"No, it was not."

"You base this opinion on what evidence?"

"There were no abrasions or broken bones, no trauma to internal organs. There was bruising when the deer fell, but nothing to indicate a collision with a vehicle."

"So, it your opinion that this deer was shot by a .22 caliber rifle, and an arrow was inserted into the entry path of the wound made by the bullet. Further, the deer was killed by the rifle shot and not the arrow? And, the deer was not struck by a vehicle. Have I accurately summarized your testimony?"

"Yes, you have."

"Is there anything else you would like to add concerning the necropsy of this animal?"

"No."

"Thank you, Doctor Tatroe. No more questions, Your Honor."

Judge Johnson said, "Counselor Purcell, your questions for the witness."

"Dr. Tatroe, the court respects your expertise and your opinions, but I do have a few questions. Are you able, or does the technology exist, to determine what amount of time elapsed between the rifle bullet entering the deer, and the arrow entering the deer?"

"No, not with any accuracy."

"I see. Of course, you have no way of knowing who shot the deer."

"No. There is no way to determine that — at least, I can't. An analysis of the rifle bore and the bullet might reveal that information, but that is not my area of expertise."

"So, Doctor, all you can really tell us is that the deer died from a rifle wound, as opposed to the arrow wound, correct?" Wil asked, anxious to make the point.

"Correct."

"Is it possible, Doctor, for a deer to collide in some way with a vehicle and not suffer any visible wound? A slight glancing blow from a fender may not break a bone, or cause an abrasion, or significant bruise?"

"Yes, that is possible. It's not probable, but it's possible."

"Doctor, is it possible for a deer to be shot by an arrow, and also by a rifle, and then be hit by a car?"

"I have not heard of that, nor have I conducted a necropsy where that was the case."

"I see. But my question was, is it possible?"

"It is possible, I suppose…"

"That's all. Thank you," Prosecutor Purcell interrupted, concluding his questioning.

"Thank you, Doctor. No more questions, Your Honor."

"Please call your next witness, Counselor," Judge Johnson directed.

"We would like to call Dr. Elliott."

After the witness was sworn in, Audrey Moylan approached the witness and began her questioning. "Dr. Elliott, please tell the jury the basic procedures that are used in conducting an autopsy."

"The first thing we do is examine the body and record extensive notes about any markings, bruises, stitches, scars, birthmarks that are on the skin. Then we take X-rays to examine the inner organs, bones, muscles. Of course, if we find a wound from a knife or firearm, or a significant bruise, we pay close attention to an X-ray of that area. In this case, a shooting, we follow the path of the bullet and remove any substantial fragments."

"Excuse me. Please define substantial," Audrey interrupted.

"In order for the crime lab to be able to trace the bullet to a firearm, they need a sizable fragment of the bullet."

"I see. And what did you find in the case of Officer Turner?" Audrey asked.

"Officer Turner died of a bullet that entered his body from the front and exited through the back near his spinal column. I was not able to find any bullet fragments."

"Did you find any other wounds on Officer Turner's body?"

"No."

"Continue explaining your autopsy procedures," Audrey directed.

"We also do a blood profile to determine whether there were any toxins in the body or if the victim had taken any drugs or alcohol or any poisoned substance. Often times samples are taken for analysis and certain organs are removed for closer study. Then, I write my report."

"So, you are looking for the cause of death, and specifically how the victim died."

"That's correct."

"When you were on the stand as a witness for the prosecution, I compared your thoughts on bullet trajectory to those of a four-year-old child implying that you had little expertise in this aspect of the crime. But, at this time I do seek your thoughts about the trajectory of the bullet that killed Officer Turner. Please explain the path the bullet took from the rifle through the victim. In other words, was the path of the bullet parallel to the floor, or at an angle to the floor? Exactly what path did the bullet take through the body?"

"The best way to describe it is to show you an X-ray of the wound path." Marie Turner and other family members lowered their heads, not wanting to see or listen to the doctor describe the terrifying few seconds that ended the life of their beloved relative.

"I believe that is exhibit 14B," Audrey said. "Could that be shown on the screen, please?"

The image came onto the screen, and Dr. Elliott commented. "Here is the entrance wound, and on the opposite side of the body is the exit wound. You can see that the path of the bullet was parallel to the floor."

"Ok, the prosecution would assert that the bullet was fired from across the road, and that the position of the shooter would be level with the barn's floor. Having said that, Dr. Elliott, I would like to have the X-ray identified as Exhibit 15A put up on the screen."

Up on the screen came the X-ray. "Can you identify this X-ray?"

"Yes, this is of the victim's chest cavity."

"I see. Can you explain the difference between the images in films 14B and 15A? They appear not to be photos of the same body. For instance, note the different sizes of the organs. I believe Exhibit 15A also shows a mass in the left lung, which is clearly absent in 14B. So, Dr. Elliott, which X-ray is of the body of Officer Turner?"

Dr. Elliott squirmed a bit in his chair. He glanced over at Mr. Purcell who was looking down at his notes. "Well, in the first place, I'm not sure the two X-rays are from two different people. I would have to go back to my lab and study the material."

"Maybe I can help you," Audrey said. "Please show Exhibit 16C, a photo of the entrance wound on Mr. Turner. You will note that the wound is to the right of the left nipple. Now, looking at Exhibit 16D, you can see the exit wound between the spinal cord and the backbone, in layman's terms. The exit wound is around the 19th or 20th lumbar vertebrae. My calculations show the path to follow an angle of approximately 60 degrees downward. Would you agree?"

"Again, I'd have to go back to my lab…"

"As a pathologist, you would need to go back to your lab in order to tell the jury that the bullet path through Mr. Turner is on an angle?" Audrey asked firmly. "You can't conclude that by looking at this evidence here in the courtroom?"

"It does appear to be an angle," Dr. Elliott replied.

"Yes, it does and if this was the angle, whoever killed this man had to have been up on a ladder at the very least. And if the prosecutor still maintains my client fired the shot, Mr. Simons would need to have been standing above the tree line across the road, and the bullet would have to enter the barn from above the door. Can you explain the discrepancy, Dr. Elliott?"

Audrey stood silent with her arms folded and silent allowing the contradiction to sink into the minds of the judge, jurors, and courtroom visitors. Neither the witness, the prosecutor, the judge, the jury, nor the visitors made a sound. After this telling pause, Audrey said, "No more questions, Your Honor."

"Your next witness, Counselor," Judge Johnson said.

"I call state police Sergeant Abramson." The sergeant in uniform took the stand and sat upright with eyes fixed on Attorney Moylan.

"What is your position within the state police?" Audrey asked.

"I am a Forensic Specialist, assigned to the State Police Crime Lab in Grayling."

"So, it would be your job to match a rifle's bore to a bullet fragment if one would have been provided to you by Dr. Elliott, correct?"

"That is correct."

"Did you find a match to the rifle belonging to the defendant?" Audrey asked.

"No."

"Did you find the bullet that went through Mr. Turner's body?" Audrey asked.

"We found two bullets. One matched a rifle belonging to the defendant, but we haven't found a weapon that would match the second bullet."

"Were any fingerprints found?" Audrey asked.

"Yes, on the door handle of the barn."

"Whose prints were they?"

"Mr. Richards."

"Prosecutor Purcell, your witness," Judge Johnson said, as Audrey took her seat behind the defense table.

"Sergeant Abramson, is it your conclusion that this killing was no accident?"

"It was not an accident."

"It was deliberate murder, wasn't it?"

"It appears that it was. It was not a suicide, if that's what you mean."

"Simply put, someone fired a rifle, the bullet struck Mr. Turner, and the projectile exited his body. Correct?"

"Yes, that is correct."

"I have no more questions, Your Honor."

"The court will recess until 10 a.m. tomorrow," Judge Johnson said. "The jury is reminded not to talk to anyone about this trial. Do not read any newspapers and do not watch any television news while this court is in session. This court is adjourned," the judge declared, bringing the gavel down on the bench.

Lou drove home to Grand Haven following the day in court to attend an important Knights of Columbus meeting. After the meeting, his cell phone rang while he was still at St. Pat's Catholic Church. Carol informed Lou that he had received an important call from a Mr. Eric Richards in Trout City, and she gave him the call-back number.

Lou called Eric Richards.

"Mr. Richards, this is Lou Searing in Grand Haven. My wife said you tried to reach me."

"Yes, my son Taylor wants to talk to you."

"Ok."

"Here he is."

"Hello."

"Hi, Taylor, this is Mr. Searing. How are you doing?"

"Ok," Taylor replied, in a most somber manner.

"I understand you want to tell me something?" Lou said.

"Yeah."

"Ok, I'm listening, son."

"I have my grandpa's gun," Taylor said, quietly and slowly.

"His gun?" Lou asked, wanting to be sure he heard correctly.

"Un-huh. He threw it in the creek."

"I see. When was this, Taylor?"

"On our way to Mrs. Gunderson's house."

"Ok. You said you have the gun?"

"Yeah. I told my dad, and he took me to where grandpa threw it, and I found it."

"So, your Dad has the gun, now?"

"Un-huh. But, Mr. Searing?"

"Yes, Taylor."

"I don't want God to be angry with me."

"Oh, son, how could that be?" Lou said. "You are a fine young man."

"Mrs. Fees, my Sunday School teacher says if you lie, God will be angry. I did hear a shot, but I said I didn't. I did see a policeman after the two came to Grandpa's house. I said I didn't."

"Well, you're being honest now, and that's good. I'm proud of you, your dad is proud of you, and I'm pretty sure that God is very happy with you."

"Mr. Searing, I think my grandpa killed that officer."

"I'm sorry, Taylor. I'm very sorry." There was silence and Lou thought he could hear muffled sobbing. "You are a fine boy. Thank you for talking with me. Everything will be OK. Do you understand, Taylor?"

"Yeah."

"Can I talk to your dad now?" Lou asked.

"OK."

"Goodbye, Taylor. Thanks for calling."

Eric Richards was now on the line. "Mr. Searing. He wanted to call you. He trusts you."

"I appreciate that. Does your dad know about this, Eric?"

"No. Taylor told me about dad throwing the rifle into the creek about an hour ago, and we just got back from finding it."

"Do the police know about this?" Lou asked.

"No, Taylor only wanted to talk to you, sir."

"I see. Is Taylor going to be okay?"

"He's scared right now," Eric said, his voice breaking. "We're both sort of having a good cry."

"He's seen too much, heard too much," Lou said. "It takes a lot of courage to do what he has done. He needs to be in a safe place. Would you object if Taylor came to Grand Haven and stayed with Mrs. Searing and me for a while?"

"Are you sure that would be okay?" Eric asked.

"Yes. That can happen. Would he be willing to come here?"

"I can ask him and call you back. You really would be willing to care for him for a while?" Eric again asked, thankful that Lou and Carol could protect his son.

"Yes. We have a dog, Samm, who would make him feel very special, and we live on the shore of Lake Michigan. He can take some quiet walks, and, of course, we can care for him and provide a safe environment. I haven't asked Mrs. Searing, of course, but she would never say no to helping a child. He's a fine boy."

"Thank you very much," Eric said sincerely. After a deep breath, he asked, "What do we do now?"

"I'll drive up to bring Taylor here to Grand Haven. You pack some clothes and things he enjoys. You call Judge Patterson and tell him that you have the rifle, and ask him to contact me by cell. Do not give the rifle to the police, the sheriff, anyone. Personally hand it to Judge Patterson. Don't tell anyone about this, and if you have, don't answer any questions. What I'm asking you to do is very important. Do you understand?"

"Yes, I do. Ok. You'll be here in a couple of hours?" Eric asked.

"Yes."

"You know where I live?"

"Yes, it's in my records."

"Thank you, sir."

"You have a fine young man there. He'll be okay. But how are you doing?"

"It's kind of rough. Dad just isn't himself. He used to be so honest and community-oriented. But now, like a kid turning into a teenager, he's just become somebody I don't even know."

"Well, I give you credit for allowing Taylor to call me and to trust me. One more thing: how does Taylor know me and how would be know he could trust me?" Lou asked.

"You wrote a book for children, right? He liked your stories, and he said he liked you."

"Interesting. Well, I'm very glad you called, Eric. Thank you."

"It was the right thing to do."

"See you soon."

Lou got into his car and headed north. From his car he first called Carol to explain the situation and to officially get her okay to care for the boy. He then called Judge Patterson to explain what was happening and what he had directed Eric Richards to do. Finally he called Audrey to explain what had happened, the specifics of Taylor's call, and his plans to bring Taylor to Grand Haven.

NOVEMBER 23

At approximately 10:15 a.m., the bailiff asked all in the courtroom to rise as Judge Johnson entered. After she sat down, she spoke, "Good morning, everyone. Thank you for your prompt arrival. I apologize for the slight delay in the morning's proceedings, but I had to handle an urgent matter. Miss Moylan, please continue."

After consultation with Judge Beekins, and Zeke himself, attorney Moylan believed that it was in Zeke's best interest to testify.

"We wish to call to the stand, Mr. Zeke Simons."

Zeke, wearing a dark suit, rose and approached the witness stand, was sworn in, and took his seat. He provided his full name and address, and then he took a deep breath, anticipating not only questions from his attorney, but also from the prosecutor.

Audrey nodded toward Zeke, "Mr. Simons, please tell the jury what happened on the opening day of bow season last October 1st."

"Before the first light of day, I encountered an elderly man who claimed my friend's land for hunting. He had a .22, and we had an argument about rights to hunt on the Wilds' property. He finally left and headed north toward the federal forest.

"While I was bow hunting after daybreak, I saw a buck, but it bounded away before I could draw my bow. An hour or two later, I heard a rifle shot, but didn't know where it came from. Around noon I went to Mickey's to get a burger. While I was there, I heard the same man talking kind of loud to some guys, bragging that he had shot a 12-point buck near the Cherry County line. That was where I had been hunting, so I figured he was the guy who shot the buck.

"When the guy left, I asked the bartender who this older man was, and he told me his name was Howard Richards. I called Judge Patterson to report the poaching, and he said he would handle it. I found out where Richards lived and drove out there, expecting to see the police investigating this poaching, hoping to see the man arrested. I parked a ways down the road from Mr. Richards' farm, and hid behind a tree across the road from his house. The police, or rather sheriff's deputies, arrived. I watched Mr. Richards talk to the two officers and then give them money. When the deputies left, I was furious that they hadn't even looked for the deer. Also, I thought they were taking a bribe, so I called Judge Patterson to complain. He begged me not to do anything rash, so I called the DNR to report the poaching. They sent an officer, Tim Turner, who talked to Mr. Richards. They walked into the barn, and then Mr. Richards went to his house and came back with a rifle and what looked to be an envelope. I got very angry and while the two of them were still talking in the barn, I aimed my rifle toward Mr. Richards and fired it. I saw Mr. Richards come out of the barn with the rifle, go over to the officer's vehicle, and then go into his house. A short while after that, he left with a boy. I ran across the road, went into the barn, and saw the officer lying on the barn floor, apparently dead. I ran out of the barn and down the road to my pickup and drove away."

"Mr. Richards testified he was not in the vicinity of his home when Officer Turner visited. Are you certain that the man in the barn was Mr. Richards?"

"Yes, the man was Mr. Richards."

"You testified that you fired a shot from across the road before crossing over to look in the barn?"

"Yes, I did."

"What were you aiming at?"

"Mr. Richards. I was so angry, I was out of control. Here was a guy who had illegally killed a prize buck, who was getting away with poaching, and bribing officers to boot. I guess I flipped out and thought I could get some justice."

"When you were aiming at Mr. Richards, could you see Officer Turner and the deer?"

"Vaguely," Zeke replied.

"You fired one shot and only one shot?"

"Yes, one shot."

"No more questions, Your Honor." Audrey walked to the defense table.

"Prosecutor Purcell, your questions."

"Thank you, Your Honor. Mr. Simons, would you say you have a temper, one that gets the best of you on occasion?"

"Yes."

"So, your being upset with Mr. Richards was not the first time you have acted inappropriately when you were angry."

"Correct. It was not the first time."

"You said that you had been to Mickey's."

"Yes."

"And did you consume any alcohol while there?"

"Yes."

"How much did you drink, and what did you drink?"

"I had three beers with a hamburger and fries."

"Three beers. What size were the beer containers — cans, bottles, pitchers?"

"Bottles, 12-ounce bottles."

"So you consumed 36 ounces of beer, correct?"

"Correct."

Purcell seemed a bit perplexed. "Mr. Simons, by your own admission, what precipitated your intense anger was your belief that Mr. Richards killed a deer with a rifle. So, why did you take a rifle when you hid in the trees across the road from Mr. Richards' home and barn?"

Zeke paused and then he said, "I wish to exercise my right to invoke the Fifth Amendment, on the grounds that I do not wish to incriminate myself."

"I see. You have admitted to firing the rifle, so I ask, why would you fire a rifle in the direction of a person, much less in the presence of a DNR officer?"

Zeke paused, and again he invoked the Fifth Amendment. His action had been planned with Audrey in advance. They agreed that Zeke needed to take the stand in order to place Howard Richards at home when Tim Turner was shot.

Purcell sighed. "To summarize, you had consumed 36 ounces of beer, and you were across from Richards' barn with a loaded rifle. You knew well the law against firing a rifle — or any weapon for that matter — in the vicinity of a home. You were willing to take that risk, simply because you were furious with Mr. Richards. You fired the rifle, intending to kill Mr. Richards, but the bullet struck the conservation officer. Is my statement true?"

"I was trying to scare Mr. Richards, and I don't know if the bullet struck anyone else."

"Thank you. I have no more questions at this time," Wil said, walking toward his seat.

"Attorney Moylan, any further questions?" Judge Johnson asked.

"No, Your Honor."

"You may step down, Mr. Simons.

Call your next witness Miss Moylan," Judge Johnson said.

"The defense calls Forensic Scientist Adam Carlson."

"Mr. Carlson, you have been with the state police for how many years?" Audrey asked.

"Twelve."

"At this time, what are your responsibilities?"

"Crime scene investigation."

"When did you receive a request from Sheriff Sherman?"

"I received my orders from the Post Commander. I don't know exactly when his request came in."

"Ok, then, when did you head for the Richards home?"

"It was around 6 p.m. on October 1st. I'd need to check my log book to get the exact time of my assignment."

"That's close enough. Were you able to find any evidence at the scene to explain the death of Officer Turner?"

"Two bullets were found in the barn. One of them matches a rifle belonging to Mr. Simons, but we haven't found the rifle used to fire the second bullet."

"Was there anything in Mr. Turner's vehicle that served as evidence?"

"There was a log book in which he had written '4:37, arrived at Richards home to investigate poaching.' All other items in the vehicle were routine law-enforcement equipment."

"According to the record of the DNR vehicle monitoring system in Lansing, we know that Officer Turner arrived at 1:37, correct?" Audrey asked.

"That would correspond to the call from Mr. Simons."

"Please comment about the letters that were written near the body on the dusty floor of the barn."

"There appeared to be two zeros linked together like in cursive writing, followed by what appeared to be the letter P, but it could have been an F, or maybe a B."

"Were these written by the deceased?" Attorney Moylan inquired.

"We believe so, because the forefinger of his right hand was dirtier than the other fingertips."

"You found his microphone attached to the right shoulder of Officer Turner's uniform?"

"That is correct."

"Has any communication record from that been analyzed at this point?"

"Yes, it has, and there was no dialogue on the recorder. It appears that Officer Turner did not activate the microphone."

"Nor the video in his car, correct?" Audrey asked.

"Not at the time of his arrival, but there was video recording later."

"I understand," Audrey said, looking at her notes. "Finally, did you find any markings in the barn area that could have been the result of Mr. Simons' shooting a rifle from across the road?"

"No, we did not."

"I'd like to go back to the arrival time in Officer Turner's logbook. Did you subject that notation to any tests?"

"Yes, we did."

"And you found?"

"We found that Officer Turner could not have made the numeral four."

"Why do you say that?"

"While the ink was the same, the recorded time was 1:37 because the depth of the indentations in the paper plies was uniform across the notation. However, it is my opinion that the markings changing the 1 to a 4 were not made by the same person, or at the time of the initial notation. The change is much lighter, not in ink color, but in the impression into the pad."

"Please explain to the jury, detective."

"Well, we can tell the pressure used by the writer, because the indentation, if I may call it that, appears on paper underneath the top page. Our diagnostic tools allow us to see the indented image, sometimes four or five pages below the top page, and this is true in this case. However, we can see an image — or indentation may be a better word — below the change in the first numeral. We found little, if any, indentation in the change to a 4, and this implies to us that two different people wrote in the log."

"Thank you, Detective. I would like to remind the jury of the testimony of Howard Richards, his way of making a 4 and Mr. Turner's way of making a 4.

"No more questions, Your Honor."

Judge Johnson said, "Counselor Purcell, your questions?"

"Thank you. Mr. Carlson, you have investigated many murders over the years, correct?"

"Yes."

"Is it your professional opinion that Mr. Turner was killed by a rifle shot?"

"Yes, it is."

"Was the rifle fired into the front of his body, or could it have been fired from behind him?"

"The entrance and exit wounds on the body clearly indicate the bullet entering the front of his body and exiting through the back."

"Have you ever investigated a murder where the assassin claims he never intended to fire his weapon and in fact aimed it away from the victim?"

"Yes, many times."

"What could cause such a discrepancy?"

"The greater the distance the shooter is from the target, the smaller the change of aim required. "

"I'm not sure I understand. Please elaborate."

"The farther back someone is from a target, the smaller the arc a gun must move to shift its aim from the intended target to another direction," Adam explained. "So, given his distance from the barn, if Mr. Simons moved his rifle a very small angle to the right, the rifle bullet would actually go farther to the right than he might expect.

Plus one needs to consider other factors such as wind, any distraction, or how angry the shooter was."

"Could drinking three beers, as described by Mr. Simons, possibly cause a slight discrepancy in his aim?" Wil asked.

"Definitely."

"In the matter of the writing analysis, while I accept your findings regarding the depth of the pressure of the writer, is it possible that the change, as you call it, could have been made by the original writer?"

"Not in my opini…" Mr. Carlson began.

Prosecutor Purcell interrupted. "But, it is possible, correct? I mean the officer could have seen his error and simply made the change softly? Is that possible? That's all I'm trying to determine."

"I suppose it is possible."

"It is my understanding that you took plaster casts of some tire tracks on Mr. Richards' property."

"Correct."

"What were the results when you compared that evidence to tires on vehicles involved in this case?"

"The cast moldings that we made were an exact match to the tires on the truck registered to Mr. Simons."

"I believe you have a visual display of your findings?"

"Yes. On the right of the display is the cast of the right front tire of Mr. Simons' truck and in the photo on the left is the tire tread from Mr. Simons' truck. The markings noted by an A, B and C indicate that the two are an exact match."

"This is sort of like having a truck's fingerprints. Is that safe to say?"

"Yes. A good analogy."

"So, you are comfortable in saying that Mr. Simons was on Mr. Richards' property?"

"I have no idea. I can't testify to where he was but I can testify that the tire tracks belonging to Mr. Simons' vehicle were on Mr. Richards' property."

Audrey knew the evidence was inadmissible because it was collected the day after the incident at Howard's home, but she let it go. After all, there is no question that Zeke was at the property.

Counselor Purcell looked toward Judge Johnson, "Your Honor, I would like video Exhibit J shown to the court, please."

Within a minute, the video was seen by everyone in the court-room. "Mr. Carlson, is this a video recording taken from Office Turner's vehicle?"

"Yes, it is."

"As you can see, Mr. Simons enters the barn with his rifle, and in a matter of seconds, he exits the barn with his rifle."

"Is anyone else in the video?" Wil asked.

"Officer Faccio is seen entering the barn a few hours later."

"Thank you. No more questions, Your Honor."

"Counselor Moylan, any further questions?"

"Yes, Your Honor," Audrey replied, rising with notes in her hand.

"Trooper Carlson, how is the camera in Officer Turner's vehicle activated?"

"It can only be activated from inside the vehicle."

"Could it have been activated by remote control?" Audrey asked.

"No. The toggle switch has to be physically moved."

"So, since Mr. Richards has testified that he wasn't there when Mr. Turner was killed, who could have thrown the toggle switch?"

"I don't know."

"How about Mr. Simons?" Audrey asked. "Would my client want a video of himself entering and exiting a barn when he thinks someone inside might be dead?"

"Not likely."

"Right, it isn't likely, is it? But isn't it more likely that Mr. Richards might flip the switch?"

"It could be."

"You recall my client's testimony that Mr. Richards walked over to the vehicle and stayed there for a short while, long enough, I imagine, to flip that switch and change the 1 to a 4 on the log report. Is that possible?"

"It is."

"But, Mr. Richards testified under oath that he was not there. Quite a mystery, isn't it? Numbers change, and a video recorder is mysteriously activated. Two acts that make no sense for my client to do. I didn't see a ghost on the witness list. Would a six-year-old boy, Taylor, run out of the house and flip a toggle switch? How about the dog, Rudy? He seems pretty smart. Maybe he flipped the switch. I don't think so. It appears the only one who could have flipped the switch was Howard Richards." Audrey turned to the jury and the silence was deafening.

Mr. Carlson glanced over at the jury, to see that each juror was seriously considering Audrey's reasoning.

"Did you see Mr. Simons with the vehicle on Mr. Richards' property?" Audrey asked.

"No, I did not."

"Finally," Audrey began. "I accept your finding that the tires match, but I do not accept an assumption that my client was in the vehicle when the tracks were made.

"So, it is possible that someone could have borrowed my client's truck or stole my client's truck and isn't it very possible that my client wasn't on Mr. Richards' property at all."

"That is possible."

"And, I'd like to ask when you took the cast of the tire marks."

"October 2nd, at approximately 11 a.m."

"So this is the day after Officer Turner was shot, not the day of the shooting. Correct?"

"That is correct."

"So we had better not jump to any conclusions that the tire marks were made in conjunction with the murder of Officer Turner. Wouldn't you agree?"

"Yes, I would."

"Thank you."

"No more questions, Your Honor."

"Mr. Purcell, any final questions?"

"Thank you. Is it possible for Mr. Simons, when he came across the road, and before going into the barn, to approach the vehicle, change the one to a four and flip on the camera?"

"Yes, that is possible."

"Thank you. No more questions."

"I believe we have a few more witnesses for the defense and then closing statements," Judge Johnson said. The court will adjourn for lunch and reconvene at 2 p.m."

The afternoon session was delayed, but court was back in session at three o'clock. The judge asked Miss Moylan to continue with her next witness.

"I call Harriett Gunderson to the stand."

Harriett came forward, took her oath, and nervously sat down. She wrapped her handkerchief around her trembling hand.

"Harriett, please try to relax. I only have a few questions, and then we'll be finished."

"I've never had to be a witness before."

"We know. I only have a few questions. Did Mr. Richards visit you the afternoon of October 1st?" Audrey asked.

"Yes. Howard and Taylor took me to dinner," Harriett hesitated. "It was an early dinner, but we had dinner."

"Did Howard say anything about a man being shot at his farm-house that afternoon?"

"No."

"Did he act different or strange that afternoon?"

"He changed my clock."

"He changed your clock? Why? Was it off the actual time?" Audrey asked.

"It was fine. I don't know why he did it. But you asked if he acted different, and yes, he did."

"How well do you know Mr. Richards?"

"I've known him all his life. We were in the same school, and, well, we've known each other all our lives."

"Does this seem out of character to you, Mr. Richards being accused of murder, having poached a deer…"

"Objection!" Mr. Purcell shouted quickly rising to his feet. "Mr. Richards is not on trial. The questions should pertain to Mr. Simons' behavior only."

"Your Honor, I am trying to establish Mr. Richards' personality traits, which may help me defend my client by showing a clear and reasonable doubt that Mr. Simons committed the crime for which he is accused," Audrey responded.

"Objection overruled. Continue."

"Harriett, please answer the question."

"Howard is not the same man he used to be."

"In what way?" Audrey asked.

"In a lot of ways, but he's still my friend. He's good to me. And, I'll tell you this, no matter what, he is not a killer. He respects life. He was brought up a God-fearing Christian. No, he's not the same, but he didn't kill anyone."

"Thank you. No more questions," Audrey said, wishing her witness had not offered an opinion about Howard and his possible murder of Mr. Turner.

"Counselor Purcell, your witness."

"We have no questions, Your Honor."

"Next witness, Miss Moylan."

"The defense calls Lillian Adams."

Lillian, the 66-year-old neighbor of Harriett Gunderson, slowly approached the witness box, took a seat, recited the oath, and took out a hanky in case she began to get emotional.

Audrey began, "Mrs. Adams, I'd like you to think back to the afternoon of October 1st. Do you recall going over to see your friend, Harriett Gunderson?"

"Yes, but I only remember because of her kitchen clock."

"Please explain."

"Well, I noticed the kitchen clock was off by a few hours," Lillian said.

"You went into the house, then? Was Harriett there?"

"No, but I check on Harriett frequently. She tells me to just walk in, and so I do if she doesn't come to the door when I knock. So, yes, I went into the house and looked for her. I noticed the clock was off by a few hours. The electricity had not gone off, and the digital numbers on her VCR machine showed the correct time."

"Did you ask her about this?"

"The next day, yeah."

"How did she explain it?" Audrey asked.

"She couldn't. The clock was back to normal, and she said she didn't change it. She did say that Mr. Richards and his grandson stopped by to take her to dinner. I thought that odd because I was there about 2:30 in the afternoon."

Audrey moved closer to the witness stand. "You're a good friend of Harriett's, aren't you, Mrs. Adams?"

"I try to be."

"You know her quite well, don't you?"

"Yes, I would say so."

"For whatever reason — age, lifestyle, health — Harriett often is inconsistent with behaviors and memory. Is this a safe statement?"

"Yes."

"So, with Harriett, isn't it possible that she changed her clock and didn't remember doing it? She could have gone off to lunch, thinking she was going off to dinner, or to have coffee and a piece of pie, mid-afternoon. This would not be atypical for her, would it?"

"Oh, no, Harriett, poor woman, has a lot of problems. All I'm saying is that the clock was off, and she said she was taken to dinner, when it must have been the middle of the afternoon. Whether it's true or not, I don't know. I'm just here to tell you what I heard and saw."

"We understand, and thank you for coming down here," Audrey replied with a smile. Mrs. Adams reminded Audrey of her mother. She turned to the judge. "No more questions, Your Honor."

"Prosecutor Purcell, your questions."

"I have no questions, Your Honor."

"Is this next witness your final, Miss Moylan?

"I have two witnesses, Your Honor. First the defense calls Dr. Dillon."

Dr. Dillon came into the courtroom, approached the witness box, took his oath and made himself comfortable in the witness chair. This was not the first time that Dr. Dillon had to testify; he was good at it, and he enjoyed the experience.

"Dr. Dillon, please provide the court with your credentials."

RICHARD L. BALDWIN

"I received my medical degree from the University of Michigan and my specialized pathology training at St. Louis University in Missouri. I am part of the crime-site investigation team in Grand Rapids. I perform autopsies that concern deaths occurring in Kent County. I have performed hundreds of autopsies and have testified in courts from local to State Supreme Court levels."

"Thank you. Your credentials are most impressive, Doctor," Audrey said nodding and smiling.

"Earlier the court heard Dr. Elliott testify that he wrote the autopsy report for Officer Turner and that his report contained a number of X-rays which he personally chose for the report. I would like you and the court to turn your attention to the screen to the right of the judge. This particular X-ray supposedly shows the path of the bullet through the body. Am I correct?"

"Yes."

"This film shows the path of the bullet as parallel to the ground, assuming the victim was standing. Would you agree?"

"Yes, but there is one problem."

"What is that?" Audrey asked, knowing a bomb was about to fall.

"This X-ray isn't from the autopsy of Officer Turner."

"It is not?"

"No. At the top right of the frame, you can see a number. This number should match the number assigned to the body when the victim is brought to the morgue for autopsy. In this film, the number doesn't match the number on the autopsy report nor does it match the other films. If you examine plates four and five, indicating the entry wound and the exit wound, you will find that these photos are of Officer Turner, but there is a 60 degree downward angle from the entry wound to the exit wound."

Audrey concluded. "If the shot that killed Officer Turner was fired from across Peavine Road, the rifle would need to have been fired from above the tree level. And, furthermore the bullet would have to have come through the barn wall to reach Officer Turner. Am I correct?"

"Yes," Dr. Dillon replied. "That would be my interpretation."

"Interesting. Thank you, Dr. Dillon. Your witness," Audrey said looking at Wil.

Realizing that he could dig the hole deeper by asking questions of Dr. Dillon, Wil simply said, "I have no questions, Your Honor."

"Your next witness, Miss Moylan."

"I would like to call Eric Richards to the stand." Her announcement caused some hushed comments throughout the audience. After all, what could Howard's son offer the defense?

Eric took the oath to tell the truth and sat down uncomfortably in the witness chair.

"Mr. Richards, for the record, please state your name and address."

"My name is Eric Richards, and I live at 1241 First Street in Trout City, Michigan."

"For the record, you are the son of Howard Richards, the owner of the property where Officer Turner was murdered, correct?"

"Yes."

"You are also Taylor's father, correct?"

"Yes."

"In fact, you have agreed to testify because of Taylor, correct?"

"Yes."

"Did Taylor say something to you that pertains to this case?" Audrey asked.

"Yes. He told me that my dad may have killed the officer." The courtroom suddenly erupted from silence into murmurs, gasps, and comments of out-right disbelief.

"Quiet, please!" Judge Johnson ordered.

"Exactly what did Taylor say, Mr. Richards?"

"He told me that Dad threw one of his rifles into some bushes by a creek down from his house on their way into town on October 1st. We went out there and found the rifle in the creek."

"What did you do with the information and the rifle?" Audrey asked.

"I called Mr. Searing."

"Private Detective Searing?"

"Yes. He was the only one that Taylor trusted with the information. Taylor was scared because he knew he would get the belt from his grandfather for saying anything."

"'Get the belt'?" Audrey asked surprised at this comment.

"The belt is how my dad makes sure young people tow the line."

"Did you know your father hit your son?" Audrey asked.

"I suspected it, but I never knew for sure till Taylor told me."

"You suspected it because…"

Eric interrupted, "Because he threatened me with it, but my mom wouldn't allow it."

"I see, but with your mother gone now, there was nobody to stop him."

"I guess so," Eric reasoned.

"So, thanks to Taylor, we now have the weapon, a brave young boy who was willing to let the truth be told while fearing pain. You've a wonderful son, Mr. Richards," Audrey said, smiling and nodding at him and at the jury.

"I know I do. Thank you."

"No more questions. Your witness," Audrey said looking at Mr. Purcell.

"No questions, Your Honor."

"Are there any more witnesses for the defense?" Judge Johnson asked.

"We have no more witnesses, Your Honor. The defense rests."

Judge Johnson leaned back in her chair and said, "This seems like a good point to break for the day. Once again I remind the jurors that they are not to talk about this trial with anyone, and I mean anyone, not even among yourselves. Do not watch or read any media presentations regarding this trial. We will reconvene at 9 a.m. tomorrow."

Now more than ever, Janet, Vince, and Josh knew that they needed to do something to pull the city together, or at least to motivate Trout City High School students. They met again at McDonald's to further their plans for a Community Leader Day. Janet reported that she had the support from the high school principal. Vince said that his government teacher thought the idea was excellent, and he had offered his help for making the day a reality. Josh reported that the Key Club would help promote the idea.

"Looks like we've taken the first step," Janet said.

"I think the best way to proceed is to put together a list of jobs we want to shadow," Vince said. "Is that the right word? Seems like I heard that on TV."

"Next, we need to contact the city officials, to see if this is okay with them," Josh added.

"Good idea!" Janet said, chuckling. "Can you imagine thirty high school kids showing up, announcing, 'Hey, what are you doing in my office? I'm the sheriff today! Or whatever." All three laughed.

"That would be the first and last Community Leader Day event," Josh said.

"Since we are the leaders," Janet mused. "It seems like we should have our choice of who we want to shadow for a day."

Vince responded, "We can either have students apply to be assigned to a particular public figure, we can draw names of potential participants from a hat, or we can make random assignments."

"Sounds good!" Josh replied.

"I think it's important for the day to have local radio station and newspaper attention, with photos and interviews," Janet said. "We want this to be fun as well as educational, and we want the citizens to see kids in a positive light. Then we should hold a follow-up session where the students make suggestions for improved government."

"I think the event should be limited to seniors," Josh suggested. The others nodded their approval.

"We ought to have a luncheon that day to thank the city officials. That would give the kids and all the officials a chance to talk and get to know one another," Vince said.

"Very good ideas, guys," Janet replied. "This is shaping up better than I ever imagined."

The trio divvied up some organizational responsibilities and agreed to get right to work.

"What about a speaker for the luncheon?" Janet asked.

"Great idea! Who should we ask?" Josh wondered.

"How about the Governor?" Vince suggested.

"The Governor?" Josh asked, laughing out loud. "Right. Why not go for the President while we're at it?"

"Hey, we shoot for the top," Janet replied.

"How about we ask the President of the National Rifle Organization? Maybe he would come to our town."

"Give me a break!" Josh exclaimed. "What could entice somebody that busy to come to our little city to give a speech?"

"There are a lot of hunters up here," Janet pointed out. "Almost everyone has firearms. I think people would come out to hear him. We'd need to open it up to the public, and we'd have to charge them for lunch. No doubt the NRO president has a speaking fee, and it's probably a lot higher than we could ever raise. But, I'll go on the Internet and find out."

That evening Janet made her request via the NRO web site. The next evening she was shocked to receive an acceptance of her invitation. Since the event was being planned by a school group, the NRO president waived his speaking fee, and he told Janet that there would be no transportation costs, either. He would include their event as part of a long-overdue vacation to visit relatives who lived in Kalkaska. Janet sent a reply e-mail expressing her sincere thanks and promising she would send further details about the event.

NOVEMBER 24

There was a dusting of snow on the ground, and winter was in the air. People filed into the courthouse for what they believed would be the final day of the Simons trial. There would be closing arguments, and most hoped it would take only a short time for the jury to reach a verdict.

At precisely 9 a.m. Judge Johnson entered her courtroom.

"Good morning. The prosecution will now offer its closing statement," Judge Johnson directed.

Prosecutor Purcell rose with notes in hand and approached the small podium. He paused, looked into the eyes of the jurors, and began. "Ladies and gentlemen of the jury, the deliberate killing of a human being is a sad event. As humans, we value life, and we are saddened when one of us is taken senselessly, especially one whose job is to protect us from criminals, and who is a respected member of the community. Officer Turner was a husband and father, the father of a disabled son.

"When you consider the act of murder, you need to identify three things: a victim; a means of causing death; and a motive for the killing. This case offers all of these components. A man was killed by a bullet from a deer rifle. By his own admission, only one man shot a deer rifle that afternoon, pointing the rifle in a direct line with an open barn door. The defendant, Zeke Simons, says he only wanted to scare Mr. Richards, but he wasn't content simply to fire the rifle into the woods, or into the air. He fired the rifle toward two men — a most irresponsible act — and that bullet killed Officer Turner.

"So, we have a victim, Mr. Turner. We have a means of causing death, the firing of a rifle. And there is a strong motive, extreme anger, which had been building in Mr. Simons' mind all afternoon. His anger started before sunrise when he confronted another hunter. It was rekindled in Mickey's, and intensified when two officers from the sheriff's department apparently accepted bribes. His anger finally came to a head when Mr. Simons believed that Mr. Richards was also going to pay off Officer Turner. In fact, he was only offering his hunting tag, but his rage drove the defendant, Zeke Simons, to kill Officer Turner.

"Granted, the defense has been able to show that Mr. Richards may also have behaved inappropriately, but the facts are solid. Mr. Simons, a man who within the hour had consumed 36 ounces of beer, and an angry man in the woods with a rifle in bow season, admittedly fired a rifle. That man was so out-of-control that he hadn't enough sense not to fire a rifle near a residence, even with an officer a few hundred feet away. Zeke Simons, acting inappropriately and illegally, fired the shot that killed Officer Turner.

"There is no reasonable doubt here, ladies and gentlemen. Two men were in conflict, and Officer Turner got in the middle of it. His life ended. I see no other course of action on your part than to decide, based on the evidence presented here that the defendant murdered Officer Turner. I ask you to return a verdict of Guilty."

"The defense will now provide their closing statement. Miss Moylan?" Judge Johnson said.

Audrey, without notes this time, rose and slowly approached the jury. She stood in front of them much like a choir director would lead a choir. She began with a low-key, yet serious, tone. "When this trial began, I said I would provide you with substantial evidence to cause you to have no doubt about the innocence of my client in regard to the murder of Conservation Officer Timothy Turner. Some of that evidence concerns the behavior of Mr. Howard Richards. We know that Mr. Richards lied to you when he said he was not near his home or barn when the victim was shot. We know this from the testimony of Zeke Simons, and by the testimony from Mr. Richards' grandson, Taylor. You heard testimony from an experienced investigator of crime scenes that Officer Turner's log book was tampered with, when the numeral 1 was changed. You know a change was made, because the pressure from the lines changing the 1 to a 4 were substantially weaker than the other numbers. Obviously, someone other than Mr. Turner changed the time. Then you heard Taylor Richards say that his grandfather was home when a second person arrived after the deputies' visit. How do we know that, beyond the boy's word? Because he indicated that soap operas were on television, and the soaps are presented between noon and 3 p.m.

"Mr. Richards thought he had the perfect alibi for being away from his home, but he didn't know that his grandson would testify, thinking the fear of a belt would be enough to silence the boy. Mr. Richards wasn't aware of the sophisticated technology regarding writing analysis. There was a reason for Richards not to do what normal people would do in an accident of this nature: call 911, assist the victim till help arrived, tell the truth to the authorities. No, there were good reasons for his behavior, and that should raise reasonable doubt that Mr. Simons killed the officer.

"You see, Mr. Richards doesn't respect the law. It is common knowledge he lives in his own world, free from responsible citizenship. He has no understanding of law and its role in protecting men, women, children, and the environment from irresponsible people and their immature behavior. Mr. Richards also knew that Officer Tim Turner would likely arrest him for poaching. That arrest would be a threat to his freedom. He also wanted revenge against my client for having had the courage to report his poaching. So, the way out of this dilemma was to do the same thing he did the last time he was threatened: he decided to take the law into his own hands, take control, and eliminate whatever was threatening him.

"Previously, the threat arose from local boys destroying mailboxes, personal property of people on Peavine Road. This time it was a no-nonsense conservation officer who was about to arrest him for an obvious violation of the law. That would have caused problems, the most significant of which would be to end his domination over people in this area. It would deny him the camaraderie of his friends at Mickey's, not to mention all the drinks they bought him, and it would deny him unlimited freedom living in his own world.

"I am fully aware that Mr. Richards is not on trial here. Mr. Richards has not been charged with murder, but my client has. Mr. Richards is not even a suspect in the death of Mr. Turner, as my client is. A man was killed in a tragic accident — or maybe it wasn't an accident. But the reality is that my client, Zeke Simons, is on trial for his life. Yes, there is a victim, and a weapon, but what is missing in relation to this crime is a motive. Why would Mr. Simons kill Officer Turner? There is no reason for my client to want the man dead. The officer was the one person who was acting on my client's claim of poaching. On the other hand, my client has been truthful when providing his testimony. He was at the scene, he was furious, and he fired his rifle. But he did not commit murder and you have patiently listened to a significant amount of testimony that should have raised a reasonable doubt.

"The prosecutor would have you believe that the bullet from Zeke Simons' rifle killed Officer Turner, but no evidence proves that. The fatal bullet came from above the officer and not from a position parallel to the ground. The evidence points instead to someone trying to cover up his presence at the crime scene, someone acting in an uncaring way by not calling 911 while a man died of a gunshot wound on the floor of his barn.

"I do know that the behavior of a man not on trial in itself provides evidence that Mr. Simons did not kill Officer Turner. Ladies and gentlemen of the jury, I ask you to accept your responsibility in this matter of life or death for my client and respond to a great deal of doubt by returning a verdict of Not Guilty. Thank you."

"Prosecutor Purcell, you are allowed a rebuttal. Do you wish to use it?" Judge Johnson asked.

"Yes, Your Honor," Wil said, standing and walking toward the jury box.

"Proceed, then."

"Thank you, Your Honor," Wil said, glancing back at Judge Johnson. Facing the jurors he began. "Ladies and gentlemen of the jury. Weapon, rifle; victim, Conservation Officer Timothy Turner, an outstanding officer of the law; motive, extreme anger; murderer, the defendant, who admitted to being at the scene, and admitted firing a shot in the direction of the victim. You have all the evidence you need to bring justice to this community, closure to the Turner family, and justification to our fleet of law enforcement personnel. Contrary to what the defense would have you believe, there is no doubt. The man responsible for this tragedy, the person guilty of this crime, is Zeke Simons."

Wil remained standing, looking each person in the eye, doing his best to cement into each brain the simple words: Victim, Motive, Weapon, Evidence, and Guilty.

Lou Searing was also seated in the courtroom. He was on the lookout for anything out of the ordinary and Jerry Tomlinson fit the bill in several ways — his wrinkled and dirty clothes, his nervousness, and his facial expressions. Jerry's behavior was sufficiently odd that Lou decided to sit beside him during the last day of the trial.

Jerry Tomlinson had come to the courtroom each day. On the first day, he carried a pair of pliers in his pocket to see whether the metal would trigger an alarm, but nothing had happened. That day he watched carefully where Zeke entered the courtroom, where he sat, and that he exited through the same door he had entered. On the second day, Jerry brought in ten shells in his pocket, to check for any sensing device, or whether a trained dog would alert a bailiff to the gunpowder. Again, no alarm was raised. Today he had waited outside to see how Zeke arrived at the courthouse: in a car, or in a van? He watched to see if Zeke was outside for any length of time between getting out of the vehicle and entering the courtroom.

On the final day of the trial, Jerry Tomlinson brought his revolver. He had run through his plan several times in his head: he wanted to act inside the courtroom, remembering the jury in his trial telling the judge he was guilty, and Zeke smiling, making a fist and pounding it in the air to signify his victory. In this courtroom, Jerry would have the last word, just as the jury foreman announced the verdict. No matter the verdict, as soon as it was read, Jerry would have his revenge, and Zeke would know, finally, what it felt like to have his world disintegrate.

As he listened to Prosecutor Purcell speak, Jerry Tomlinson reached into his pocket, feeling the warm metal of a loaded pistol. His heart beat faster with the excitement growing toward the moment when the jury would return a verdict. He smiled, thinking he also would deliver a verdict, not with words, but with action.

∞

"Ladies and gentlemen, you have heard the closing arguments from both sides," Judge Johnson began. "Now it is your responsibility to retire to the jury room, choose a foreman, discuss the evidence, and return with a verdict. Once I have instructed you on the law related to this matter, the bailiff will escort you to the jury room, where you will begin your deliberations."

After the instructions from Judge Johnson, the twelve jurors filed out of the courtroom and into the jury room. Most of the visitors left the courtroom to await a verdict.

∞

The jurors took their seats around a table. One man went directly to the coffee pot. "Anybody else want a cup?" No one responded, so he poured himself a cup and sat down.

"Guess we need to choose a foreman," Larry Adderly, a retired barber, said.

"You want to be it?" Mrs. Jacobs asked Larry.

"No thanks. I don't hear well and besides, that kind of thing is not my cup of tea."

Jake Hermans, the owner of the True Value Hardware Store in town, spoke up. "I'll do it, unless someone wants the job." Jake was well-known in the community, having been the mayor several times before. He was an elder in the First Presbyterian Church as well as chair of the marginally-successful United Way Campaign.

"I think you'd do a good job, Jake. I say Jake's the man," said June Williams, a young mother of twin girls. Eleven heads bobbed up and down, and the jury had a foreman.

"Well, that was some trial," Jake said. "We sure have a cast of characters: a farmer, and probably a poacher, to boot; a big city attorney; and lots of experts. I've served on juries before, and it seems to me we can do one of two things. We can take a straw vote to see where we stand and then talk about the case, or we can just say what's on our minds and vote the verdict later. Anyone have any preference for one over the other?"

"I'd like to take a straw vote," replied June. "I'm curious."

"Ok, I see some heads nodding," Jake replied. "You want a voice vote, a raised hand vote, or a private hand-written vote?"

Brenda Thatcher, a middle-aged beautician suggested, "Let's do a hand-written vote."

"Fine." Jake folded a piece of paper and tore enough sections to give everyone a square. When he had finished, he gave directions. "Write down 'guilty' or 'not guilty', fold the paper, and send it down to me. Don't put your name on it, just your vote."

Everyone did as Jake had directed. He tallied the votes and then announced the results. "Our straw vote is as follows: seven vote guilty, and five vote not guilty. It looks like we've some thoughts on both sides of the issue. Let me remind everyone of what the judge said. The prosecutor has to prove beyond a reasonable doubt that Mr. Simons killed Officer Turner. The defense doesn't have to prove that Zeke Simons didn't kill Officer Turner. I think juries get hung up on which side proved guilt or innocence, but that isn't our job to decide.

If we decide that we have a reasonable doubt that Zeke Simons fired the rifle shot that killed the officer, we would have to find him not guilty of the crime. But, if we believe that the evidence was clear that he did kill the officer, we'll have to hand down a guilty verdict."

"I have a lot of doubt." Meredith Blackman, a clerk in the IGA grocery store was frowning. "I mean, old man Richards was lying through his teeth. He said he wasn't at the barn, but I'm convinced he was. If this Zeke killed the officer, why would Howard think he had to lie? Why wouldn't he come right out and call 911 and get some help and then explain what happened? There's a reason he's lying and making up a story. That right there is enough reason for me to doubt that Mr. Simons killed the officer."

"I'll take the other side to make my point," Susan Lawrence, a single mother of two, replied. "Zeke was the only one who admitted he fired a shot. So, a man is killed by a rifle shot, and the only one who admits to firing a shot was Zeke. A man is killed by a rifle, and a rifle is fired from across the road in the direction of the victim. One and one makes two and having Zeke fire a rifle toward the victim sure makes him look guilty in my eyes. Now, why this old man thought he had to lie about not being there is a mystery, but the rest seems straightforward to me."

"But he didn't aim at the officer," Jackson Wilson, a local banker objected.

"After 36 ounces of beer, who knows what Zeke saw when he looked down the barrel of his rifle?" asked Wally Baker, a mailman.

"Howard is a liar, so don't use anything he says to try and sway my thinking," Meredith stated flatly.

"I don't mean to change the subject, but one thing keeps eating at me: Why did Howard Richards have to lie?" Brenda asked. "Why did he leave, only to return after the police and ambulances were there? Why didn't he call 911? What kind of a human being leaves a wounded man to die? And, if he did change the one to a four, why did he? All of this signals guilt to me. If Howard wanted to prove his innocence, why didn't he do what Meredith said, just call 911 and explain to the police that the officer was shot? And besides, if he wanted to frame Zeke, why didn't he stay put and say, while he was talking to Officer Turner, a shot came from the woods, and it struck Officer Turner. Please, somebody make some sense of his lying."

"I see what you mean, but everybody who knows Howard knows that he's strange," Jackson replied. "He is a liar, and we all know that. He should have been sent to an asylum years ago and we all know he's crazy. So, if I am looking for 'normal' behavior, I won't look to Howard. I'm sticking to the facts, as the prosecutor said: a man was shot; another man said he fired a shot in the direction of the victim. Therefore, I can only conclude that the shot that killed the officer came from the rifle fired by the defendant. Case closed. Let's vote."

"Not so fast, there," Jake said. "We've got a lot of people to hear from."

"I know, but to me this is a simple case, and we should just get the vote done and get on with our lives," Susan said.

"Anyone else want to comment?" Jake asked.

"I have something," June Williams said thoughtfully.

"That's what we're here for. Go ahead," Jake replied.

"I just want to put everyone on guard. No matter what anyone on this jury says, after hearing the testimony and comments from both attorneys, I assure you that under no circumstances will I cast a guilty verdict." The rest of the jury stared at her, surprised that June would take a strong stand. "The defense has convinced me that there is reasonable doubt. And there was no witness to the crime."

"There was too!" Wally responded loudly. "The witness is the defendant, and he said he fired his rifle in the direction of the officer. How much more of a confession do you want, for crying out loud?"

"There will be only a 'not-guilty' vote from me," said June. "That's all I have to say. I mean, the X-rays were wrong, and then some ghost turns on a camera. It's a mess."

"I'll speak for the other side, even if I'm all alone; there will be nothing from me besides a 'guilty' vote," Wally said angrily.

"Is that because of the kick-back you got, or is it what you really believe?" Meredith asked Wally. After a short silence, Meredith continued, "I got money to vote 'guilty' and I assume others of you did as well. Well, there isn't a dollar amount that can give me peace of mind. I don't know who killed Officer Turner, but I have a whole lot of doubt that it was Mr. Simons."

Before anyone else could comment, Jake said, "Your vote was bought? Is that what you're telling us?"

"That's right," Meredith replied. "Don't tell me this is a shock to everyone. I know for a fact that each of us was paid to vote 'guilty'. You don't have to admit it, but you know it is true."

"Do we tell the judge about this?" June asked.

"Absolutely not!" Brenda exclaimed. "I like living in a house that's not on fire. Nobody says anything to anybody!"

"I took the money because I need it, but I'll tell you this: I will vote my conscience," Meredith said firmly. "As far as I'm concerned, the money is to make sure I give a more serious look at a guilty verdict, but that's all."

"I am convinced, based on the evidence that the defendant is guilty," Jake said. "You heard the judge say that we can only consider the evidence. We may have thoughts about this case, and we may want one outcome over another, but all we can look at and consider is the evidence. The evidence for me is that the man had been drinking, and he fired a shot within a few feet of the victim by his own admission. I mean, how much more evidence do we need? Hey, folks, are your oars in the water? Isn't one and one making two here?" Several heads were nodding.

"But what about all the lying?" Meredith asked. "What about the cover-up?"

"I know, I know. But to repeat, what are the facts in the murder?" Jake asked. "A man under the influence of alcohol shot a rifle in the direction of the victim, and the victim died."

"But Howard did nothing to help Officer Turner. He even made up a story to prove he wasn't even at the place when the officer arrived." Meredith kept trying to convince the other jurors of her doubt. "How devious and inhumane can you get?"

"I agree," Jake replied. "But look at the evidence…"

"Yeah, I know, a man who had been drinking admitted firing the rifle, and the victim died."

"That's right," Jake said. "You know, to be honest, I don't trust Howard Richards, either. I don't even like the man, but I can't let that get in the way of the evidence. I really would like to find the defendant not guilty, and maybe he isn't guilty. But, based on the evidence, I really have no other choice than to find him guilty of the crime." Several heads were nodding. "Does anyone have anything to add?" No one spoke.

Foreman Hermans spoke up. "I'm going to send slips of paper around again, and I'd like each of you to vote "G" for guilty and "N" for not guilty. Does everyone have a pen or pencil?" They all nodded.

A few minutes later the ballots were sorted, with the "G" pieces on Jake's right and the "N" pieces on his left. When the 12 votes had been tallied, there were no "N" votes.

"Thank you, members of the jury; I believe we have made a just decision. Will someone knock on the door to signal the bailiff that we're ready to return the verdict?" the foreman asked.

The judge informed the attorneys that the jury was on its way to the courtroom to issue their verdict. People who had been waiting in the hall, or who had gone outside to have a smoke, quickly returned to the courtroom and took their seats.

Lou came into the courtroom with Judge Beekins. After looking over the people present, Lou again felt uncomfortable about the guy in the second row. He whispered to Judge Beekins, "I'm suspicious of that guy in the brown coat; I'm going to sit next to him."

"Good idea," the judge replied. "He does seem strange. Maybe he came in to get out of the cold. Listening to court cases is like watching a live soap opera right before your eyes."

"Could be a street person trying to get warm, but something tells me he could use some watching." Lou quickly walked to the second row and sat down.

The bailiff spoke up. "All rise. The Honorable Judge Johnson presiding."

The judge walked to her seat and sat down. The jury was escorted into the courtroom.

Without any pomp or circumstance, Judge Johnson asked, "Ladies and gentlemen of the Jury. Have you reached a verdict?"

"We have, Your Honor," Foreman Jake Hermans replied, rising to offer the decision.

"What say ye?" Judge Johnson asked.

"We the jury, find the defendant guilty." Amidst the gasps and immediate hum of comments, Jerry Tomlinson quickly rose, turned, and walked toward the door. Lou watched him closely, alert for any odd behavior. For weeks, Jerry's plan had been to kill Zeke Simons, but he had a niece about the age of one of Mr. Turner's nieces sitting near him and he decided he just couldn't have her witness such a terrible act as a killing. When he glanced at the little girl, he changed his mind and knew instantly that he could not carry out his mission. There would be another opportunity at sentencing, but for now, Zeke would live.

Defense Attorney Moylan decided not to poll the jury. She had expected a guilty verdict, and that is what she got. Audrey was sure the case would be appealed, and eventually Howard Richards would be tried for perjury and murder. The new evidence could be entered at that time.

The judge thanked the jurors and dismissed the jury. She brought her gavel down on the bench and said, "Case closed."

Zeke, in a state of disbelief, remained seated with his head in his hands. Seated with her father and her friend Tricia, Angie sobbed uncontrollably. Prosecutor Purcell smiled as if he had just won a blue ribbon at the county fair. One more case won on behalf of the people, he thought. Winning was satisfying.

Audrey put her hand on Zeke's shoulder and whispered in his ear, "This is far from over. Be patient. I'll appeal. Any judge in his or her right mind will overturn this verdict. It's upsetting, but you will be exonerated." As Zeke was led away, she walked over to Wil Purcell and shook his hand.

Lou and Judge Beekins looked at one another. Judge Beekins shook his head, mumbling, "Incredible decision." Lou nodded in agreement.

At home in Dansville, Lucy Duerr was watching Court TV while babysitting for a friend. As soon as the verdict was read, she saw a familiar figure get up out of his seat and walk out the door. She knew Jerry from a weekly group therapy session she attended at the Ingham County Office of the Human Services Department in Lansing. He had missed a couple of meetings lately, but she wondered why he'd never said anything about going to northern Michigan to attend a trial.

Lucy knew something of Jerry's problems with the law; he'd said a lot in therapy about his hatred for Zeke Simons. He had also mentioned in the group session that he needed help with his strong need for revenge.

Since the baby was sleeping, Lucy called Sue, another member of the therapy group. "Did you see Jerry Tomlinson on TV?"

"What show? Jerry Springer?" Sue asked with a laugh. "Or maybe it was COPS. Was he getting arrested for something?"

"No, neither of those. He was on Court TV," Lucy replied.

"You're kidding. What was he accused of?" Sue asked.

"He wasn't on trial or on the jury. He was just sitting in the courtroom. As soon as the verdict was read, he jumped up and walked out."

"It's a wonder that character didn't jump up and shoot somebody," Sue said. "He's got so much hatred and anger bottled up inside him. He's like a lightning rod in a summer thunderstorm: one spark, and he'll explode with emotion."

"I know, but all he did was get up and leave."

"Where was this trial?" Sue asked.

"I missed the city, but it's up north somewhere."

"Who was on trial?"

"That attorney from Mason," Lucy replied. "Zeke Simons. He was accused of killing a conservation officer. His wife must be beside herself.

"I would think so," Sue replied. "I know I couldn't handle it. What was the verdict anyway?"

"Guilty. Mr. Simons killed a conservation officer."

"Guilty?" Sue asked, stunned.

"That was the verdict."

"That can't be right," Sue said. "He wouldn't kill anyone!"

"Well, we know better than most what out-of-control emotions can lead to, right?" Lucy asked.

"Yes, I guess you have a point there," Sue replied.

"Listen, I've got to go," Lucy said, ready to bring the conversation to an end. "I'm babysitting for a friend and I hear the baby waking up."

"Okay, we'll tell Jerry he's famous because he's been on TV. Not many in these parts can make that claim."

"Or want to," Lucy added.

While the population of Trout City was not as concerned about Zeke's conviction as it was over the poaching trial, a few of the citizens began to realize that Howard Richards was not the model citizen he appeared to have been in the past. Some folks may not have been convinced that this downstate attorney was innocent, but they certainly had their doubts about the level of justice in their community.

NOVEMBER 25

Everyone involved in the trial was with relatives or watching the Lions on TV and eating their Thanksgiving dinner. Lou and Carol and Taylor were in Grand Haven. Angie Simons was with her mother and father in Bad Axe. Zeke was alone in a jail cell. He was served a hot turkey dinner with all the trimmings. While Zeke was thankful for many things, he was not thankful for the dilemma he was in.

NOVEMBER 29

The first school day after the Thanksgiving break was Community Leader Day in Trout City. The town had taken the program to heart, for most folks thought it was a good idea. The newspaper had done a series of articles highlighting several students and the officials they would be paired with. The high school paper also featured the event, and an assembly was held to explain the activity and the benefits everyone expected.

At precisely 8 a.m., the students reported to their mentors for orientation and to get a glimpse of what life was like in the day-to-day world of running a community. Throughout the morning, the students encountered several opportunities to learn about local issues and how community leaders responded to the challenges they faced. It was an exciting and positive morning for Trout City.

At the noon luncheon, the banquet hall was filled with tables decorated by the Culinary Arts Department of the Cherry County Vocational Skills Center.

Janet, as president of the Student Council, welcomed everyone to the luncheon and introduced the high school Mrs. Sagala, who began the program.

"Thank you all for coming to our Community Leader Day Luncheon. Today, thirty members of our senior class are role-playing, or 'shadowing', our city leaders to get a basic understanding of what is involved in running a city. Janet and her committee deserve a round of applause." Janet was pleased with the ovation and introduced Vince and Josh who stood for another round of applause.

"We decided on this meal to give community leaders and students a chance to get to know one another in an informal setting. Janet, please introduce our speaker."

Janet approached the microphone and began with confidence. "Our speaker this afternoon is Mr. Wendell Babbitt, an influential leader in Washington, D.C. He is president of the National Rifle Organization, which boasts thousands of dues-paying members. How many people are members of the NRO? Please signal with applause."

The room filled with spontaneous applause such that people undoubtedly joined in who were not members, but who simply wanted to be a part of the atmosphere.

"Please join me in giving a big Trout City welcome to Mr. Wendell Babbitt."

Babbitt was greeted with a standing ovation. To many in the room, Wendell Babbitt was more popular than the President of the United States. He thanked the crowd twice for their applause before the people settled into their seats.

"Thank you, Janet, and greetings to everyone. And, a special greeting to all of you who are members of our fine organization." Once again, there rose a round of applause and whistles. "I am happy to be here. My stepmother, whom I haven't seen in almost five years, lives in Kalkaska. So, when Janet invited me to speak to you, I welcomed an opportunity to visit your wonderful state, to visit my stepmother, and to spend some time with real red-blooded Americans, those who fully support our right to stand with our forefathers and demand the right to bear arms!" Once again, the audience burst into applause, whistles, and shouts of support.

"This morning I participated in your Community Leader Day program. The person who 'shadowed' me was Connie Wright. We talked about my responsibilities in the NRO. I shared some of my e-mails with her and I showed her some of my correspondence so she could see what kind of letters I had to answer. We talked about leadership, and the attributes of a leader. I learned from Connie, and I hope she learned from me.

"I think the Community Leader Day program is a marvelous concept, and I want to acknowledge Janet, Vince, and Josh — students who saw a need and did something about it. That's leadership. It does little good to identify a problem or an injustice and simply say, 'This is not my problem', and then spend time complaining to others about how this or that isn't working. Leaders work to solve problems and resolve issues that make life better or easier for others. I can't define a leader more clearly than that, whether we're talking about a general in the army, the President, a mayor, a sheriff, or a parent. A leader tackles problems and issues that make life better or easier for others.

"Other important attributes of a leader are ethics and morality. These big words simply mean doing the right thing, doing what is ethically and morally right.

"My message to the young people participating in today's activities is always to meet a challenge with a strong sense of morality, of doing the right thing in spite of any obstacles you face. Stand up to any form of corruption, because corruption takes our rights away. We see it in today's terrorist activity. In order to fight the people who are threatening us, we have given up some of the freedoms for which our forefathers fought so hard.

"The leaders of Trout City face the same challenge: you must be model citizens. You must be individuals the public can look up to, for if you are not, people will disrespect you and the government you represent.

"The future of your city, state, and country belongs to our youth. They need good examples so they will grow up to respect government and see the good that it can do for people who live in a civil society. I hope all of you young leaders have the courage to stand up to all that is wrong with our society, because it is your city, your state, and your country that you will leave to your children and grandchildren.

"It has been an honor to be with you today. I can assure you that the National Rifle Organization will always defend your right to bear arms. And, furthermore, our organization will continue to be a model for this country and the free world in demonstrating leadership of the people, by the people, and for the people. Enjoy your afternoon."

The audience stood for sustained applause for Mr. Babbitt. They felt good about what they had heard, and they appreciated the strength of character of the man who had spoken. The students couldn't wait to get back to the business of civic leadership, so the city officials took their high school seniors back to their work sites for a few more hours of role-playing.

In the city offices, the students felt a sense of power, sitting in leather chairs behind big desks, or riding in law enforcement vehicles full of technical equipment and weapons to assist in any difficult encounter. There was power everywhere. If it didn't come with a title, it came with attractive offices, equipment, prestige, and being in demand by the people you were serving.

Student Mary Burkett, prosecutor for the day, found it fascinating to shadow Mr. Purcell. She listened to his advice to his underlings, learned about a number of cases that would be coming to court in the near future, and took a tour of the courtroom and a judge's chambers.

While Mr. Purcell stepped out of his office briefly, Mary, seated at his desk, saw the phone message light blinking. Because she was being brought into the real life of the Prosecutor, she hit the message button and heard, "Wil, you'll get the payoff for keeping the case out of court. Nice work. This should give you and the Mrs. a wonderful trip to Hawaii this winter." Mary hit the save button, and the tape quickly rewound. She decided not to mention the message when Wil returned.

Student Luke Thornton was mayor for the day. While the mayor stepped out of his office to talk with a citizen about a sensitive issue, Luke looked through a stack of letters on the mayor's desk, wondering what type of letters a mayor would receive.

Typical letters voiced complaints about various problems, and some invited him to speak to service organizations. But then Luke came to an unusual letter, addressed to the Mayor as 'Confidential'. But, hey, Luke Thornton was the mayor for a few hours, so the letter was his to read, right? His eyes followed the typed lines. 'I ask that the city officials stay clear of the gray wolf-poaching issue. Several thousand dollars should show our appreciation for your stand in opposition into any investigation into such alleged behavior. I hope this little 'tip' in your pocket will keep the investigation nonexistent in your area." The letter was signed, "With warm regards, David J. Lewis, President, Hunters United Against Nature's Destruction of Deer Herds."

Luke quickly buried the letter in the stack, deciding not to mention it to the Mayor when he returned.

Tina Russell was the sheriff for the day. Her biggest thrill was wearing a visitor's badge and a heavy belt, complete with a container of Mace, a walkie-talkie, and a cell phone hanging on her hip. She had a hat, too, and got to ride in the Sheriff's car, listening to the radio lingo of the law enforcement world. It all seemed quite glamorous.

She was waiting in the car while Sheriff Sherman responded to a domestic dispute when a message came across the cruiser's computer from the dispatcher. The message was from Max Bell. Tina read, "Sheriff, it looks like Howard's 'not guilty' verdict in the poaching trial is going to be appealed, and likely overturned. If this happens, a gray wolf-poaching episode is sure to be investigated next, and you don't need the public outcry that would cause. I'll need your help clearing him, and you know I'll make it worth your effort."

It was obvious to Tina that she wasn't supposed to see that message. She decided not to say anything to the sheriff when he came back to his car.

Theresa Rojas was thrilled to be the editor of the Trout City Times Herald for a day. She wanted to be a journalist, and this was the perfect chance to look into the world of publishing, specifically newspaper publishing. The editor, Ron Otto, showed her a number of stories he was following and pointed out some of the difficult decisions he had to make each day. Theresa hung on his every word, asking tens of questions: How did he decide on an editorial? How did he remain unbiased when he felt strongly about an issue?

Around 2:00, Mr. Otto had to attend a meeting to question a writer he believed was plagiarizing — taking material from another publication — and claiming it as his own. Theresa's presence at the meeting wasn't appropriate. He directed Theresa to become familiar with the stories that were not from the Associated Press or the controlling publishers so that when he came back, the two of them would decide what stories to print in the morning paper. He promised one of the stories would be about her experience as editor for a day.

The editor had shared e-mails throughout the day as a means of teaching Theresa some of the realities of his job. While he was out, an e-mail appeared on the screen. She saw no reason not to open it. She read, "Mr. Otto, I am writing to ask you not to publish the story by your reporter, Larry Weeks, about the vanishing gray wolves. His story supposedly exposes a poaching ring operating in our area. He sexually harassed me during the interview, and if you run his story, I will take him and your paper to the Supreme Court if I have to. You can expect a huge payout, because I recorded the interview, and he hasn't a clue. I repeat: if you publish the article, I will bury you, Larry Weeks, and your paper. If you don't, I'll not follow through on my harassment charge. Am I understood? The ball is in your court."

The e-mail was not signed and Theresa didn't want to know who the person was anyway. She hit the 'Save As New Mail' key, deciding to keep this attempt at blackmail to herself.

Zeke did everything he could to be isolated in his cell. As some inmates go on hunger strikes, he became totally silent. He didn't start any conversation, and he didn't respond to anything said to him. During exercise time and group time such as meals, he stayed by himself when guards were present, and when they weren't, he generally stayed close to the largest number of men, thinking that if he were attacked again, those around him would break up the altercation.

DECEMBER 1

Two days after the Community Leader Day, the 30 seniors who participated in the activity met at school. Positive comments far outweighed the negative. In fact, the only negative comments were related to some students not feeling welcome, or leaders being reluctant to share information about the ins and outs of their jobs. One minor official had agreed to be a part of the program, then had gone to an out-of-state conference, leaving the student to meet with a secretary who had no clue as to what the day was about or how to involve the student.

Near the end of the debriefing, an anomaly came to light. The principal asked, "Was there anything that you experienced that you found troubling?"

Victor Silas, who had been assigned to the Director of Animal Control, said that he had learned there was suspicion that gray wolves were being poached; the office had picked up three carcasses in the previous month. Their radio-controlled collars had been cut, the wolves had been shot and left to die, and there had been no attempt to bury them. In two of the three cases, the heads had been cut off and taken away, presumably to become trophies for someone's den.

As soon as Victor said, 'gray wolf', it triggered the memories of three others who recalled their own experiences, but no one spoke up. However, each privately told Janet what had happened.

As Student Council President and the instigator of this project, Janet brought together the five students who had heard something involving gray wolves. They met in the school conference room after classes. Janet used Mr. Babbitt's speech to reinforce the need to bring morality and ethical behavior into the issue before them.

As each student shared the bits of information he or she had stumbled upon, the fact of gray wolf poaching in their area became evident. Once the pattern was clear, the collective decision was that they needed to act, but what to do was not obvious. Each student felt that going to their adult mentors would not help, because they were apparently part of the problem. The group might find support within an environmental organization, but those groups were not in a position to take action to end the illegal activity apparently tolerated within Trout City.

One of the students suggested they bring in Reverend Evans. "I think he could suggest a course of action that would be appropriate. He's a community leader who would take us seriously and guide us to do what is morally and ethically right."

"I'm glad you have such high regard for Reverend Evans, but I think he is another part of the problem," Janet said.

"A part of the problem? How is that?" the student asked.

"Well, the student who was assigned to Reverend Evans is not here today. While she told me what happened, she didn't want to be a part of this group, nor did she want to share her experience. I promised her I would not repeat her story, but I do feel that Mr. Evans is not part of the solution. I also ask each of you not to start any rumors, because this student fears some sort of retribution."

"Man, is this city corrupt, or what?" Vince blurted out.

"I don't know if the city or county is corrupt, or whether we simply stumbled onto an issue that is lurking below the surface. I imagine every community has some secret in a closet that people are not proud of, and maybe this is ours," Janet said.

"Well, we're about out of community leaders who could suggest the moral and ethical thing. We can't go to the editor, the sheriff, the mayor, the prosecutor, or a prominent religious leader," Josh said.

"Right, and who is to say that the adult we do share it with isn't involved in the mess," Janet added.

At this moment, Mary Burkett recalled seeing a letter from a student on a University of Michigan College of Law letterhead that had been sent to Mr. Purcell, the prosecutor. The letter was apologetic in nature, but the writer thanked the prosecutor for speaking with him about the death of two students in the mailbox-smashing case.

"Maybe that should be our course of action!" Janet said with some enthusiasm.

"What course? Am I missing something?" Mary asked.

"Well, this person at the U of M would be outside our community, and he would have the resources of the College of Law at his disposal. He has some interest in our community, or he wouldn't have come up here to look into that terrible incident. Maybe our help could come from this student!" Janet said, while the others nodded in agreement.

"How would we go about finding out who this was?" Luke wondered aloud.

"This person also wrote in the letter that something should be done about a speeding ticket that was issued that he believed was totally unwarranted," Mary offered.

"That is our entrée right there. There must be a record of that ticket, and there can't be too many issued to people from Ann Arbor," Mary said, pleased to be able to offer a solution to the matter.

"We'd have to go to the sheriff, and he's going to wonder why we want this information. That won't work," Janet said.

"Why couldn't we contact the dean of the Law College and say we are trying to locate a student from the college who may have been researching a legal matter up here?" Mary asked.

"There are hundreds of students in the Law College," Janet replied. "I don't think that would work, either"

"I know what we can do," Mary said in a burst of positive energy. "I could contact the secretary in the prosecutor's office and say that I'm thinking of going to the University of Michigan to become a lawyer. While at the Community Leader Day program, I saw that Mr. Purcell had received a letter from a law student at the U of M, and maybe she could find out who wrote the letter, so I could request an interview!"

"That might work," Janet responded. "Do the rest of you agree?" Everyone nodded.

"I can use my cell phone right now, and we could have our help in a few minutes."

Janet rang Mr. Purcell's office and asked the secretary for the name on the U of M student letter. A minute or so later she heard, "I checked our mail log, and that letter was written by a Mr. Scott Anderson."

"We've got our contact!" Janet reported to the group.

She opened the phone again, checked with information, called the University of Michigan Law College, and then asked for a Mr. Anderson. She left a voice mail message: "Mr. Anderson, this is Janet Abs, president of the Student Council in Trout City, Michigan. It is very important that I talk with you. Please contact me as soon as possible. My number is area code 231-555-6485. Thank you."

$$\infty$$

That evening Scott returned the call.

"Hello, Janet?"

"Yes. Mr. Anderson?"

"Yes. How can I help you?"

"Well, we've got a mess up here in Trout City" Janet replied.

"Yeah, I found it sort of a crazy little town, too."

"I know, and I'm embarrassed."

"So, what can I do for you?" Scott asked.

"We know you are a law student, and we are wondering if you can give us some advice about getting our town back on track."

"Why would you, a student, be calling me, instead of an adult in the town? Don't get me wrong, you are probably more mature than most in Trout City, but you have to admit that my question is legit."

"Oh yes, it is. Well, I'm the Student Council President, and I also was a leader in our high school's Community Leader Day program, which is over now and was successful. We brought in the leader of the National Rifle Organization and he gave a great talk. Anyway, while some of us were shadowing officials, we accidentally uncovered some strange information. Once we pulled it all together, it added up to what looks like corruption with a capital 'C'."

"Please continue. You've got me curious."

"It seems so widespread that we don't know who to turn to, since many of the officials in our town may be part of the problem."

"Uh-huh."

"One of our students was assigned to the prosecutor. She remembered seeing a letter from you thanking Mr. Purcell for some information he provided. So, we tracked you down, so to speak."

"OK. How do you imagine I can help?" Scott asked.

"I don't know, really. I have no specific plan or request. We just think, you being a law student and all, you might have an idea about how to get an apparently corrupt town back on track."

"I see."

"We don't know whether to go to the Governor, to the '60 Minutes' television show, or maybe our legislator or senator. We were sort of hoping you could tell us where to start."

"Janet, let me think on this a bit," Scott said, not sure he wanted to get involved. "I have your phone number, and I promise I'll get back to you. I want to ask a professor or two for thoughts, and I have a few student friends who may have some advice."

"Ok, thank you very much!"

"You're welcome."

Scott thought this was about as close to reality as a law student in public administration could come.

DECEMBER 2

The next morning, Scott arranged for a meeting with Professor Beekman in the Michigan Union in the heart of the campus. He explained what he had learned from Janet. For a few seconds there was total silence while Professor Beekman thought. When he spoke, his concern was for propriety. "We want to do this in a way that would not embarrass Trout City.

"My first inclination would be to initiate a media blitz that would throw the town into chaos and set it back on its heels for years to come. But a more rational approach may be to help the community overcome this mess quietly; and get back on track to becoming a law-abiding city. Nobody needs to get the citizens up in arms, perhaps literally, or to bring a lot of negative publicity to a tourist area that needs growth as much as anyone."

Then, as any wise professor would do, Beekman left the solution to the student. "What we need to do is determine how best to accomplish this. Any ideas?"

Scott listened as his mentor set the stage. Here was Scott's test, in a non-academic arena, outside of stacks of law books, over a cup of coffee in a student union.

"You've taught me to study precedent, so I suppose the first thing to do is find out whether there has been a similar situation that I could use to learn how the problem was handled elsewhere.

"Further, we need to determine precisely what the problem is," Scott continued. "I think Janet has identified the symptoms, but I should know who and what is involved before I even think about precedent, or how to resolve the situation."

"Very good, Mr. Anderson," Professor Beekman said. "You've learned your lessons well."

"My first thought would be about protocol," Scott began. "Our system of laws and policies and procedures are all based on protocol, going up the ladder, so to speak. In addition to understanding the problem and seeking precedents, we also need to identify the appropriate protocol," Scott added.

"Meaning what, Scott?" the professor asked.

"I mean, maybe this thing ought to be looked into by the FBI, or maybe the state police have jurisdiction. And no doubt the State Bar has some procedure to follow when a member is accused of inappropriate behavior. We need to know how the problems are supposed to be fixed and how to follow that procedure, unless the corruption makes it impossible somewhere along the line."

"Good thinking. Anything else occur to you?" Professor Beekman asked.

"I guess I'm wondering if it is even proper for me to get involved. I'm not an attorney yet. Even with your expert advice, I'd hate to get us in a jam because of some asterisk in the law I didn't know about."

Professor Beekman recognized an opportunity for reality to replace fiction. "Scott, this is a 'win-win' opportunity, and those don't come along very often. If you tackle this problem, if you successfully guide Trout City toward becoming a law-abiding community, I will call this your comp exam. I think you'll learn more by helping this community than you would in any written or oral examination."

Scott thanked Mr. Beekman for his encouragement, and then both men went off to their separate pursuits.

∞

Keeping track of news pertaining to Zeke Simons' conviction became an obsession with Jerry. He collected newspaper articles, and he even kept a journal recording every detail he learned via the Internet or through phone calls to several informants in the Trout City area.

With the appeal date for Zeke's conviction trial for Officer Turner's murder fast approaching, Jerry took renewed interest in the case. He felt he really could kill Zeke, should he be able to buy his way out of justice, a path that Jerry had not been able to follow.

In reality, Zeke Simons and Jerry Tomlinson were quite similar. When each perceived injustice, he acted in an immature way to right the wrong. The difference between them was that Zeke had the services of a good lawyer and a tremendous amount of know-how behind him, and Jerry had nothing to draw on but pent-up anger and frustration.

Jerry knew that if Zeke were set free, it would be his duty to see that justice was served. This time Jerry would not fire at Zeke in a crowded courtroom, but on Zeke's way to freedom. Yes, that would be perfect. Just when his victim was celebrating victory, thrilled to be free, Jerry would snatch away that freedom, and the victory would be Jerry's to celebrate. If the system didn't work, then he would have to do the job, and this time he wouldn't hesitate.

DECEMBER 3

Scott Anderson began his behind-the-scenes work, searching the Internet for cases involving corrupt government officials. He searched nationwide, but he paid more attention to those cases tried in the Sixth Circuit, since those would hold precedent for Michigan. Another search using 'poaching' produced scores of cases throughout the country.

After three days of intense research, Scott came up with a classic case in Indiana. From what he knew of Trout City, the situation in a community near Fort Wayne seemed like a perfect match. There, the city had called upon the county, which handed the problem off to the legislators, who appealed to the governor to take control and bring the city around. The process to resolve the mess in Indiana seemed too long and involved. While that worked in Indiana, Scott thought Trout City needed a simpler and better solution.

Next, Scott found a similar case in Idaho that had been solved by citizens. When they learned of the corruption, they launched an extensive recall campaign targeting the politicians involved. This approach took some time, but eventually all the corrupt officials were booted out of office and replaced with law-abiding citizens.

As with the Indiana case, the Idaho resolution didn't seem like the best plan for Trout City; there might not be sufficient population base to replace the corrupt officials with proper citizens. In fact, from what Scott could learn about the people of Trout City, the recall petitions probably would not lead to weeding out many of the officials. The politicians were popular with the power-brokers, and one segment of the general citizenry was apathetic, and didn't recognize a problem.

Then Scott found a case in Arizona where a similar situation had been handled by professional groups. The professional organizations disciplined their members and in some cases, revoked memberships and/or rescinded credentials. In the Arizona incident, the associations had sanctioned the sheriff, the medical examiner, a prosecutor, and a pathologist.

In all three cases, while corruption was rampant, murder was not a factor. They presented white-collar crime, bribery, and underhanded practices, but no murder. Scott concluded that the Trout City situation was unique, in that there was a strong criminal element: homicide. None of the successful solutions in Indiana, Arizona, and Idaho would completely address the troubles in Trout City.

Only one official in Trout City seemed totally free of corruption — Judge Patterson. The people respected his tough demeanor and were proud of him, but many thought him too rigid and conservative. Scott set up a conference call with Professor Beekman and Judge Patterson to seek their advice on a solution to the mess in Trout City.

Professor Beekman began. "Judge, how are you today?"

"Well, considering all that has happened up here, pretty good."

"Let me explain why I am calling."

"Please do. I'm curious, as you can imagine," Judge Patterson replied.

"Yes, I can. We got a call from Janet Abs, a senior at your high school."

"Oh, yes, I know Janet. She's quite a talented young woman."

"Yes. She and her fellow students came upon some information during their Community Leader Day program. They combined their experiences and came up with an apparent pattern of bribery. This correlation, reviewed in relation to the criminal cases involving Mr. Simons and Mr. Richards, paints a picture of wide-spread corruption."

"That seems to be the situation at the moment, I agree."

"Janet has asked one of my students, Scott Anderson, to get involved. I have agreed that Scott should take on the Trout City problem as a comp final for the term, so he has been researching the options. Part of his strategy is to talk with you, as the one leader who seems above reproach, and who has the respect of the citizens of Trout City. That's why we are calling."

"I see. Well, thank you for your confidence in me. Plenty of people around here don't see eye-to-eye with me, but I'd like to think that I'm free of misconduct. And we do need help up here, that's for sure. I'd like to think we could solve this ourselves, but maybe Janet is wise in seeking expert help from non-biased professionals."

"Good. Our main question for you is, what do you think needs to be done to turn Trout City around?"

"Before I answer that, let's be sure we're both on the same page. Who is on your list of 'corrupt' officials?"

"So far, we have the sheriff, the prosecutor, the mayor, a minister, and…"

"The mayor? You really think the mayor is corrupt?" Judge Patterson interrupted. "You must have information I don't."

"We've learned that he accepted money to keep trials for poaching gray wolves out of the courts."

"Really? That's a surprise to me. The mayor is the last man I would expect to be involved in such a scheme. He actually took the money?"

"Please allow me to clarify that statement. We can't say he took the money, but he was offered the money, and there have been no court cases filed in or around Trout City involving the poaching of gray wolves. We jumped to a conclusion there, Judge. Sorry."

"I suppose others that you mentioned would be possible, but I'm still a bit surprised at your accusations."

"There could be more, but those are the ones we have identified from what Janet told us after talking with the students who were paired with these officials for their Community Leader Day."

"I see."

"Is anyone trying to address the problems now?" Professor Beekman asked.

"No. A few citizens have come to me with complaints, though the town is hardly in an uproar, but I'm concerned, and I've been thinking of some strategies."

"Let me switch subjects. What is your take on the Simons trial?"

"Attorney Audrey Moylan is guiding Zeke through the mess," Judge Patterson replied. "She appealed the guilty conviction, and I expect the Appeals Court will find him innocent of all charges."

"Could the jurors have been bribed in the trial?" Professor Beekman asked.

"I don't know, but I suppose anything is possible. Do you have evidence of that?"

"No, but we do have a pattern of bribery as a means to an end and since a guilty verdict was handed down, one can't help but wonder whether the verdict was bought," Professor Beekman said.

"I see. Have you had any contact with Lou Searing?" the judge asked.

"Never heard of him. Who's he?" Professor Beekman asked.

"He's a private investigator working with Zeke's attorney, Audrey Moylan," the judge replied. "He's working hard to find further evidence into the murder investigation."

"I think we need to touch base with him. Does he know of our work?" Beekman asked.

"I doubt it. He would only know if Janet told him, and I don't even think he knows about Janet."

"Seems like one hand should know about the other, right?" Professor Beekman proposed.

"Most definitely."

"Lou may have information critical to our work, and vice versa."

"I'll ask Lou to contact you, and I'll give you his cell phone number before we hang up in the event you want to contact him."

"OK. Thank you, Your Honor. Back to our original reason for the call: do you have any plan for cleaning up the corruption in Trout City?"

"Not really, and the main reason is that I don't think the citizens care about corruption. Also, stirring this particular pot may make matters worse. This is no reason not to take action; I just want whatever action we take to lead to a definite change."

"Agreed. Ok, we'll look forward to talking to Lou Searing, and we'll continue thinking about a good approach. But, if it is all right with you, we'd like to have the benefit of your thinking on whatever we recommend."

"Most definitely," the judge responded enthusiastically. "I appreciate your involving me."

"We'll be in touch, Judge."

"Yes, we will. Thank you for your help."

After the call ended, Professor Beekman remarked to Scott, "I hope you are paying attention to what's going on here." Scott looked at him confused. "This is valuable communication. It's generally not a good idea to crash someone's party and take over. What happened today is key to problem-resolution: finding someone on the inside who is knowledgeable, who has the trust of the community, and with whom you can work. Because of that call, we now know of another player in all of this: Lou Searing. And I'll bet he'll have information that will help us. The major players in our drama now appear to be Judge Patterson, Lou Searing, and Audrey Moylan."

"And you and me," Scott added.

"Yes, you and me, for sure."

DECEMBER 4

Lou was spending the day in Trout City. He'd noticed one thing about Zeke's trial that seemed askew: the strange-acting man in the courtroom. He arranged with Court TV to receive a video from the trial. From that, Lou was able to get a sense of the man, not complete by any means, but good enough for identification purposes. He had a gut feeling that it was important he find out who the man was.

Another puzzle to Lou was the source of the bribes corrupting Trout City. From what he knew of Howard Richards, he wasn't wealthy, but he must be paying big bucks to convince officials to do what he asked. Any official's career and reputation would be ruined, once that bribery was uncovered.

It seemed a poor assumption that Howard had money, unless he was an old skin-flint whose heirs would discover he had millions, but that was highly unlikely. A more likely scenario was that, while Howard probably received only Social Security, he had savings or stock put away for a rainy day. Still that hardly seemed enough to pay off several county and city officials in order to enjoy living outside of the law.

RICHARD L. BALDWIN

Also, the possibility that Howard's source of money was a worthy cause was out of the question. If anything, Howard was getting money from someone who supported what he was doing, and better yet, who didn't want law or government officials to interfere with illegal activities.

Since Howard was poaching, it made sense that he was supported by other poachers. When Lou accessed the Internet to research poaching in Michigan, the one poaching target that stood out was the gray wolf. There was a fair amount of deer poaching, but for people banding together to pursue a cause, the poaching of the gray wolf was unique.

Lou found a web site that took him to the DNR office in Crystal Falls in the western Upper Peninsula, where counting and tracking records of gray wolves were maintained. Apparently people in general often confused the gray wolf with the coyote. He called an investigator with the Crystal Falls office.

"I'd like to speak to the officer most knowledgeable about gray wolf-poaching activity," Lou asked.

"That would be Officer Gunn. One moment please."

A few seconds later Lou heard, "This is Bart Gunn."

"I'm Lou Searing, a private investigator from the Lower Peninsula, calling to find out some information about gray wolf poaching. I understand you know the most about this."

"Yes, I suppose I do. What do you want to know?"

"I'll get right to the point. Is an organized group of people poaching the gray wolf? I mean like an illegal network, or something like that?"

"I am sure there is, but, to the best of my knowledge, they are underground. I don't find any official recognition of such, but my investigation to date leads me to believe there is an organized group behind the poaching."

"What do you mean 'your investigation to date'?" Lou asked.

"We've been able to put radio signaling devices on many wolves up here, and we can tell when they stop moving. When we track the signal, we often find the collar thrown off into the woods, but sometimes the collar is still on the wolf carcass."

"Why are these people poaching?" Lou asked.

"They maintain the wolves are thinning the deer herd."

"Are they?"

"Wolves prey on deer, but I personally don't think they're 'thinning' the herd to any appreciable extent. There are plenty of deer up here, enough for excellent hunting and for nature to flourish in a survival-of-the fittest environment."

"Do they offer any other reason?"

"Well, farmers don't like them," Bart added. "A farmer can shoot a wolf if the animal is actually killing farm animals, but to be honest, that isn't a problem up here. At least I don't know that such killing is a problem up here."

"So, this group of alleged poachers, do you think they have money and a plan to eradicate the gray wolf population?"

"I wouldn't be surprised. You see, a mounted gray wolf head is worth quite a bit. It's a status symbol in that it's illegal to kill a wolf. So, to have one in your den or hunting cabin indicates you're a man who stands up to the law while protecting the farmer and the hunter."

"I see. But you don't know of a named group?" Lou asked.

"No, I don't. Why are you asking?" Bart inquired.

"I'm investigating a murder case in Trout City involving someone allegedly poaching a deer. But, more importantly, a conservation officer was murdered while investigating the poaching."

"Oh, yes, I've heard about that case."

"The man who apparently poached the deer probably has a connection — or I believe he has a connection — to money, and I suspect it might be a group of poachers elsewhere who support him."

"Very likely," Bart replied. "Actually, now that you mention it, we've recently had a couple of reports of gray wolf poaching downstate."

"Is that right?"

"Yeah, some gray wolves were spotted in the Lower Peninsula a few months ago, and about a month later, one turned up dead. About a week after that, another was found dead. Those are only the ones brought to our attention, but there could be several more."

"Did they have those radio collars on?" Lou asked.

"No, but we've seen the carcasses, and the wolves were shot. And, in both cases, the heads were cut off, so I imagine they're hanging in someone's den by now."

"Thanks for your help. Again, my name is Lou Searing. My cell is 555-678-5555. I'm going to keep working on my hunch that some group is funding this downstate poacher. If you hear any more about poaching in this area, or if you discover an organized group, I'd appreciate your contacting me. OK?"

"Yes, and please let me know if you learn anything."

"I'll do that. Thank you, Officer Gunn."

"My pleasure."

Lou hung up the phone and checked the Yellow Pages for taxidermists. He took out his notepad and wrote down the names, addresses and phone numbers of the four he found listed, thinking he would visit each and ask a few questions.

The closest taxidermist to town was Rusty Miller. When Lou entered the shop, he was struck by all the trophies that lined the walls. A tall man appeared from a back room. "Mr. Miller, I presume?" Lou asked.

"That's right. What can I do for you?"

"I'm looking for the best taxidermist in Michigan to do some work for me, and I'm wondering if that might be you?"

"I don't know about 'best', but I think I'm pretty good. Look around and judge for yourself."

"I thought you did work for sportsmen. Are all these trophies yours?" Lou asked.

"Yes, my pride and joy."

"Really? You're quite a hunter."

"Yes, I am. I've been to most parts of the world. I've been on many wild animal safaris, and what you are looking at pretty much represents the game that's legal to hunt throughout the world."

"It is a mighty fine collection. I will say that."

"Thanks. Enough about me — what do you need?" Rusty asked.

"Actually, I'm doing a little advance work for a friend of mine who hunts almost as much as you do. I work for him actually. He lives down in Portage — big corporate exec. He's buying some property up here and he sent me to find some merchants with whom he can deal. He doesn't want to take the time to find his own people — that's my job."

"I see. Well, I'd be glad to serve him. Here's my card. If he wants to call or stop in, I'd be happy to talk with him about my fees, amount of time needed to do the job, mounts — things like that."

"No, you'll be dealing with me. Like I say, he doesn't take the time. I'd bring you the animal, you'd mount it, and I'd take it to him. He's kind of strange that way."

"OK, whatever."

"I presume, looking at this display, that you have mounted large and small animals," Lou inquired.

"Yes, I have."

"Have you ever mounted a gray wolf?"

"No, I haven't. Hunting gray wolves is illegal in Michigan you know. Your boss doesn't poach, does he?"

"My boss takes whatever animal he wants, when he wants it, where he wants it."

"Well, I'm not your man," Rusty admitted. "I don't mount illegal game. It's not like me to throw money away, though I need it as much as the next guy. But if you're looking for a guy to mount illegal game, you need to talk to Mike Summers. He's about five miles east of here on Nichols Road. Mike doesn't care what the animal is — he'll mount it. You gotta pay big bucks, but he'll do it. Me? No way."

"What do you mean by 'big bucks'?" Lou asked.

"Well, at least two thou. He's the only one that'll do it, so there isn't a free market, but a poacher can turn around and sell it for at least double that."

"We may give you plenty of business on the legal game," Lou said. "I like your work, and you seem like a good guy."

"Like I say, if you want legal game mounted, no one can match me. If you want illegal mounted, you gotta find Mike — he's got no conscience."

After getting specific directions to Nichols Road, Lou shook Rusty's hand, walked to his car, and headed for Taxidermy by Mike

Summers. Unlike Rusty's shop, there were no trophies mounted in the small pole barn. Once in the door, he was approached by someone.

"I'm looking for Mike Summers. I hear he is one fine taxidermist." Lou said.

"I'm Mike Summers. What do you need?"

"I'm trying to find a taxidermist who will mount a gray wolf," Lou replied.

"Yeah, I'll do it."

"Good. Listen, I'm finding you for a hunter friend of mine who lives in the Lansing area. He knows it is illegal to take a wolf, but he did and he'd like it mounted."

"Yeah, he's not the only one."

"Really?"

"Yeah. They're not a popular animal around here — got a bad reputation. Being an animal, the wolf needs to eat, and what he likes to eat are deer, and sometimes farm animals. Those things can run in packs and take a farmer's small herd of animals in a night. Hunters don't like them either."

"Yeah, well, listen, can you give me any of your satisfied customers so I can call them and find out how they like your work? My friend is very picky about the quality of work. He'll also want to know your price."

"The prices are fair, but I don't give out names of customers. People up here don't like giving out personal information."

"That's too bad, because my friend researches the people who do work for him. If he likes your work, you could be making a lot of money in the next few years."

"Can't give out names. Sorry."

"Not even one happy customer?" Lou asked.

"Nope. Won't do it."

"Then can you give me the name of another taxidermist around here who would do a good job of mounting a gray wolf?"

"I think you're looking at him. The other guys don't mount illegal game, and I don't blame them. Normally I wouldn't, either, but I've got four kids and a wife, and times are tough and it's not me killing the animal. All I do is mount it, and if that makes me a criminal, so be it."

"I see. Do you know a man named Howard Richards?"

"Yeah, everybody knows Howard."

"Have you done any work for him?" Lou asked.

"Yeah."

"Pays you pretty well, I take it?" Lou asked. "At least that's his reputation with those I talked to."

"Yeah, he pays. But he pays me more to keep my mouth shut than to mount his poached game."

"Poached game. Howard's a poacher?" Lou did his best to sound surprised.

Mike laughed. "You've got to be the only person in the world who'd be surprised by that. Everybody knows he poaches game."

"Maybe an occasional deer," Lou replied. "I imagine accidents occur all the time."

"His shooting is no accident."

"Deer and wolves — what else?" Lou asked.

"Oh, let's see. He's also brought in some exotic animals, but I don't know where he got them."

"You got a business card I can take to my friend? I think he may want to give you his business. I'll certainly put in a good word for you."

"Thanks," Mike said, handing Lou a card. "If I can help your friend, have him give me a call."

"Will do. Thanks, Mike."

Bingo! The gray wolf connection, Lou thought as he walked to the car, feeling satisfied with what he'd learned. As far as he knew, Mike Summers didn't realize the information he had given, even after being paid to keep his mouth shut.

Lou needed a search warrant. He wanted to get Howard's computer if he had one, and anything else that might link him to an organization willing to pay him to keep this poaching operation quiet.

After Judge Patterson heard what Lou had discovered, he issued a search warrant. Officer Faccio picked up Lou, and they drove down Peavine to the Richards farm. Rudy was acting as watchdog quite well, and Rudy wasn't alone; someone was in the house when Lou and Ginny arrived. But, unlike previous visits, Rudy was on a chain and not a threat. Inside they found Howard's son, Eric, who was gathering up some of Howard's belongings. Eric understood the search warrant and offered no resistance.

Lou wondered if Eric was at his father's home to destroy incriminating evidence, but that didn't seem to be the case. Eric said he was looking for financial information, bills to be paid, insurance policies, birth and marriage certificates, things like that. No reason was given, and Lou didn't ask.

Lou and Ginny got right to their search. They found no computer and no file drawer. A bedroom which Howard had turned into a den/office was a total mess, with no organization whatsoever. Papers were piled high all over the place.

The object of Lou's search was bank statements and/or written communications showing any connection between Howard and an illegal support group. After an hour of searching, Ginny uncovered something interesting, not in the den, but in a box under Howard's bed. The box contained photos, dozens of them, all depicting the killing of gray wolves. There were shots of men in hunting clothes holding up severed gray wolf heads, some hunters smiling with radio-tracking collars around their own necks, and others raising their right arms with the two-fingered 'V' for victory.

Lou was fairly confident that, even though they were stupid enough to have their pictures taken, these men wouldn't be so dumb as to allow their names to be connected with these photos, but he turned over a photo and hit pay-dirt: a clearly legible caption read, "Jim, Rick, Kelly, Ed and me poaching wolves." Since Howard wasn't in the photo, Lou figured Howard must have taken the shot. In other photos, Howard was alone with a slain wolf, or shown with one or two of the other men.

As far as Lou and Ginny were concerned, they had found the mother lode, though there was no evidence of cancelled checks or correspondence from an organized group. The best thing was that, when Lou and Ginny completed their search, no one could tell that the two had been there for it was simply impossible to mess up Howard Richards' home.

Lou did strike up a conversation with Howard's son, Eric. "Looks like your dad's in some trouble, young man."

"Yeah, I reckon what he got away with for years is coming back to bite him. He's getting old, and his act is wearing thin on people, and it should. I used to be very proud of him when I was a kid. He was a leading citizen around here. He was an elected official, revered in town. He was 'top banana' for quite a long time. But when Mom died, I don't know, he just seemed to change into someone I didn't know."

"Too bad," Lou replied.

"Yeah, my theory on it is that he had lost his influence, his power, his popularity, and he missed them. I suppose the only way he thought he could capture some of that status again was to use illegal means to get the same rush. He started drinking more, spending a lot of time at Mickey's, and he let his appearance and this place go to pieces.

"You know that mailbox mess? That seemed to be a turning point for him," Eric continued. "He got attention for that. I don't think he meant to kill those kids, but he got a lot of support for standing up to them. I think it reminded him of the days when he could control the city council, not with payoffs, but with influence and political savvy. Now, he can't do that, so his power comes from guns and finding illegal activities to give him that sense of control.

"I really didn't want my son staying with him, but he's free child-care, and I need every buck I earn to keep my house warm and food on the table. I figure, he raised me, so he's probably okay for my son, a few hours at a time. Most of the time, Taylor is in school, but on sick days, I needed childcare and my dad would do it."

"Times can be tough," Lou said.

"Yeah, they are."

"We found some photos of your dad; can I ask you a question?"

"Sure, I guess so."

"Do you know any of the men in this picture?" Lou asked, handing Eric the photo of the four men with dead wolves.

"I can't help you. I've never seen any of them," Eric replied, giving the photo back to Lou.

"Did your dad ever talk to you about poaching?"

"No, but he wouldn't. He knew I'd turn him in if I knew anything first-hand. I'd hear some rumors once in a while, but I never heard it from him or saw any evidence of it. And, you know, I understand his keeping it from me. He is my father, and he wants to be a good man in my eyes. I think that's important to him. So I think he would go to extremes to keep me from learning about poaching. I really do."

"Thanks for talking with me. I'm sorry about all of this happening in your family."

"Yeah, me too." Eric walked away with his head down.

Lou and Ginny gathered the photos into an envelope, retrieved their coats, and closed the door behind them, driving away in Ginny's DNR 4-wheel-drive vehicle.

"That trip was well worth the effort, wouldn't you say, Lou?"

"You betcha! But, like a lot of things you find, it simply brings up more questions, and the search goes on."

Lou asked Ginny to stop at a print shop so he could scan the photos. He then sent a copy of them to Bart Gunn in Crystal Falls hoping that he would recognize one or more of the men.

DECEMBER 10

Citizens of Mason opened The Lansing State Journal to read, "Local Attorney Freed: Appeals Judge Overturns Circuit Court Decision." The story summarized the events of the previous three months, ending with the finding that Zeke Simons had been wrongfully accused and convicted of murder. The last line in the story was a quote from Zeke: "I've always believed in the justice system of our society. I'm thankful to be free."

As Jerry read the article, his desire for revenge grew stronger. The system didn't work for him because he didn't have the money or the connections to get help. So, for Jerry, the system still didn't work. Zeke was one of the reasons it didn't work, and Zeke would have to pay the price.

Jerry unexpectedly met Susan in an aisle at the Mason Meijer store. "I'll be at therapy next week, but not the week after."

"That's too bad. I enjoy seeing you there," Susan said with a smile.

"You do?" Jerry replied, surprised that anyone would enjoy seeing him.

"Yes, you've a sense of humor. Those sessions tend to be depressing, but you usually have something funny to say."

"Well, you'll have to get along without me, Susan. I'm going up north."

"Taking a vacation? Are you going skiing or something?"

"No, going up on business," Jerry replied. "Yup, I got to take care of business."

"Really? I didn't know you were in business. You never bring that up in therapy."

"It's personal. There's a lot I don't bring up in therapy!" Jerry started fidgeting, looking away from her at the canned goods.

"OK. Well, nice seeing you, Jerry. Hope you have a successful business trip and a Merry Christmas. See you in a couple of weeks."

"Yeah, I'll have a successful trip, for sure. A lot of planning has gone into it." Jerry's story that he was going up north on business was going to be his ace in the hole. He would kill Zeke Simons right there in Mason, and Susan could support his alibi.

To give a firmer impression of a trip north, Jerry told his landlord that he'd be gone for a few days. He went to the post office to stop his mail, but he didn't stop home delivery of the newspaper, planning to let the morning editions pile up outside his door.

He would indeed head north, but only after Zeke Simons paid for sending him to jail and ruining his life. The killing would not be random, but well-thought-out and methodical, with no slip-ups. Jerry had spent days studying how to abduct and kill, the pros and cons of each method. Poisoning was slow, but he didn't need to be present to kill. Shooting was easy, but it left too much evidence around. Staging an accident was good, but that could backfire.

After considerable study, Jerry's plan began to take shape. Zeke Simons jogged alone every morning, and his route was predictable: down the street from his house, through a strip mall area, past the elementary and middle schools, around the high school track, through a wooded area, and then a turn to retrace his steps back to the house.

The wooded area would be the perfect place to kill, Jerry mused Like a desperado in the old West, Jerry planned to wait till Zeke came jogging right into his trap, and then a silenced revolver would stop him dead in his tracks. It would be a few hours before his body was found, and by then Jerry could be in Trout City, in Mickey's, with plenty of witnesses. Or, maybe it would be better to abduct him when he jogged past the strip mall. No stores were open at that hour, so no cars were in the parking lot. It seemed too good to be true. Jerry pondered his options — pick him off in the woods, or kidnap him in the strip mall parking lot and kill him somewhere out of town.

DECEMBER 17

The leader, June Walker, a psychologist, began the next therapy session, "Our discussion topic this week is getting a hold on our emotions. This is difficult, but important, because we often notice that people take advantage of us because of our problems. Can anyone offer an example of this?"

After a few moments of silence, Frank Thomas, one of the men in the group spoke up. "I think I know what you're talking about. I used to have a paper route and one day some guy said to me, 'Never grew up, huh? Having a paper route usually goes out of style around high school.' I wanted to kill the guy! In fact, I thought about a lot of ways to hurt him."

"Yes, that's a perfect example," Miss Walker responded. "We often allow what others say or do determine our actions, and when we do this, we create more trouble for ourselves. For example, Frank, what did you do after that man made the rude remark?"

"For the next week, I took the sports section out of the paper before slipping it into his newspaper tube." The others laughed, and a few gave him a high five.

"Then what happened?" Miss Walker asked.

"I got fired."

"Fired?" Susan exclaimed. "For that?"

"The guy called and complained every day. My boss talked to the foreman of the printing press and found out it was impossible for a paper to be missing a section. And, for it to happen randomly, and at the same house... well, it had to be me. And it was, so I was history."

Therapy group members expressed disappointment. "There it is," June replied. "You got angry, took some action, and it hurt you. That's what I'm saying. Now, what would have been a better way to handle that?"

"Just don't pay any attention to the jerk," Susan said.

"Exactly," the therapist replied.

"Yeah, but it's not that easy. When someone ruins your life, you can't just forget about it," Jerry Tomlinson said.

"Ruins your life?" June countered.

"Yeah, take me, for example," Jerry began. "This lawyer, he prosecuted a case against me, and sent me to jail, and it ruined things. For you to just say, 'Don't pay attention to the jerk', that makes no sense to me. Then there's no justice. That just isn't fair."

"But life is not fair, Jerry," the therapist said. "It wasn't fair for that man to say what he did to Frank. It wasn't fair for Frank to take out the sports section of the man's paper. It wasn't fair for Frank to lose his job. Life is not fair, Jerry. That's one thing we're trying to learn in this group."

"It's not the way I was raised," Jerry replied. "My mom was always punishing me, and it was always when I did something that she didn't think was fair. 'That's not fair, Jerry!' she'd shout, and then give me a whipping. If I heard, 'That's not fair', once, I heard it a million times, and it was always followed by a whipping. So when I see something that's not fair, like my mom, I'm going to give it a whipping."

"Right, and like I said, when you do that, it's going to come back to bite you," Frank remarked.

"Not if I'm smart enough to stay far enough away from whatever is going to bite me! Know what I mean?" Jerry said.

"That's a nice thought, Jerry, but sooner or later, it comes back to bite you," June repeated and the others nodded. "That's 'karma.'"

"'Karma?' What's that — some martial art or something?" Jerry asked.

June responded. "No, karma means that, if you do something nice, something nice will be done for you. But if you do something that is hurtful, something hurtful comes back to you. It's sort of a boomerang for behavior."

"I don't believe any of that crap. I believe that if anyone crosses you, you cross them, and I'll cross that lawyer Simons."

"I know that's what you believe, and that's why you're in this group," June explained. "We're trying to help you realize that good behavior will be rewarded in some fashion, and you won't be getting into trouble. That's what we want you to understand."

"That's crazy!" Jerry angrily got up to leave the room.

Mary Nichols shouted after him, "Jesus taught us that 'an eye for an eye and a tooth for a tooth' is wrong, Jerry Tomlinson! We're supposed to love our enemies!"

"Oh, shut up, you fruitcake!" Jerry shouted, as the door slammed behind him.

Suddenly Susan made the connection between Jerry's presence at Zeke's trial and the fact that he had a need to get even with him. She feared that Zeke soon might pay a price for "messing" with Jerry's life. The only question she had was what, if anything, she should do about this mess. She could be quiet and wait for disaster, or she could speak out and deal with the consequences of becoming involved.

Lou called Professor Beekman. "Professor? This is Lou Searing. I understand you and at least one of your students talked with Judge Patterson recently regarding Trout City."

"That's right. We became involved after a high school student, Janet Abs, contacted one of my students. She and fellow students came upon information implicating a number of city officials in illegal activity. Janet hoped that since we were removed from the situation, we could offer some help. Anyone local they might have approached might be part of the problem."

"I haven't heard of this student. Is she someone I should talk to regarding poaching or murder?" Lou asked.

"Most definitely. From what I understand, the students found evidence of wrong-doing in city government. She never mentioned you, so she probably doesn't know about your investigation, either."

"Could you bring us together?" Lou asked.

"Be glad to."

"Thanks, professor. Now, what can you do for me, or what can I do for you?" Lou inquired.

"I think we need a meeting of the minds, Lou. If Judge Patterson, you, my student Scott Anderson, Janet, and maybe a few of her peers and I could meet, each sharing what we know, we should be able to come up with a strategy to solve a lot of things."

"That's a good idea," Lou replied. "Where and when?"

"Well, a central place for all of us would be Clare. We'll find a day and time when all of us can be there. I'll call the Doherty Hotel to book a conference room. Anything I missed?" Professor Beekman asked.

"Nothing I can think of. I'll wait to hear from you."

DECEMBER 21

While snow swirled around downtown Clare, Michigan, the people invited to the meeting arranged by Professor Beekman and Judge Patterson sat at a table in Conference Room B at the Doherty Hotel.

Judge Patterson began by stating that, on behalf of Trout City, he was thankful that those around the table were interested in the welfare of the town. He hoped an open discussion of what everyone knew would lead to a plan or strategy that might turn things around for the city.

Janet spoke up, "I want to thank you all for coming, too. After the Community Leader Day program, a number of our students' observations revealed a pattern of behavior. At first, we believed that a number of city leaders were involved in bribery. But, a letter to our mayor from a group calling themselves, 'Hunters United Against Nature's Destruction of Deer Herds' really tipped us off. That letter suggested the mayor would come into a lot of money if he successfully blocked an investigation into alleged poaching of gray wolves."

Lou perked up immediately. This was the first indication that a specific group was involved in poaching and was paying people to further their cause. "I am a private investigator looking into the murder of Officer Turner on behalf of my client, Zeke Simons. I've uncovered poaching of gray wolves, and I've been trying to find a connection between Mr. Richards and this group. What you've just said, Janet, is a great lead for me. Do you have a copy of the letter?"

"No." Janet responded. "Luke Thornton, mayor for the day, found the letter in a stack of correspondence our mayor had suggested Luke look over while he attended a meeting. He thought that Luke should read the mail, to get some idea of the issues that a mayor faces. I am sure of the name of the organization because Luke noted it on a piece of paper."

"Was there a signature on the letter?" Lou asked.

"Yes, it was signed by an Ed Wible," Janet replied.

"Great information," said Lou. "Was there any indication of copies?"

"No."

"How about a return address?"

"Luke didn't say. Sorry."

Audrey Moylan spoke up next. "I'm an attorney representing Mr. Simons, and I was convinced, as was the appeals judge, that my client was innocent of murder. I also believe my client was put through a kangaroo court. Either the jurors were paid, or the jury had made up its mind well before the trial began. The evidence clearly should have planted doubt in their minds, given the inconsistencies between Mr. Richards' testimony and his behavior."

Lou's cell phone vibrated on his hip. "Excuse me. This call might relate to what we are discussing." A few nodded as Lou rose to step outside the conference room.

Judge Patterson was speaking when Lou entered the room less than a minute later. A few looked up, thinking Lou would not have time to complete his conversation, and the judge stopped in mid-sentence.

Lou punctured the silence when he said, "Zeke Simons is missing. Mason Police suspect he's been abducted."

To a person, Howard Richards came to mind. Most upset was Audrey Moylan.

"What happened?" she asked.

"No details, just that he's missing," Lou replied.

While everyone else thought of Howard Richards first, Lou also remembered the stranger in the courtroom. Lou first called Judge Beekins in Bad Axe, thinking he might know what had happened being close to Zeke. The judge was not in his office, but Lou had his cell phone number. On the third ring, Judge Beekins answered.

"Judge, this is Lou Searing."

"Yes, Lou."

"I just got a call that Zeke is missing."

"Yes. We're reeling from the news."

"What happened?" Lou asked.

"As I understand it, he was abducted by three or four men."

"Just snatched off the street and driven away?" Lou inquired.

"That's the best way I can describe it. Apparently it happened about an hour ago, in broad daylight, in the strip mall parking lot outside Mason. A witness said that Zeke was jogging and a vehicle pulled up, three or four guys jumped out and forced him into a van, and they sped away. I'm on my way to Mason now to see Angie, and I hope to learn more. But as I understand it, the only witness is fuzzy on what she saw. It happened so fast, she only got a glimpse when they were shoving Zeke into the vehicle."

"I'm sorry judge. I know Zeke's like a son to you."

"Yes, he is. Thank you, Lou."

"Please pass on any word you get," Lou asked. "You've got my cell phone number, right?"

"Yes, and I'll see that you get any details."

"OK. Thanks, Judge."

While Lou and the judge were on the phone, Mary Burkett from the group therapy session was calling the Mason police. "I have some information about that missing man, Mr. Simons."

"Yes, ma'am. What can you tell me?" a lieutenant asked.

"I'm pretty sure who did it. Jerry Tomlinson took him."

"How do you know this?" the officer asked, remembering that an audiotape recorded every phone conversation.

"Jerry said that Mr. Simons had wronged him, and he'd get him. Jesus said to love your enemies, but Jerry couldn't. Jesus said to turn the other cheek, but Jerry didn't. Karma is what got Jerry Tomlinson and Zeke Simons. Jesus said, 'An eye for an eye and a tooth for a tooth' is not good. We need to love, and Jerry won't love." Mary's voice grew hard. "Besides, he called me a fruitcake."

"May I have your name and address, ma'am?"

"Mary Burkett. I live in a group home near the bowling alley, but I don't know the address."

"Ok, thank you, Mary."

The officer knew about the group home, and presumed Mary's mental condition. He was inclined to dismiss her words, except that he knew any information in a missing-person case was by definition, good. You never knew when or how the right piece of the puzzle would fit into the larger picture.

The officer decided to check on Jerry Tomlinson, who was also familiar to him from previous encounters. He doubted Jerry was capable of abducting someone, nor did he think Jerry had any friends who might be involved with him, but he wanted assurance that Jerry had not been near the strip mall when Zeke had been kidnapped.

Audrey stepped out of the conference room to make a phone call, but she wasn't able to get any word about Zeke's whereabouts. The group looked to Judge Patterson to resume his comments, but instead he asked Lou to share what Judge Beekins had told him. Lou presented everything he knew to the group.

"This is disturbing news, to say the least," Judge Patterson agreed. "However, I think we should continue with our meeting. Before the break I indicated that we have some unethical behavior going on in the sheriff's department and in the prosecutor's office. These incidents may be linked to bribery. I can't prove that at the moment, but Howard Richards is the prime suspect in this matter."

"I heartily agree," Audrey Moylan offered.

"I'd like to offer some thoughts," Professor Beekman said. "While I would ordinarily allow Scott to speak for himself, he was mistreated during a traffic stop in Trout City. He's aware of his rights and the local laws, and this incident would support the judge's assertion of wrong-doing related to law enforcement. However, my main concern at this point is not the courtroom trials and procedures, although they are important, but what remedy may be right to resolve this mess. I'd like Scott to comment on his work so far."

"Thank you, Professor," Scott said. "I've done a thorough review of the literature in public administration misconduct. Many of the cases involve bribery of numerous government officials. Three approaches to resolution seem to have worked in the involved communities. In no particular order of importance, they are: petitioning to recall and vote the officials out of office; removing the officials from their positions by action of certifying bodies — the Bar Association, medical licensing boards, and the like; and firing by the City Commission. You folks know your community best, so you would know which of these three would be most effective. You'd also know whether any of them would work."

Janet responded. "As far as I am concerned, they may all work, but they would take time. Maybe that's OK, but there must be a faster way to get us back on track."

Audrey spoke next, "I'm not a citizen of your town, but I know that unless something stops the bribery, nothing will happen at all. Money would control the outcome of any of those approaches. My guess is that, in the case law, the communities themselves wanted to be clean and legal, and I'm sorry to say, I'm not sure that's true in Trout City."

The judge spoke up, "I may have a solution. I think we should appoint a grand jury to look into all of these matters, to address the bribery, the unethical courtroom activity, the inappropriate activity of town officials. They should operate secretly and fairly quickly."

Professor Beekman nodded, thinking the judge might have hit on the answer. "Who orders a grand jury to convene in a town-government situation like this?"

"Usually a lower court judge does in a preliminary hearing," the judge replied.

"Maybe that is the answer," Janet replied. "But can't some higher government officer see what's going on and come in and 'clean house'?"

"That does seem logical, Janet," Judge Patterson replied. "But unfortunately that does not happen easily or often. There is concern for autonomy, an assumed initiative for city and county governments to solve their own problems,"

"Perhaps that's true, but if the people don't want to solve the problem, somebody has to be decisive," Janet reasoned.

"One would think so," the judge replied. "But once you move out of the local area, you definitely bring politics into the matter. If legislators get involved, they are subject to the same bribery, and if the governor gets involved, who knows what forces might be working at that level?" the judge replied.

While the discussion was helpful, Lou was anxious to get his hands on the letter from the Hunters United Against Nature's Destruction of Deer Herds. He could use the Freedom of Information Act to get it from the mayor's office. But that would take time and the request might well be denied. "Excuse me, but I need to see that letter Luke talked about finding in the mayor's office. Is there any quick way I can get that?"

"The mayor's secretary used to work in my office," the judge replied. "In fact, we go to the same church. Let me see what I can do. Would the rest of you mind if I called right now?" Everyone agreed, then listened as he placed the call.

"Jackie? This is Judge Patterson."

"Yes, Judge."

"Jackie, I need some help, and I want to keep this between the two of us. I understand the mayor received a letter within the past month, from a man by the name of Ed Wible. I'd like you to fax a copy of that letter, and any response to it, to the Doherty Hotel in Clare. Can you do this for me?"

"Yes, Judge, but it may take a little while."

"Thank you. I'll be waiting."

"Are things going to happen around here?" Jackie asked.

"I'm afraid so. You won't get hurt, I trust."

"I wouldn't think so," Jackie replied.

"Thanks, Jackie."

The judge explained that the relevant letter would be faxed soon. Lou went to the front desk of the hotel and asked that the faxed material soon to arrive from Trout City be brought to Conference Room B.

The idea of a grand jury captured the interest of the people at the meeting.

"Would all of us need to tell the grand jury what we know?" Janet asked.

"I expect that would be the case," the judge explained.

"Could I speak for my fellow students?" she continued.

"That would be up to the judge and jury, I presume. My guess would be that each one would be asked to testify."

A knock on the door interrupted the discussion, as a hotel clerk brought in two faxed pages. The judge read the letter and passed it to Lou and the others around the table.

"Judge, what outcome would you expect from the grand jury?" Professor Beekman asked.

"Well, based on what we know at this point, I would expect a number of trials to take place outside the county in the matter related to Howard Richards and Zeke Simons. I presume, also, if they find out who is offering bribes, that those people would be tried as well. I would expect full disclosure to the public, and the prosecutor would lose his job, as would the sheriff and the mayor. The minister would likely be reprimanded by his church; I haven't heard of any illegal behavior, only inappropriate pastoral care, so that would be up to a church council. I'm not familiar with the organizational structure of the Nazarene Baptist Church."

"How quickly would all of this happen?" Janet asked.

"It would depend on how many witnesses there were and how much of a mess they find. It's hard to tell, but my guess is that it would wrap up in six months to a year."

Lou carefully read the letter, noting a return address in Iron River, Michigan. He was intrigued by the mayor's response which read in part, "Thank you for your letter. To the best of my knowledge, no investigation into poaching the gray wolf has taken place in and around Trout City. I will see that it doesn't, either. You have nothing to fear. All is under control. If such an investigation arises, I can assure you that the resolution will suit you."

The participants continued their discussion of problems in Trout City, strategies to deal with them, and their hopes for the city's future. After an hour and a half, they adjourned, promising to think about options and to communicate via e-mail once an acceptable approach to dealing with the problem had been identified.

The Mason police had to take Mary's call seriously no matter how suspect, for it was their only lead. Jerry wasn't at home, and his buddies at the bar where he usually hung out had no idea where he was. After a state-wide alert was issued for his vehicle, Jerry was pulled over by the state police on U.S. 127, ironically, near Clare. He refused to answer any questions and would not cooperate with the officer. He did give the trooper his driver's license but he said nothing and followed no directions. As a result, he was handcuffed, patted down, put in a Michigan State Police trooper's vehicle, and taken to the Clare County Jail for booking and questioning by a detective.

While Jerry sat in a jail cell, the van carrying three men and Zeke Simons crossed the Mackinac Bridge and headed west into the Upper Peninsula. Bound and gagged, Zeke was secured in the back of the van like a piece of luggage. Any attempt to move was futile.

The Mason police had also contacted the Ingham County Community Mental Health office and spoken with June Walker, the psychologist. They told her Jerry was a suspect in the disappearance of Zeke Simons, and that he had been apprehended near Clare.

"I'm very concerned," June said. "Can I go to Clare — be there for the questioning? I really think I can help. In his condition, he could say things that are not true and that will damage him. He has a lot of anger and while he's intelligent, he can't handle stressful situations. I think you'll get a lot further if I'm with him. He knows me, and I think he trusts me."

"It's quite a drive for you, but it might help," the officer replied.

"For Jerry, I'll do it. I only ask that he not be questioned until I get there."

"I'll see what I can do."

"OK. I'll start out for Clare," June said. "I'll give you my cell phone number in case you need to reach me."

"Yes, ma'am."

The Mason police officer called the state police and explained why psychologist Jane Walker wanted to be with Jerry. The trooper indicated that interrogation had begun, but the suspect was not talking, even in the presence of an attorney who was assigned to him. "We'll wait until the therapist arrives."

"Thank you."

Lou called Conservation Officer Bart Gunn to ask whether the name Ed Wible meant anything to him.

"It sure does," Bart replied. "He is one militant animal, let me tell you! Talk about the militia being difficult a few years ago — this man is dangerous! We've not caught him doing anything illegal, but when a problem comes up, Ed Wible is the first person mentioned."

"Has he been poaching gray wolves?" Lou asked.

"Not to my knowledge."

"Have you heard of Hunters United Against Nature's Destruction of the Deer Herd?" Lou inquired.

"No, that's a new one to me."

"Well, Ed Wible and that organization could be the source of your gray wolf-poaching activity. Where does he live?" Lou asked.

"He's got a small place outside Iron River, really a trailer out in the woods. He lives alone, sort of an angry hermit who causes some problems when he comes to town."

"Have you any vehicle information on him?" Lou inquired.

"Drives a Jeep, as I recall."

"Do the names Jim, Rick, or Kelly, mean anything to you?"

"In relation to Ed?"

"Yes, or to poaching wolves."

"No. Like I say, I don't have any leads on poachers, except to know they're active."

"Well, I have some poaching photos with the names Ed, Jim, Rick, and Kelly written on the back. They were found in the home of Howard Richards down in Trout City. Those photos, along with a bribery letter to the mayor of Trout City from Ed Wible, seem to paint a picture of the group you want to get to know."

"Ok, thanks."

"I'll scan the photo and send it to you electronically," Lou said. "Also, while I have you on the line, a man from Mason, Zeke Simons, appears to have been abducted. His whereabouts are unknown, but I suspect his absence has something to do with Howard Richards and maybe these poachers are in revenge mode, since the appeals judge reversed his guilty verdict and set Zeke free. This will probably lead to Richards' arrest in the murder of Officer Tim Turner."

"It's all got to be tied together, Lou," Officer Gunn agreed.

"I think so too. We need to put two and two together, or to try to stay one step ahead of a good clue. If I were you, I'd keep an eye and ear open for some activity up in your neck of the woods. We don't have a description of the vehicle, but I know every law enforcement person has a few informants. Please ask for information about this Ed

Wible and the others. Zeke could very well be in your county, and if he is, I fear that, like a gray wolf, he may be dead. These guys could be poaching man and beast."

"Ok, Lou, I'll be asking around. Stay in touch, and I'll do the same."

The van carrying Zeke entered Escanaba and stopped at a fast food place. There was no fear of Zeke making any noise or making a break; he was tightly bound and he couldn't make a sound if he wanted to.

The men wanted to be at Ed's hunting cabin by nightfall, and at this rate they would make it easily.

Officer Gunn immediately called his supervisor, who in turn called the state police, relaying what Lou had said, and explained what Lou thought might happen. Ed was known to the law enforcements agencies, and they knew he had a small house in town and a hunting trailer between Iron River and Iron Mountain. The police had been to both places on more than one occasion for numerous citations, from DUI to petty theft.

City, county and state law enforcement officers met at McDonald's on the eastern edge of Iron River to discuss the possibility that Ed and his buddies would bring Zeke Simons to Ed's home territory.

They decided to set up two stakeouts as soon as possible, one in town, and one at Ed's hunting trailer. The plan was to have four men from a county SWAT team at the trailer and a couple of troopers in an unmarked car near the house. If there were any action, it would take place in the country and not in town. The men at the trailer would wait in the woods, and the two in town would stake out the street near the house to see who showed up.

"All of this might be a waste of time," Bart said.

"Maybe, but then again, we might be able to stop a killing and finally catch this guy. There isn't much that would give me more joy," one of the state troopers replied.

Within an hour, the county SWAT team was in position, surrounding the small hunting trailer deep in the woods. After dropping the men off, the driver of the SWAT van positioned the vehicle so that he would know when any other vehicle headed down the county road toward Ed Wible's property. The SWAT team had an assortment of equipment at their disposal, including a bullhorn and nighttime field glasses, which would allow them to observe anyone who approached the trailer after dark. The team was prepared for peaceful surrender or all-out assault, depending on the response of the suspects.

About two hours later, under cover of darkness and a cloudy sky, Ed Wible, driving a dark blue van, turned onto the county road leading to his trailer. He had no idea he had been spotted.

The SWAT team driver put out the call on his radio. "Vehicle en route to your location. Dark blue or black van, license number TST-336. Unable to determine if any passengers on board, over."

"10-4, I read you. We're ready."

Less than five minutes later, the headlights of the van were visible from the trailer. The vehicle slowly came closer, its headlights bobbing up and down, signaling an uneven and bumpy road. Confrontation of some sort seemed inevitable.

"Team alert! Team alert!" the commander said. "Suspect vehicle almost to destination. Fire only if and when fired upon. We want this man and anyone in the vehicle. Repeat, fire only if fired upon. We have no indication that the subject has violated any law."

Trooper Harris mumbled to himself. "Right! Name me something in the books that SOB hasn't broken."

The vehicle stopped about fifty yards from the trailer, and the headlights went off. Positioned with infrared field glasses, the SWAT commander wasn't able to see anyone getting out of the vehicle, nor could he see why the vehicle had stopped. All he could do was keep the suspect in view and wait for movement.

Ed Wible and his party suspected that they might be ambushed by the law. They had stopped short of the trailer for security. They, too, had infrared binoculars. More often than not, these were used for nighttime hunting, but on this particular night, the men were searching for humans.

Ed knew the lie-in-wait routine. The SWAT team was well-trained such that no one was visible. In order to lure anyone out, in case an officer was waiting for him to drive up, Ed turned around in a small clearing near the trailer and slowly drove back to the county road, out of view of the trailer, before turning on his headlights. He would wait there for ten minutes or so, hoping that anyone back by his trailer would come looking for him. The standoff continued as the SWAT team commander quietly alerted the three men: "Suspect vehicle has left the area. Stay in position until ordered otherwise."

∞

While the SWAT team waited in the western Upper Peninsula night, June Walker arrived at the Clare County jail. After she met the sheriff and deputies waiting to question Jerry Tomlinson, Jerry was brought from his cell to the interrogation room. June's suggestion was that only she be in the room to start with; bringing Jerry into a setting with many people he didn't know would threaten him, and he likely would clam up, as he had done earlier in the day.

When Jerry was escorted into the interrogation room with June, he seemed unresponsive and stoic.

"Hi, Jerry," June said with a pleasant smile. "I thought you might need me, so I came to help."

There was no response; Jerry only stared at the floor. "Please take a seat, Jerry," suggested June. He sat but continued to look depressed. June sat next to him quietly for a few minutes. Then, very softly, Jerry said, "Karma."

"Yeah, it's not fair," June replied, thankful that Jerry had said something, anything.

Jerry looked up. "Why am I here?" he asked in a manner implying he really didn't know.

"Didn't they tell you?" June asked.

"Something about Zeke Simons — I dunno."

"Mr. Simons is missing, Jerry. Several men forced him into a vehicle in Mason and drove off. The police got a tip that you might be involved, so there was an alert out for you, and when you were spotted, you were pulled over." Jerry offered no response.

"Did you have anything to do with this, Jerry?" Miss Walker asked.

"No."

"I didn't think so," June replied sympathetically.

"It's Eddie and his friends," Jerry said, in a low, almost unintelligible voice.

"Eddie and his friends?" June repeated, hoping to encourage more words.

"They did it. I said I didn't want any part of it. That was right after you told me about karma." Jerry was becoming agitated, speaking faster, his voice growing louder. "I didn't do nothing, but I got stopped, thrown against my car, handcuffed, and threatened. I didn't do nothing, and yet I get karma! Bunch of crap!"

"I'm sorry, Jerry," June said. "I really am." Jerry didn't respond, but continued to stare at the floor. "Who is Eddie, Jerry?"

"Not going to say!"

"Why not? You might be able to save a man's life."

"He didn't save mine," Jerry replied matter-of-factly. "He didn't help me."

"That's in the past, Jerry, and you know you committed that crime. It's Zeke's job to represent the people you harmed. You do realize that, don't you?" Jerry was quiet again for several minutes.

"How do you know this man by the name of Eddie?" June asked.

"I met him in a bar in Trout City. He asked me lots of questions about Mason. Said he wanted my help taking Zeke down. He wanted me to ride with him, and I was going to — except you said that I'd get karma if I helped kill a man."

"Where's this Eddie from?" June asked.

"The U.P. He said he'd give me a mounting of a wolf's head for helping him." Jerry smiled slightly. "That'd be something most people don't have hanging in their homes. I'd like that. That would impress people — a wolf's head."

"I see."

"I was going to kill Zeke when he got out of jail," Jerry admitted, his voice getting louder. "They said he didn't kill the officer and was free to go. Nobody told me I was free to go after my trial. It isn't fair! It isn't fair!" He sighed deeply. "Karma isn't fair."

"Where were you going when the police pulled you over?" June asked gently.

"I don't know. Where am I now?" Jerry asked.

"You're in Clare."

Jerry looked about, surprised. "Where?"

"Clare, Michigan, in the middle of the state."

Jerry obviously was not himself, June realized. She believed he had spoken the truth as he saw it, but he needed a doctor and medical care, not incarceration.

The sheriff and an investigator had monitored the conversation between Jerry and June, and they realized that Jerry hadn't broken any laws. As long as he would be with the therapist and would not be driving, Jerry could be released.

In the autumn darkness west of Iron Mountain, the standoff continued. Ed Wible had seen no indication that the police were in the area. Believing the coast was clear, he drove toward his trailer.

Once again the SWAT team went to alert status. Ed Wible pulled up to the front of the trailer; three doors of the vehicle opened, and the driver went to the back to open the rear door to the van. Two men followed, and the three pulled and lifted Zeke out and into a standing position.

The SWAT commander knew that this was certainly an abduction, and the bound and gagged man was undoubtedly Zeke Simons. Whatever happened, protection of the victim is paramount in a successful mission. Unknown to Ed and his accomplices, three rifles were fixed on them, with crosshairs over their chests, whether they were standing still or moving.

The commander faced a major decision at this point. He could confront the men while all were still outside, but one or more suspects might escape in the darkness. It could also lead to injury of the victim, as the three might panic. On the other hand, if the three were totally surprised, they might simply surrender without a struggle.

If the commander allowed the men to go to the trailer, they would have a hostage and bargaining power. They might also burn the trailer down taking Zeke with them. On the other hand, the kidnappers would be confined and unable to escape, and negotiations could proceed from a confined place without threat of escape. The decision was a difficult one, and it needed to be made very soon.

The commander decided to wait a while to see what might develop. Two of the men took the victim into the trailer and turned on a light, leaving the driver, thought to be Ed, and one other man outside. They were rounding up bags of what looked like groceries and rifle cases. That was another thing to consider: there might be a lot of ammunition in the trailer.

Suddenly, the commander shouted. "Police! On the GROUND! On the GROUND! Get down!!!"

From the rear of the van, Ed shouted, "COPS, COPS!" The door to the trailer slammed closed. One SWAT team member immediately appeared with his rifle aimed at the men. The police definitely had the upper hand.

Inside the trailer, the two men turned lights out, pulled drapes over the windows, locked front and back doors, and pushed a sofa in front of the door. Zeke, still bound and gagged, was simply shoved to the floor while the two men grabbed weapons and took positions at the two windows facing the drive.

Ed and his accomplice were handcuffed, patted down, and tied to trees fifty feet from the trailer. The commander called for backup, and presently sirens could be heard approaching from the main road.

The two men inside were not aware of the two SWAT team members with rifles aimed at the windows. The officers had been ordered not to fire because of the threat to the victim held hostage inside the trailer.

Negotiations were at a standstill. The police had captured the leader and one of his accomplices, but the victim was held by two armed, cornered men, who could either surrender peacefully or force a shootout.

As more police cars and an ambulance arrived on the scene, the two men inside the trailer realized they were out-gunned. If they surrendered, they might live; if they put up a fight, they probably would die in a hail of gunfire. They quickly came to the conclusion that living was more important to them than a murder charge. The poaching gig was up, but a few years in jail beat a lifetime in prison, and actually, they hadn't been all in favor of supporting that hick, Richards, in the first place. Ed would probably expect them to die in a shootout, but that wasn't their idea.

Zeke heard the commotion, but he had no idea where he was, or who was involved. He had heard very little in the back of the van during the trip because of the material wrapped around his eyes and ears.

One of the men removed Zeke's gag and blindfold. "We're in a lot of trouble here the man said to Zeke. "I'm going to turn the porch light on and wave this white handkerchief for surrender. You're going to lead the way. If anyone fires a shot, I'll lift this gun in your back up to your head and blow you to kingdom come. You understand?" Zeke nodded.

They turned on the porch light and opened the door quietly and slowly. Zeke inched forward, while behind him, one of the men waved the white handkerchief and shouted, "We're coming out! We're coming out!"

As soon as all three were clear of the trailer, the man threw the revolver off to his right and raised his hands. "Down! On the ground! Hit the ground!" the commander shouted.

The paramedics immediately moved toward Zeke. Along with a detective, they removed his binding rope and tape. They checked his vital signs; other than a rapid heartbeat and high blood pressure, he seemed to be okay. He was helped onto a stretcher, and lifted into the ambulance, which set out for the Iron Mountain hospital. The detective riding with him assured him that the ordeal was over. He also called police headquarters to report that Zeke was safe and en route to the hospital. The commander of the operation contacted Angie Simons to give her the good news.

When the SWAT commander entered the trailer to look for evidence, he found the mounted heads of five gray wolves on the walls. And a search turned up incriminating photos showing the four men posing with their trophies hanging from a deer rack beside the trailer.

The SWAT commander was satisfied. Zeke was safe, and four poachers were now in custody in a county whose justice system was intact and where bribery was not an option. There would be trials for poaching and for kidnapping, and, after an investigation, other charges might be brought against the men.

The day the standoff took place in Iron Mountain, an article written by one of the students involved in the mailbox-smashing incident appeared in the Trout City High School newspaper.

All You Have to Do is Look UP
By David Peterson

I find it ironic that a recent trial in our county court caught the interest of some of the top legal minds and investigators in the state. Yet, for all their intelligence, and all their research, all anyone, including the police, DNR, the defense attorney, and private investigator Lou Searing had to do to solve the crime was look up. Howard Richards tipped his hand when he successfully rigged an overhead trap to kill two of my friends while we were destroying country mailboxes. Yes, I learned a painful lesson in respecting the property of others, but I also learned that a man's character and method of operation can be predicted by his past actions.

I no longer destroy the property of others, and I do not trespass, either. But I'll bet my last dollar that if anyone in this case simply looked up, in addition to looking around, he'd find a rifle rig above the barn door, and the shot from that rifle positioned there probably killed Officer Turner.

Furthermore, he would see that Mr. Simons had nothing to do with the killing. Richards framed Mr. Simons as revenge for reporting his poaching to the authorities. But, what was the motive for Officer Turner's murder, you ask? Why would Mr. Richards want Officer Turner dead? For the same reason he wanted me and my friends dead: he wanted control. He could control most people with bribes, but the real hero in this tragedy, Officer Turner, was not interested in a bribe. Officer Turner was about to arrest Howard Richards for poaching, ending the long reign of power he'd enjoyed in Trout City.

The gig was up — or, in this case, the rig was up — and with one shot, Mr. Richards snuffed out the life of the officer who would follow the law and bring an end to his power and framed the man who reported the poaching. May I suggest that someone simply look up in Howard Richards' barn? Maybe he'll find the truth in this case. Richards' guilt should be obvious.

I've lived in this area all my life, and I know that writing this article may lead to my being shunned by this community. If I don't voluntarily leave, I will be harassed to the point where I have no choice. Punishment leads to either escape or aggression, so I will escape. I would like to thank our school newspaper sponsor, Mrs. Williams, for having the courage to publish this statement.

Welcome back to freedom, Mr. Simons!

When Danny, standing at the bar in Mickey's, read the letter, he flashed back to his conversation with Howard Richards nearly three months before. The last words Howard had said were, "Gotta set up."

DECEMBER 22

Lou drove from Clare to Trout City after spending the night in the Doherty Hotel. After reading the article in the previous day's high school newspaper, he made plans to go to Howard Richards' barn with Ginny Faccio and Judge Patterson. When they arrived, they immediately went to the barn and looked up, but they saw nothing odd.

"Lou, lie down where Officer Turner was lying and look up," Ginny suggested.

Lou did as she asked and remarked, "I don't see anything out of the ordinary."

"Hmmm" said Ginny. "Let me have a look." As she lay down on her back, her eyes were immediately drawn to a bracket on the upper left side of the door, above the pulleys for opening and closing the door. "What's that bracket for?" she asked, pointing to the strange protrusion.

Both Lou and the judge looked above the door. As soon as Lou saw the angle of the bracket, and followed the angle to the figure of the judge standing where Officer Turner would have been, it hit him. "A rifle was secured to the bracket, aimed where someone would stand while inspecting the carcass. It accounts for the bullet trajectory of 60 degrees," Lou reasoned. The two nodded in agreement. "The kid was right. Howard Richards used the same setup on the conservation officer as he did on the students. Apparently, if you act contrary to the laws in the County of Howard, you pay, and in this case, like the students, Officer Turner paid with his life."

Ginny was seeing it too. "It all makes sense now. Officer Turner wrote letters in the dust on the barn floor with his right hand, and the OO and the P we found were undoubtedly his attempt to tell us to 'Look Up'."

The three stood in amazement as the case came together. Finally the events of October 1st were fully understood. On that day, Howard Richards had been poaching man and beast.

The bracket assembly in the barn, the autopsy review by Dr. Dillon, the work of Dr. Tatroe, the observations of the Trout City High School students, Scott Anderson's efforts, and the work of Ginny Faccio and other law enforcement personnel allowed Lou Searing and Audrey Moylan to put the pieces of the puzzle together. The real story could finally be told, with the goal being justice in Trout City.

DECEMBER 24

It was Christmas Eve in the Searing home in Grand Haven. The Searing children, Scott and Amanda, and their families were on hand for a delicious meal, the writing of the traditional note to Santa Claus, and the ritual of putting out cookies and a Diet Coke for Santa.

During dinner, Scott turned to his father and remarked, "According to the papers, you've solved another one."

"I can't take the credit, son. It was the work of a lot of people. But, you know who really gets the credit? A group of high school students. They saw clues and drew conclusions. It was amazing to see these young people work together. It is true that I helped with some of the evidence in the murder trial of Mr. Simons, but cleaning up Trout City — all that is the doing of those young people. They'll be fantastic future leaders, wherever they decide to live."

"Your father is very humble. He was the reason the case was solved," said Carol with a smile.

"Grandpa, when I grow up, I want to be a detective like you!" Jackson said with pride, and everyone laughed.

"Well that's nice, Jackson, but I'm sure you'll find a job that is much more satisfying and rewarding than that," Lou responded.

"But you saved a man's life," Carol said.

"Yes, I guess I did. But enough about me! May I have the potatoes and gravy down here, please?"

EPILOGUE

A grand jury was convened, and, after several weeks of interviewing witnesses and reviewing evidence, announced their findings. At play were a band of well-funded wolf poachers. They involved an old friend, Howard Richards, in their criminal activity. With their substantial resources, Howard had been able to use his influence in the county to bribe a number of people so that poaching could continue unchecked.

Zeke Simons was a major interruption in this smooth use of power. Zeke had to be eliminated, lest the kingdom tumble. Howard figured he could kill the conservation officer and make it look like Zeke had inadvertently killed him. Using this strategy, he could escape the crime. He changed the time of arrival in the log book, activated the camera inside Officer Turner' vehicle, and claimed he was not at home when the crime occurred.

Howard had paid the pathologist to write up a phony autopsy report on Tim Turner. This would help prove Zeke's guilt, especially since the casts of the tire tracks were supposedly evidence of Zeke's being on the property. The result would certainly be a guilty verdict, especially if the jurors were paid a hefty sum to return that verdict at trial.

What Howard didn't anticipate was Scott Anderson's involvement and the high school's Community Leader Day program. He also didn't anticipate Lou's involvement, or his decision to have the autopsy report reviewed by another pathologist. And Howard certainly didn't expect his grandson to retrieve the rifle from the creek and tell the truth of the events of October 1st.

Howard Richards was tried and convicted for the murder of Conservation Officer Timothy Turner; he was sentenced to spend the rest of his life in state prison. A finding of conspiracy and malpractice led to Max Bell's, Wil Purcell's and Harrison Corbett's loss of their licenses to practice law in Michigan. The pathologist, Dr. Elliott, lost his medical license. The sheriff was found guilty of unethical behavior and was voted out of office in a special election. The two officers who accepted bribes not to investigate the poaching were reprimanded; because they were following orders from the sheriff, they were suspended pending extensive counseling in ethical behavior. Danny Willard was fined and placed on six months probation for perjury and obstruction of justice.

Janet Abs and the other students who had the courage to speak out against unethical behavior were given keys to the city by the city manager who was appointed to fill the term of the mayor.

Taylor Richards' father, Eric, was ordered to take parenting classes and to assure that Taylor was under appropriate adult supervision outside school hours. Taylor returned to his father's home in time for Christmas, and thereafter his school work began to improve. He entered the local Big Brother program and began to flourish through interaction with appropriate adult role models.

Reverend Evans hastily accepted a call to be chaplain in the Wisconsin prison system. The Sunday school teacher, Mrs. Fees, was honored by the new pastor, whose first sermon praised her as an example of integrity and true compassion for her students. She received a standing ovation from the congregation.

Zeke Simons returned to Mason with his wife Angie. He agreed to participate in some anger therapy. He became a good friend of David Peterson, the youngster who had written the article about "Looking Up," and became his mentor, as Judge Beekins had been a supportive adult figure for him. Zeke realized he would never win a public election, so he settled down to practice law. Ironically, he never went hunting again.

Judge Patterson led community action in becoming a law-abiding area. In fact, the city presently earned the distinction of being one of the finest Michigan communities in which to live.

The Community Leader Day Program was established as a permanent program at the high school.

The band of poachers was caught, jailed, and fined a substantial amount. When asked why they had violated the law, they explained they'd acted for the fun of it to save farmers grief for lost calves and ewes and to give deer hunters a better population for their enjoyment of the hunt. Zeke chose not to press charges related to his kidnapping.

Scott Anderson received a special commendation from the Dean of the University of Michigan Law College. Later, he presented his work at the National Conference of Criminal Attorneys. Scott went on to graduate with honors, making a commitment to practice in rural towns and villages.

THE END

ST. LOUIS, MISSOURI:

Tom Hoffmeister, at five years of age, was a whiz with numbers. His game of choice was Pokemon Monopoly for Children, at first glance just as complicated as the adult version of Monopoly. There are properties to own and rents to pay, based on the number of houses purchased. There is a bank with thousands of dollars, and Tom was in charge of this game. Carol, or Nana to her grandchildren, had the patience to challenge Tom, but he always won. He bought up every available property, while still maintaining sufficient funds in his bank to stay afloat. It was not only remarkable that he skillfully played the game, but that he understood all denominations of money and the breakdown of bills to reach a pre-determined amount. "You owe me seventy-five dollars, Nana, and I'll take it in three twenties, a ten, and a five."

Lou watched the two play, his mind relieved of the recently solved case in Trout City. Now he was an assistant to his beloved Nana, who was in charge of child care while Amanda and Joe were off to California for a family wedding and their own 10th anniversary celebration. Lou could hardly believe Tom's deftness, as he seemingly anticipated each move and the consequences of his actions.

Once the game was over, Lou and Tom went outside to shoot baskets. The rim had been lowered, since Tom needed some success at putting the ball in the basket instead of shooting into the heavens; it must have seemed that way from 36 inches off the ground. Tom would dribble and laugh and shoot, dribble and laugh as Lou tried to intimidate him by blocking the shot, always allowing Tom a clear chance to lob the ball down through the net.

It was great fun sharing the day with Tom and his sister Hannah. A few weeks earlier, Lou had been deep into resolving a grave injustice; now he marveled at a five-year-old Donald Trump buying up the world, and a miniature Michael Jordan sinking shots with ease.

Life was good, and justice had been served in Michigan's North Woods. Lou was content, happy to be with his grandchildren and with Nana, the most beautiful woman in the world.